The Forbidden Book

Tim Wuebker

DEDICATION

For Dr. Donna Bauerly, who
lit a fire in me to
love literature, and
cherish free minds.
I will always be grateful for
your passion,
your verve,
and your deep compassion
for the thousands of students
whom you taught over an incomparable, fifty-year career.
Every day, I try to
live up your example,
both as a teacher
and a lover of literature.
Peace.

CONTENTS

ACKNOWLEDGMENTS

A hat tip and bow to Lindsey Weishar for her deep insights into character, plot, and language. Lindsey is a lyrical essayist and poet, and I am grateful for her wisdom.

Also, I owe deep gratitude to Grace Willy for her original and striking cover art. You are a talented artist, Grace, with a wonderful future in front of you.

CHAPTER ONE
Under the Surface

The new boy seemed fake to Rose. As if he were playing a role like a professional actor. Even his appearance seemed calculated: black hair in a sloppy buzzcut, probably done last week so it would look like his parents made him get it; school-issued khakis and red shirt, just a little too perfect, like he put them on before ironing out the creases from the package; shoes that were popular four years ago, but looking like they came from storage. And his story, that he'd transferred from DVE, the most violent school in the city? It sounded rehearsed.

"He's cute." Sophie elbowed Rose. When Rose's friend communicated with her, she did so in a combination of whispers, sign language, and their own personal code, which came from a lifetime of deceiving the authorities and knowing each other.

Probably a narc, Rose signaled back.

Or a drug dealer, Sophie replied.

Or both, Rose motioned. *Plays both sides.*

Right as Sophie laughed, Mrs. Stein stepped nearby, and Rose's phone pulsed in her pocket. Rose kept her face neutral, but she felt shades of pink.

"What have you two decided for your report?" Mrs. Stein asked. She was thirty, pretty, and for reasons Rose could never figure out, forty pounds overweight. A beloved teacher, Mrs. Teresa Stein's moods rocketed between hilariousness and despair.

"Anne Frank," Sophie blurted.

Mom! Rose thought. *Stop.* Discreetly, Rose switched

off her phone, and felt the boy's eyes on her—but when she looked up, he appeared to be concentrating fully on his book and his notetaking. *Mr. Dedicated*, she thought.

Rose knew when she was being watched, especially by a pro. *What are you writing about me?* she wondered.

"Anne Frank?" Mrs. Stein asked.

"Yes." Rose looked at Sophie, who nodded solemnly. "Anne Frank it is."

The boy wrote quickly.

As Mrs. Stein quizzed them about the details, Rose's phone pulsed again—but this time, it was Dad. Rose brushed a pencil off her desk, leaned to pick it up, shut off her phone, and caught the boy glancing down her shirt.

Or had he? When she glanced back, he was buried in his notepad.

He takes more notes than anyone I've ever seen, she thought. Mrs. Stein's World War II class was fascinating but not challenging. What was he always writing? The new boy also attended her math class, in which he did the same thing.

I want to see his notebook.

"Okay, but I have to warn you, that's a really depressing story." Mrs. Stein's eyes poured out empathy. "She was only thirteen, and she had to live in an attic. Imagine hiding in a crowded, dusty, leaking prison for two years, all the while listening for the knock on the door at the wrong time of day. All the while hearing rumors that your friends are disappearing, stolen off the streets, and not coming back. The ruler says they're being relocated to a new, modern city. It has everything. 'It's luxurious,' everyone says, because that's what the media says. 'People like you are receiving special treatment.'"

Rose and Sophie nodded solemnly. They both loved Mrs. Stein. She'd helped Rose all the way through last year, which was the worst of her life. And Rose was fascinated by the stories of ordinary people of World War II. She knew Anne Frank was a tender-hearted girl who was gassed to death at age thirteen.

"I read this!" Sophie exclaimed. "The authorities actually wanted to make the Germans angry at the Jews, so they told them the Jews would receive the best housing, rich foods, and do rewarding work. They'd have the best classes, art, music, sports, massages—"

When Rose's phone shook for the third time, she let the distress show on her face. "Mrs. Stein?" She made herself go pink, and she stood. "May I run to the restroom?" They shared that woman-to-woman glance.

"I can go with her." Sophie shot to her feet opportunistically. Rose felt a dozen girls' eyes on them—and every boy avoiding looking at them.

Except one.

Mrs. Stein nodded, and Rose and Sophie hurried out of the room. They passed the school's police officer, who was leading three unfamiliar adults in suits and two German Shepherds down the hall. Both Rose and Sophie knew what to do: make eye contact briefly, pretend the visitors were normal, and ignore the dogs, the guns, and their body cameras. They passed the restroom and instead veered into a tiny hallway with no cameras. They opened a door and dashed into the theatre room, which was empty. If they skirted along the wall, they knew the room's surveillance was poorly set up; they'd never be spotted. As they did so, Rose retrieved a key she'd swiped, duplicated, and returned, and she unlocked the prop room, and they stepped inside.

Sophie looked at her searchingly.

Rose displayed her phone. She turned on the signal jammer as they both scrutinized the prop room for anything different. Listening devices would be impossible to spot, but they might see unusual shoe prints on the dusty floor, or obvious patterns of the authorities finding a place to hide surveillance equipment. *But if they're really good,* Rose thought, *the authorities won't leave any signs. We have to trust that the signal jammer works.*

Clear, Sophie signaled.

Rose unlocked her phone—twice. Behind the start screen, there lay a second gateway to an illegal app. Rose pressed the one that looked the least interesting; it appeared to be game where you opened up one doll only to find another, and another, and another, hidden inside. She'd nicknamed it *Dolls with Layers.* Created in an enemy nation, *Layers* did not look the same on any two phones.

Mom's hands appeared—but not the rest of her. For the communication, she'd removed her wedding ring. *Nothing identifying,* Rose thought.

Rose! Let me know immediately *that you are okay!* Mom's fingers signaled.

Rose and Sophie signed.

They played the video slowly so they could read all of the hand signals.

There was a shootout in Eastgate, Mom continued, fingers talking. *Thirteen people are dead. They are diverting traffic around Eastgate until further notice. They aren't letting the media know, and they are suppressing all private communications.*

Your mom is so paranoid, Sophie whispered. *She doesn't even want them to hear her voice.*

She needs to trust the app, Rose whispered. *Dad does.*

Rose pressed her screen to transmit that she, Sophie, and the whole school were safe. *Just the usual police dogs, strangers in tailored suits with guns, and creepy new kids who pretend not to be watching us,* Sophie whispered. Rose laughed.

But they stopped laughing when Rose's Dad texted again, for the third time in ten minutes. As she started to reply, he called her instead.

Sophie and Rose stood on their tiptoes. Rose wanted to scream.

"Daddy," she said calmly.

"Are you safe to talk?" He was in his police uniform. Behind him, paramedics were hauling out bloody people on stretchers. The girls forgot to breath.

"Yes. Nothing's happening here. Are you okay?"

"Yes," he said. "Did you call your mother?"

"I was about to. Tell her not to worry," Rose said, while in the background, Dad's C.O., another former SEAL whom she had known her whole life, was yelling something. Another SEAL, Dad's friend Jack Gretton, waved at her through the screen, then disappeared. Abruptly, a wailing siren died out. "What happened?"

"Two paramilitaries decided today was a good day for a street battle." She watched the screen as her father carefully showed her where he was: in a bar with a broken picture. The shards glinted red, and Rose suddenly felt afraid: *Is that blood?* She wished that he would—and also wished that he wouldn't—show her what was on the street. *Corpses?*

"They're going to try hard to keep anything from getting out. The first official story will be that nothing happened," Dad said. "Listen, this doesn't matter. Your mother just wants you to be extra alert today."

"I will, Daddy."

"To anything."

"I will."

"If anything happens, I want you running out of that

school."

Rose was silent.

"I mean it, Rose. Don't try to save anyone."

She did her best to keep her face neutral, and to not look at Sophie for reinforcement.

"Rose?"

"I'm not leaving people behind, Dad."

"Rose, you make sure you're okay first."

"What about Hans? He's on the opposite end of the school."

"Your brother knows what to do. We've gone over the map together. You, Hans and I have identified every exit, every secure room—"

The school had a shockingly high number of hidden steel vaults built in case of attack. They were built during the Fracturing Era, but most students—and even most teachers—didn't know about them. The vaults were illegal. The map Rose's father had was illegal. Dad sharing it was illegal. Through the police department, Dad had acquired the map, and combinations to the unknown vaults, which he made Rose and Hans memorize. And then he destroyed the police's records.

"What if I have a clear shot?"

"I don't care, Rose. You run."

"What if there's only one of them?"

"There's never just one of them," Dad said.

"Dad, why did you train me if—"

Abruptly, a man in the background started screaming, "Oh. Oh my God. Oh *God!*" And a woman shrieked. Sophie absorbed their fear, started shaking, and Rose could tell the blood on the walls, like a child had flung paint, was getting to her.

"I have to go," Dad said.

"What happened here? What *happened*?" the woman wailed as the man steered her away.

"I love you," Rose said.

"You escape," Dad said, and clicked off the call.

Sophie was trembling. "Do you think more than thirteen died?"

"He didn't say," Rose said, but thought, *Yes.*

"Did you see those people on the stretchers? And the paramedics?" Sophie was clutching onto Rose, now.

Rose felt like freaking out herself because one victim had been convulsing, and the paramedics were splattered with blood.

"Oh my God!" Sophie was trembling. Rose hugged her.

"Let me call my Mom," Rose said. She hoped that would calm Sophie down.

"This is horrible!" Sophie whispered, shivering, shooting to her tiptoes. Rose tried to give her a reassuring look—

—but when Mom answered, she looked both haggard and panicked.

"I love you, Mom," Rose said.

"Rose. Thank Heaven." Mom looked beside herself. In the kitchen, Rose saw her four-year-old sister, Inge, mixing vegetables they'd grown themselves. Nearby in a pan, sat a chicken, freshly killed and cleaned. Her dangling hair touching her chin, Inge lit up the instant she saw Rose.

"Why didn't you respond?" Mom asked.

"I'm sorry," Rose said.

"You're in class." Mom nodded. She was talking to herself as much as to Rose. "Hi Sophie."

"Hi." Rose could tell Sophie was trying to compose herself.

"They have strict phone rules," Mom recited.

"Which everyone breaks," said Sophie.

"Mom, I really didn't mean to scare you," Rose murmured. She couldn't take her eyes off of Inge, who started singing to herself.

"I'm sorry I get so rattled," Mom said. "I should trust that you'll be safe." Except that her gaze was skittish, and Rose knew what Mom said before: *The school only has six armed guards. What if a paramilitary shows up?*

"We're way out here, on 45th Street, miles from anything," Rose said.

"I know."

"Eastgate is over ten miles away."

"I know."

"Every road is monitored."

"I know." But Mom's breath froze, and she had that dam-about-to-burst look that Rose dreaded.

"Mom, if anyone comes near, we'd have plenty of warning. Dad would drop everything and—"

"Honey, they got into Eastgate. *Eastgate.* That's not supposed to be possible. They got past electrified barbwire and private security. Your father—"

"Mom, we'd all just run from the school and hide in woods and hills."

"—says they have more firepower than the police!"

"Mom—"

"They're the second most fortified location in the city—"

"Right!" Rose exclaimed. "So why don't we just—"

"Sweetheart!" Mom blurted, noticing what Inge was doing. The four-year-old had the bowl too close to the edge. Mom dashed over.

"So why don't we just leave?"

"Honey, be careful," Mom told Inge. Inge reached to pull the bowl back to where she had it. "Sweetheart, it will fall."

"Mom, you said it yourself," Rose plowed on. "Murder is rising. Everything is getting more expensive. It's not safe. We can't afford anything. Why don't we—"

"Inge," Mom said.

"I'm chopping!" Inge said. Despite herself, Rose smiled.

"We can't just abandon your grandparents," Mom said.

"Let's take them with us," Rose whispered.

"How? And what about your aunts, uncles, and cousins?" Mom began. "Inge!"

"Dad would like to get out," Rose said.

Inge yelped, and the bowl fell to the floor, scattering salad everywhere.

"I have to go," Mom said. "I'm sorry. We'll discuss this later. I'll try not to bother you so much at school. I love you."

"You're no bother. I love you," Rose whispered, and then clicked off.

Sophie whispered, her face inches away. "Can your family get out?"

"I don't know," Rose said. "I want to try."

"Where would you go?" Everyone knew that the neighboring nations were shockingly violent, run by tyrants.

"I don't know."

"How would you get your grandparents out?" Sophie asked.

"I don't know! I just wish they would let us try to figure it out." Rose fluttered her arms. Her grandparents were slow, and in poor health. "Let's go back to class."

"When we step outside this room, we have to pretend that we don't know anything," Sophie said miserably.

Rose nodded.

"I wish they'd put it on the news," Sophie said.

"But they won't."

"People are dead, Rose!"

"Dad didn't say that." But she recognized the accumulation of details: the number of sirens. The wailing pedestrians. The shattered glass on the pavement, the bits glowing like stained glass because they were refracting blood.

"Who did this?" Sophie asked.

"Sophie, we have to go."

"Do you think it was *them*?"

"I don't know," Rose said. "We have to—"

"It was them."

"Okay, it probably was." Rose held her friend's shoulders. "You're an actress. Put on your I-walked-my-friend-to-the-restroom-because-she—well, you know—and-we-stayed-too-long-because-we're-teenagers-who-are-getting-away-with-something face and *let's go*."

Sophie's gaze dropped to Rose's pocket, inside of which Rose hid her plastic gun. Sophie nodded. She closed her eyes, breathed, and then opened them. She was now a different person. Rose smiled reassuringly, and they slipped out of the prop room, and into the empty drama room.

Rose opened the door to the narrow hallway. They crossed the threshold—

—and ran into the new boy.

Sophie startled.

He looked them up and down, drinking them in. When he didn't look away, Rose shuddered. *Creepy!* She thought. He was leaning against the wall, his back to the longer hallway from which this was an offshoot. He was on his phone.

"Don't tell anyone." He winked.

The girls were frozen. *I should say something*, Rose thought. But she knew what Sophie was thinking:

Was he listening in?

He couldn't have, Rose would have replied. *We locked the door behind us. And walked to the back. And whispered.*

But the authorities had all kinds of listening devices. Rose's Dad was always updating Dolls with Layers to keep ahead of them. "I'm not *feeling* well." He smirked. "That class sucks, right?"

Sophie fixated on his phone. "Don't get caught," she said.

"Don't worry." He nodded. "I just had to text my girlfriend."

"Mrs. Stein's class is actually really cool," Rose said. She wasn't sure why, but she felt the anxious need to change the subject.

"It's kinda boring. And fake history. Is that what they teach you, here, in your gated community?" He shrugged. "I'm Harry Dent."

"Rose."

"Sophie."

"We're glad you're at our school," Rose said.

The boy smiled wanly. "No offense," he said, but I wish I were back at DVE with my girlfriend."

"Why did you transfer?" Rose blurted. Sophie elbowed her.

"My dad says this is the last real school in the city." Harry Dent rolled his eyes. "I don't think he knows how retro it is. No offense."

"We should get back to class." Sophie looked at Rose

nervously.

"It was nice meeting you, Harry." Harry's screen flashed, and he forgot about Rose and Sophie, and started typing a response.

"Bye." Rose hooked Sophie's arm and they veered into the main hallway, and beelined for their classroom. "Do you think he actually has a girlfriend?"

"I don't know," Sophie replied. "He's obnoxious." She scratched her nose while speaking, as did Rose. They always did this; it blocked the cameras from recording their lips' motion. In case anything happened, they didn't want the police's forensics to review the recordings. But there were rumors that the observers could isolate one voice out of hundreds of noisy kids during passing periods, so they also spoke in the coded language that they started in kindergarten, which they made more cryptic as they went.

"Our star performers," Mrs. Stein said as they entered. "We are just about to read from a play that was actually written inside Nazi Germany. It's about a bride on her wedding day."

"Whoa," said George John Dasch, one of Rose's friends since kindergarten. "Is it pro-Nazi?"

"We'll see, G.J.," said Mrs. Stein. Everyone called George by his initials.

"Someone probably dies," said Davis.

"You'll find out," Mrs. Stein said, handing out copies. "I'll need those back at the end of class." As Rose took her seat, she realized Mrs. Stein had brought them from outside the school, and she wasn't going to keep her copies at St. Max's. The hair on the back of Rose's neck stood on end.

Mrs. Stein assigned parts to the fourteen students, and said, "Page thirteen."

Rose saw that her lines came first:

ROSE, as LISA: But it's my wedding.

G.J., as JONAS: Keep your voice down.

LISA: I can't.

JONAS: (In a low voice.) Listen. I appreciate what you're saying. I'm your brother. But think about how selfish you're being. Do you want to get us all killed?

LISA: I can't have swastikas in my wedding photos!

SOPHIE, AS SONJA: Wake up, Lisa!

ROSE: Those hideous, blood-red armbands. That black mark is a stain. Do you know what they stand for?

JONAS: For the love of God, Lisa, I'm begging you to not talk that way!

LISA: (Softer.) They insist that their symbols should be larger than the cross. Did you see the photos of Sonja's wedding? Jonas, I love you, but that's not what I want.

SONJA: Do you think that's what *I* wanted? Swastikas dwarfing the statues of Our Redeemer? Their predatorial eagle being larger than Mary and the Apostles?

JONAS: (harshly) Be quiet!

SONJA: You—you sound like…

LISA: …one of them.

JONAS: I'm sorry. (Opens his arms.) Sisters, come here. I love you. Do you think this is easy for me?

LISA: Where's your conscience?

SONJA: That's not fair.

JONAS: Listen to me. I know you think we're only in our parents' living room, and we're just a family having a conversation—

LISA: An argument. We're having an argument!

JONAS: —fine. An argument. But—

LISA: An argument about what we stand for!

JONAS: —but it's dangerous. You get in the habit of talking

this way, and then you'll start saying these things on the street.
SONJA: I would never talk this way on the street.
JONAS: (Shrugs; conceding the point.) Do you think I like this? That Sonja likes any of this? LISA: Some little prick who ran like a jackrabbit in the Great War, some lifelong failure and drunk who was always a nobody now showing up at my sister's wedding, and ordering everyone around because now he's a lackey in the Nazi's *Volksgemeinschaft?*

"Whoa!" Sophie said. "Is that how that's pronounced?"

"It means 'people's community.'" Mrs. Stein motioned. "The people's community remade the schools, the homes, and even Sunday dinner. They put their stamps on all aspects of life. They compelled you to say their words. Keep going."

SONJA: Some sexually frustrated, blotchy-faced coward who hid during the Great War—
JONAS: SONJA, please. That's what I'm trying to tell both of you! You can't talk that way.
SONJA: (Bitterly.) Not even in the living room where we grew up together. Where we played blocks on the carpet.
LISA: Especially in our own home.
JONAS: What is that supposed to mean?
SONJA: I think you know.
JONAS: Don't you dare call me one of them.
LISA: Aren't you?
JONAS: Take that back.
(A pause. It only lasts seconds, but it feels very tense.)
LISA: I take it back. I'm sorry.
JONAS: (Hurt. Composing himself.) I'm not saying we can't

be honest with each other. I'm just saying if we don't watch it, they are going to come for us.

LISA: (After a pause.) At my wedding?

SONJA: (Distraught. Her emotion has been building throughout this scene as she remembers what happened to her.) You made me go along with them. At my *wedding!*

JONAS: No. (Sighs. Closes eyes. The energy drains out of him.) Dear sisters, people are disappearing off the streets. You know this. No one talks about this but everyone knows it's happening.

LISA: I hated that odious little man ever since they first started marching. Ranting in public. Blaming the Jews. Accusing the Catholics of being loyal to themselves first over the Fatherland. Deriding those who live in the East. Accusing the West.

JONAS: (Low and intense.) Do you want to die?

LISA: (Defiantly.) Is that why you joined the military?

JONAS: Do you think I had a choice?

LISA: We all have a choice!

SONJA: No, we don't, Lisa!

LISA: (Turns to Sonja in stunned silence.)

SONJA: I see what your problem is, now.

LISA: What's my problem?

SONJA: You think you're better than the rest of us.

LISA: What?

SONJA: You look down on Jonas for joining the army, but all he wants to do is defend Germany.

JONAS: (Looking both ways nervously, as if glancing toward the windows.) I didn't join to defend Germany. I joined to protect this family. Not from the Soviets—and they're evil. But from *them.*

LISA: I don't look down on Jonas. I love Jonas. He's— you're—our brother. He's always tried to protect us.

JONAS: I didn't do it because I'm with *him.*

SONJA: He's not one of *them.*

(An uncomfortable pause. They all are conscious of Jonas's uniform, and his armband. Ashamed, they cannot look at each other.)

LISA: (In a weak tone.) But the end result is the same.

JONAS: (Going white.) Don't say that.

SONJA: Lisa!

LISA: (Says nothing, but looks at her brother with plaintive eyes.)

JONAS: I'm— (Goes through a range of emotions, all done in gestures and expressions, of frustration, trying to cope, and finally surrender.) The compromises I make. The things I do. I'm trying to keep us all alive.

SOPHIE: (Hand to her mouth.)

LISA: Why?

JONAS: "*Why*"?

LISA: So that we can be what for them? You all know what he turns men into. You're just mindless soldier ants. Part of his anthill mind. And we women. Maybe we have it just as bad. We're just supposed to be breeders. Breeders of new soldier ants!

SONJA: That's sick. Don't say that.

JONAS: If you say any of this outside these walls, you aren't just endangering yourself, Lisa. You're endangering us all.

LISA: "Don't say that." "Don't say that." "Don't *say* that!" That's all you ever say. And you lie for them. And you want *us* to lie for them! You think if they own us, they'll let us live. (She pauses, thinking about something he just said.) What "compromises" are you making?

JONAS: What?

LISA: You said, "The compromises I make. The things I do." What are you doing for them, Jonas?

JONAS: (Caught off guard.) I—You don't want to ask me that.

SONJA: (A shocked whisper.) Oh, Jonas.

JONAS: I— (Falls silent. They are shrinking away from him as though he were a scorpion.) I have no choice. Don't you see? (Frantically.) *None of us has a choice!*

The classroom door opened, and the three strangers whom Rose and Sophie had seen in the hall walked in.

Abruptly, Rose felt her skin grow frigid. The hairs on her arms stood on end.

The woman, who looked at least seventy and had blonde hair, motioned for Mrs. Stein to continue.

But Mrs. Stein seemed paralyzed. Rose watched their teacher force herself to breathe, put on a calm face, and fake it. *She's an actress, too,* Rose thought.

"We'll stop there," Mrs. Stein said. "Kids, take out your books. We'll have a reading quiz tomorrow—"

The usual people who would groan instead started at their desks, and avoided catching the attention of the observers.

"—over Austria's surrender to Hitler without resistance. The first nation *de Fuhrer* took over, he dominated and controlled with the people putting up no resistance whatsoever."

"Complete cowardice," G.J. whispered.

Rose ignored her bright friend, hid her playscript, and began to read *The Diary of Anne Frank*. She hoped G.J. would get the message.

Mrs. Stein walked past Rose on her way to greet the observers. Ordinarily, Mrs. Stein ran a laid-back classroom, and kids would talk. But today, everyone was silent. Randomly, Sophie's pencil rolled off her desk, and she had to stand up and walk near the new boy's empty desk to retrieve it. Out of the corner of her eye, Rose saw Sophie lean on Harry Dent's desk and take his notebook.

Sophie!

Rose watched Sophie discreetly sat down and slipped the notebook beneath her playscript, which was hidden below a chemistry textbook.

"What is this class?" one of the men asked Mrs. Stein. His voice was fake-conversational; to Rose, under the casual tone, he sounded menacing.

"Holocaust," said Mrs. Stein.

Rose realized that she could see the four adults' reflection in the window. Mrs. Stein was standing absolutely still. The old, blonde woman's eyes flitted around the room, and she was marking items down on an electronic clipboard.

"Why aren't there any cameras?" a man murmured.

"I—" Mrs. Stein startled. "We've never had cameras."

"Give us your reading list," a man said.

"Of course."

"And class rules."

Mrs. Stein nodded too quickly.

"What do you do if a student is emotionally distressed?" the old blonde woman asked.

"I comfort them," Mrs. Stein blurted.

"What does 'Holocaust' cover?" the old blonde woman asked.

Rose watched Mrs. Stein blink twice. "World War II," she began. "How Hitler and Stalin built cults of personality, and how each led to the deaths of tens of millions. And how this war shaped our world."

"Hm," said one man, sounding like no matter how hard he tried, he couldn't be interested.

"Well, this class is about violence and blame, is it

not?" the older woman said. "Are you trained to handle their distress?"

"They're resilient."

The older woman lowered her chin and raised her eyebrows.

"They're seventeen and eighteen years old," Mrs. Stein added. Rose could see the observers' faces harden. "The class comes with a warning: they know what they signed up for."

"Do you have any trained counselors on staff for these children?"

"Yes."

The old woman looked at Mrs. Stein with anger tinged with disbelief.

"Do you mind if we…" a man began.

"Of course not!" Mrs. Stein said.

Each of the three observers walked down a different row. At individual desks, they paused to see what each person was reading. It was hard to know, but did they look progressively more upset? Rose clutched the top of her book, hiding the title, and forced herself to concentrate.

Except, out of the corner of her eye, she saw Sophie hastily cover Harry Dent's notebook with her own story of a Nazi collaborator. Rose felt heartsick: *Why did she swipe that?*

The door opened and Harry Dent returned. He gave an embarrassed smile, made eye contact with an observer, and took his seat. To Rose, it looked like they recognized each other, but she couldn't be sure. Mrs. Stein immediately whispered to him that they were reading.

In the window, Rose watched him. *Is he frowning? Does he notice his notebook is gone?*

A smile crept across his face as the observers approached. *He's from DVE*, Rose thought. *He's used to this.*

Only in the last month, since the election, were the inspectors increasingly visiting the private schools.

Unbidden, Rose was flooded with a disturbing memory, and she asked herself, *Where is Müller?*

She couldn't stop watching the old, blonde woman, who was now whispering to Mrs. Stein, who looked distressed.

"Because kids need to know about the past!" Mrs. Stein whispered.

"But you're very selective."

"'Selective'?" Mrs. Stein blinked like she had dirt in her eye. But when the blonde woman didn't speak, she added, "Eleven million people died in those camps. And a lot more died in slave labor prisons after that—work camps that governments established in dozens of nations all over the world."

"We'll see," the old woman said.

Mrs. Stein went white. "We'll see what?"

"We'll see whether funds should continue to be wasted on these classes that don't move the needle."

"This is a private school," Mrs. Stein blurted. "You can't—"

An inspector was approaching her. Rose pretended to read. The man's thick fingers reached for her book, and he plucked it off her desk.

She froze. He flipped through the pages, but his eyes settled back on her as if he knew her. His brown irises floated in a sea of white; he was looking too long; she noticed he was a smoker with stained teeth and nails, and his skin was soft with fat. She had the creepy feeling that he was looking her over. She pretended to read her notes to avoid him.

Peter Müller, she thought. He was in this class, and

math. *Where is he?* Because she hadn't seen him in a week.

Except: he never missed school, as far back as she could remember. He could be provocative. He liked to say things and get a rise out of people. He spoke about the travel ban. Once, he said, "Every kid should have gun training." Rose wasn't sure if he had a crush on her, but she wasn't interested. Peter was trouble.

Where is he?

"Hello," G.J. Dasch whispered.

Rose startled. A dozen people glanced in G.J.'s direction, and then pretended he hadn't. They looked down into their books.

"Have you read this book?" G.J. whispered.

In the reflection, Rose saw the observer give her assistant a thin smile. He shook his head.

"It's about the Gestapo," G.J. said. "It's really good."

G.J., shut up! Rose thought. G.J. was too smart for his own good.

"Are you from here?" G.J. asked.

"Yes. Excuse me," said the observer, who stepped away from G.J.

"Nice chatting," G.J. said softly.

As if nothing happened, her friend went back to his book. Rose suppressed the shakes.

The observer replaced her book and plodded back to the old, blonde woman. In the window's reflection, Rose saw her raise her eyebrows at him. He shook his head.

The old woman made another check mark. "You'll be hearing from us," she said softly. "In the meantime, you might want to think about cleaning up what you think you're teaching." She led the two men out.

When the door closed, Rose watched Mrs. Stein struggle to compose herself. Then her teacher glanced at the clock.

"Oh my gosh!" Mrs. Stein exclaimed. "Class is over. You have to get to your second hour." Their school didn't have bells. Students sprang toward the door.

"Rose?" Mrs. Stein asked at the doorway.

Abruptly, Sophie collided with Harry Dent, her foot tangled with his, and they both tripped, their books flying.

"I'm sorry!" Sophie exclaimed.

"Are you all right?" Mrs. Stein asked.

"Fine," said Harry Dent, from all fours. As three cute guys helped Sophie up and one leftover offered Harry Dent a hand, others helped gather their items.

"I can't believe I did that," Sophie said to Harry Dent, who was laughing.

As they sorted out who owned what, Mrs. Stein's palms touched and she pointed her fingertips at Rose's heart. "Are you auditioning for the play?"

"I don't know," Rose said.

"We need you," Mrs. Stein said.

"That's kind," Rose said, "but my family has a lot going on."

Mrs. Stein clutched Rose's hands. "I know. And I appreciate that. I do. And we'll work to help you in any way we can. And maybe I shouldn't say this, but you're the difference between the play's success and failure."

"The other actresses are more talented," Rose said. Sophie beelined past her and out the door; Rose noticed her book stack was now short one stolen notebook.

"Not like you," Mrs. Stein said. When the last student left, and she closed the door. "With everything going on, we need to touch people's hearts."

Does she know about the deaths in Eastgate? Rose thought. *Or does this have to do with the observers?*

She suppressed the urge to ask Mrs. Stein what happened to Peter Müller.

"I would like to be in the play." Rose immediately regretted saying so. *Why do I always want to tell everyone 'yes'?*

"Go with your heart, Rose."

But what difference does a play make? Rose frowned. *Unless this isn't about the play. Unless she wants something else.*

"No promises, but I'll be there," Rose said, "unless something comes up."

"Yes," Mrs. Stein exclaimed. "It's at St. Joan of Arc's. Not affiliated with the school."

The hairs rose on the back of Rose's neck. *Not affiliated with—*

"I have to get to class," she said.

"Thank you," Mrs. Stein said.

Rose met Sophie in the hall. "Graceful," Rose said.

Sophie pulled Rose close as they maneuvered around clusters of people.

"You're not going to believe this," Sophie said.

"What?"

"His notebook? He has pages and pages of writing, and it's all in code."

"In *code*?"

"Some kind of symbolic language," Sophie was nearly *sotto voce.* They shielded their mouths from the cameras hovering overhead. "Like hieroglyphics."

"What?"

"I don't know what it is," Sophie said, "but it can't be that complicated. If it's some kind of alphabet, there aren't more than thirty letters and symbols."

"Did he write down anything from the actual class?"

"From Mrs. Stein's notes? Not that I can tell," Sophie said.

At their lockers, G.J. Dasch nodded and gave them a stark look. "Have you seen?" He displayed his phone.

Bloody pictures from Eastgate. A red-soaked woman lay bent on the floor, her stained hand reaching upward, her fingers in a rictus.

Sophie gasped. Rose noticed that his encryption program wasn't as good as he thought.

"Sorry." G.J. said. "I should have warned you first."

"Are there more?" Sophie swallowed.

G.J. nodded, and showed hem the inside: people in camouflage lay dead on the floor, some still clutching pistols.

He swiped right, and a man and a woman who both wore blue shirts and canvas hoods sprawled across each other, rigid and motionless, as though they were furtive lovers who had died that way.

"How many?" Rose whispered.

"I count at least eight," G.J. said. "I want to *take a look around.*"

"Please don't," Rose blurted, and clutched his arm. Because she knew what he meant: he wanted to hack into government data to see if he could find out more.

"I won't get caught," G.J said. "You know you want to take a look, too."

He meant, *Sneak into their system.* "But I'm not going to," Rose said. "Tell me you won't, G.J."

"Who did this?" Sophie asked.

"They're all dressed like paramilitary soldiers," G.J. said. "No civilians anywhere."

"Thank God," Rose said.

"The Yellows say Holder doesn't go far enough." Albert Holder was the nation's president. "Blues support Thompson." Vice President Hale Thompson was part of the unity government.

"Shhh." She nudged both Sophie and G.J. "Listen."

"Why?" Tears bubbled up in Sophie's eyes. "Why do they have to…to…"

Rose fought the urge to phone her mom, who had warned her to be aware of all of her surroundings, today.

I wish we'd just leave, Sophie whispered.

"Wouldn't that be great?" G.J. murmured.

If my mom would just…just… Rose whispered.

Someone had started panicking. She was freaking out, her voice rising. Rose quickly zeroed in on a sophomore who was a hundred yards down. Three older people formed a tight circle around her, the taller ones using their bodies to hide her from the lenses above, and even from far away, Rose could hear them shushing her.

The whole hall was half as noisy as usual. Her head down, Rose whispered, "Look around." G.J. and Sophie did so, and the three of them saw teens pulling each other toward their lockers, where they huddled—obviously looking at phones, but no one could actually *see* what they were doing; you had to assume it from their body language.

Rose could tell: half of the students were still oblivious to what was going on, but the other half were learning about the paramilitaries' deaths. The information was spreading through the school.

Dad said there were a dozen, but G.J. said at least sixteen—

"Listen to me." Rose lay a comforting hand on both G.J. and Sophie. "Be hyperaware. Anyone asks about these photos, act surprised, but don't lie."

"Do you think they'll tell us anything?" Sophie asked.

They'll blame the Island, Rose thought.

"Not if they don't have to," G.J. said.

"That's disappointing," Sophie said. "I expected St.

Max to not be like everyone else."

G.J. opened his mouth, and Rose felt he was about to say, *Technically, the principal won't lie. He'll just leave things out. But some of the teachers will lie.* But the heartbroken look on Sophie's face warded him off.

"Treat us like mushrooms," Sophie said. "Keep us in the dark and feed us manure."

"Preserve our childhood," G.J. said sarcastically.

"Just don't get caught alone anywhere. Always make sure you're in a crowd," Rose said. Unbidden, Peter Müller came into her mind again. *When was the last time either of you saw him?* she thought.

Last week? G.J. would answer, unsure. She already knew what he'd say. Then he would look worried, and wonder why Rose would be so foolish as to bring him up.

He was here two Fridays ago, Sophie would say. *Rose, I heard he transferred to DVE.* An obvious lie, spoken for G.J.'s benefit, to give him deniability. *We'd better—*

"Talk after second hour," Rose said. The three of them separated.

Teens everywhere were flowing through the halls, but groups were swiping through the bloody photos. Rose pretended not to notice.

She felt bone-cold. When she thought of the boy with the notebook with pages of symbols; the observers angry at Mrs. Stein; how Mom and Dad were reacting—with overwhelming anxiety—she had to force herself to keep going.

She passed Evey Stevenson—Peter Müller's on-again, off again girlfriend. Evey had hollowed-out eyes, like she always cried herself to sleep. She was trying to disguise her haggard look with concealer, but any girl could tell. Clothes hung on her like she was a coatrack; she'd lost too much weight.

Don't ask about Peter Müller, Dad's voice popped into her head.

Or Thomas Berger. She hadn't seen him in six months. *Or Klara Fogarty.* She'd made the mistake asking about Thomas Berger.

Just go about your day, Dad's voice said.

Pray, her mom urged fervently.

But thinking about Mom and Dad frustrated Rose.

Rose walked into math class, which she dreaded because her teacher always put together presentations that had nothing to do with math. He made everyone nervous. She was sure the administration didn't like this, but there was nothing they could do about it. Rose thought she was done with math, but the government changed the rules over Labor Day, and that forced her out of two electives she had always wanted to take, and into physics and math, instead.

Taking a deep breath, she entered the room exactly at the last second. Mr. Oswald Mosley looked at her, looked at the clock, and barked, "Sit down."

Rose cringed, smiled, and beelined for her seat.

"Deep fakes," he nearly shouted. His voice was a hammer. "Anyone know what those are?"

"Fake photos, fake videos," said Lane N. Chambers, a boy who worshipped Mosley.

"That's right. Usually done by people seeking to discredit authority. Watch this."

Mosley pressed his clicker. One of those sanctioned speakers from a promoted YouTube channel came on, and a woman in an orange pants suit began explaining how previous politicians, histories, and authors had whitewashed the old nation's crimes. Quietly, Rose lay her book flat on her desk and began reading, instead. Occasionally, she glanced up to make Mosley think she was paying attention.

The screen flashed, and then went black. "I understand," Mosley said, "that some doctored photos from Eastgate are spreading through the school."

Rose did not move.

"Have you seen them?" Mosley asked.

No one spoke.

"Daladier!" he barked. A boy in the front startled. Mosley waited. When Daladier didn't say anything, the math teacher said, "Well?"

Daladier shook his head.

He's lying, Rose thought.

"Suzanne?" he asked. He had a deep, powerful voice that reminded Rose of coal.

He was immobile.

"Suzanne?" he asked gently. She was one of his favorites, Rose knew, even though Suzanne had told Rose that Mosley gave her the creeps.

"Photos?" she asked.

Convincing, Rose thought. But Rose felt that Suzanne, too, was lying.

"You know, the day is coming when no one has an addictive phone," Mosley said. "The Committee for Neurological Safety issued a preliminary report on what's good for the adolescent brain, and the brain scans are irrefutable. The evidence is terrifying. One reason is, your peers fail for these obvious deep fakes." He frowned. Everyone knew he hated the foreign apps and communication platforms "because they spread misinformation." The government was in a never-ending battle to take them down, only to see them pop up again under new names, with better encryptions.

"Rose," he said.

"Yes, Mr. Mosley," she said respectfully.

"Have you seen them?"

"I'm sorry?" she asked.

His brown eyes pierced her. She shrank.

To the class, he said, "What I'm about to show you may be disturbing. If you can't handle it, turn away. But you need to know some people are lying to you. I want to show you *how* they lie, and then I want you to ask *why*."

Mosley pressed his clicker, and a photo of Shenanigans, a Eastgate bar, flooded the screen.

Broken chairs lay in pools of blood. Rose tensed. Someone gasped—

—but there were no people in the photo.

"See that so-called pond of blood?" Mosley said, pointing. "It's not even blood. First of all, the color is wrong. Second, that's too much blood. Third, look at how the floor is slanted: it wouldn't even flow from *this* area of the floor to *that*."

Several kids turned away. Rose leaned in closer. *Why not?* she wondered.

Mosley clicked to the next slide, which showed a Rorschach splatter pattern of blood against the wall. Rose froze; she saw bits of flesh.

"Another deep fake." His finger touched the screen. "The blood looks like someone poured it from a container."

But you just said, "It's not even blood," Rose thought.

"Maybe animal blood," Lane Chambers said.

"Gross!" Lena Fischer said.

"Raise your hand before speaking." Mosley glared at his eighteen-year-old students. "But you're correct." Mosley stood still, like President Holder. Rose wondered if Mr. Mosley, too, ever acted in plays. On one hand, he was highly theatrical. On the other, he never stepped out of character.

"Fake patterns, fake blood, fake photos. The question is, 'Why?'"

A chest medal pinned beneath a knocked-over chair in the photo caught Rose's eye. *An Iron Sunrise,* she realized. She'd seen those in Dad's police photos, on the news, on the internet. The Yellow paramilitary rewarded its members with Iron Sunrises for "acts of bravery and service to our nation." Although they were officially illegal, the Yellows insisted they supported President Holder and his National Unity movement.

No one spoke. Mosley's taut body relaxed, he held up two hands in surrender, and sat down in an easygoing slouch. "You won't get in trouble for saying," he said in his reassuring voice, as if to say, *C'mon, we're all friends, here.*

The Iron Sunrise. The photo, Rose realized, must have been overlooked. Because Rose *did* recognize this photo: Dad sent it to her. Only when he did, it had two dead people in it. And she had seen far too many police photos, so she knew everything Mosley had outlined was false.

They removed the dead Yellows, but they missed the Iron Sunrise, Rose thought. *How many people* really *died today?* She shuddered.

"Why do they send out fake photos?" Mosley asked.

"Fake stories," Lane Chambers blurted.

"Go on."

"They want us to believe something false," Lane said.

"What?" Mosley asked. He waited. No one spoke. "What do they want you to believe?"

No one answered.

In a calm voice, almost as though he were channeling a father telling a bedtime story, he said, "They want you to think things are falling apart. They want you to lose hope when, in fact, things are demonstratively getting better."

Isn't this math class? Rose thought.

"Of course, events have been chaotic," Mosley murmured, "but life is getting back under control. You're safe. But some people benefit if you don't feel safe."

"The damn Island," someone murmured, and a few people laughed nervously.

"Ohhh!" Mosley's arm shot out, but playfully. "No *pol*itics!" But Rose could tell he was pleased.

Now he'll say something to appear neutral —

"There are lots of people with bad motives out there," Mosley said. "People who want you to hate each other. People who want you to hate people across the metro. They doctor these photos, they know people will panic, and they send these photos around to create more panic."

"I just ignore them." Lane Chamber's face didn't move. He always reminded Rose of a patient in a psychiatric ward who had the emotional part of his brain cut out.

"Raise your hand," Mosley told Lane, but he nodded. "Delete the photos. Take designated routes when you have to drive or be out. Always have your I.D. with you. If you see something, report it. And trust the authorities. We want what's best for you." He stood up, and pressed his clicker. The screen displayed equations. Apparently, it was math time.

Rose opened her textbook to page 420.

~

When class ended, Rose strode to her locker. She hoped Sophie and G.J. would join her.

Compared to the first passing period, the halls were sepulchral. People whispered and kept their heads down. Rose didn't see any phones, but it was obvious what people were doing: swiping through photos of the bloodshed at Shenanigans. She veered into the restroom to see if her parents contacted her—

—and found a dozen girls.

They looked up warily, but petite Ruth Weinstein approached her.

Was your dad there? Ruth murmured.

I don't know any more than you do, Rose whispered. *But the photos are real.* She glanced at Suzanne Zeller and Rachel Rosendahl, who were having a loud conversation about the basketball boys. *They're doing everyone a favor, and they know it,* Rose knew. Every student suspected that the school—or the state—hid listening devices in the restrooms. Rachel and Suzanne's conversation would drown out everyone else's whispers.

At least four people are dead, Ruth said.

Rose flashed one finger, then three.

Thirteen? Someone's mouth made the word, but without sound.

Maybe more, Rose said. *Blues and Yellows.*

But Eastgate is restricted, Ruth said, dismayed.

Rose nodded. Every person who entered the premier shopping and entertainment district passed through metal and toxin detectors, and was subject to getting frisked and even detained. Her parents hadn't taken her to Eastgate in three years.

At least thirteen people, Rose confirmed.

As she and Ruth whispered, Rachel grew louder. "We could win state!" Rachel said to Suzanne.

"Do you have a crush on Mark?" Suzanne asked.

Rachel laughed mischievously. "No," she said.

"Good," said Suzanne.

"Why?"

"Because then *I* stand a *chance!*" Suzanne's laughter trilled up an octave.

She checked her phone. No updates from her dad. Just a note from mom to check on her younger brother, Hans.

How did they get in? Ruth asked.

Some people on the force are blatant about how much they hate the Yellows, Rose said.

Are you saying someone let *the Blues in?*

They had to have. Eastgate was heavily fortified.

Are you worried about your dad?

Yes, Rose admitted. Dad was tough, an ex-SEAL, as were his buddies on the force, but he was forty-five years old. Mom was heartsick that he still put himself on the streets.

There's a manpower shortage, Dad had said to Mom, just last night.

You have four children, she repeated. *What will happen to them if something happens —*

Mom never finished that sentence.

Ruth nudged Rose. Rose shook herself; she realized for an instant, she had drifted away.

"He'll be okay," Rose said. What Dad lost in agility, he made up in know-how.

Ruth tried to smile reassuringly. *How do they get the guns?* she asked.

I don't know, Rose said. Dad thinks there are lots of guns already hidden within Eastgate. *The nearby neighborhoods had always had bloodshed, even before the fence went up.* Before the Fracturing.

Do you think the police let them in? Ruth asked.

Rose shook her head. *I think it was the army.*

What's the difference? someone else in the restroom

asked.

They don't get along. The army bosses the police around.

Rachel pointed at her watch. They needed to go.

What do we do? Ruth asked.

Be aware, Rose said. *Stay connected.*

The girls spaced out how they left, only two or three laving at a time so as to not attract attention. Rose was grateful to Rachel and Suzanne, who kept breathlessly discussing the basketball boys. Rose was the last to leave.

She hurried for her locker. She and Sophie had lunch; they only had two minutes to arrive. As she shot around a corner, she nearly ran into the old, blonde observer from Mrs. Stein's World War II class.

"I'm sorry," Rose said softly, and stepped out of the observer, and her two assistants' path.

"Whoa!" the old woman laughed. "Slow down!

She sounded fake to Rose, who weaved herself into a stream of kids, and made it to Sophie, whose arm she hooked, and with whom she strode to the cafeteria. They found two empty seats and unpacked their lunches. Only a handful of kids ate what the school sold; everyone had been saving money ever since the Rose entered high school.

"How was science?" Rose asked.

"Garbage," Sophie said. "Mrs. Brennanlicht spent ten minutes lying to us about how the photos were deep fakes."

"So did Mosley," said Rose.

"I know what your dad sent you," Sophie said, "and we've all seen more from people at the scene. I think they—" the Blue and Yellow paramilitaries— "were shooting at each other for half an hour before the police showed up."

Rose nodded. From being her father's daughter, she figured as much. And most people believed the paramilitaries outnumbered and could outgun the police, and that was because the army didn't want the police to have too much firepower.

"Is the school telling the teachers to lie to us?" Sophie asked.

Rose tensed, opened her hands, and shook her head in bafflement. But then, her intuition told her something. "Mosley and his friends are supporters of the authorities," she said. "They're always talking about 'the greater good.'"

"I hate this," Sophie said.

"I'm worried about S.T.," she whispered, switching Mrs. Stein's initials.

"Because they observed her class?" Sophie asked.

"That, and she's going ahead with the play."

"The play?" Sophie asked. "I thought the school canceled it. We can't afford it."

Rose shrugged. The play was easy to do with a plain set and a few props—the principal just didn't want the notoriety.

"She moved it off-campus."

"Off-campus? Where?"

"A church basement. She's putting on a separate play here. As a distraction. To make everyone think everything is normal."

Sophie couldn't hide the pain on her face. "She'll get caught."

"I know," Rose said.

"The kids who participate, the parents who come watch—"

"She isn't going to advertise it," Rose said. "She'll just use word of mouth. It's underground theatre. She told me yesterday that not even the actors will know the play's title. You only get the parts of the script that you're in. And you have to memorize your lines while you're at rehearsal—you can't take the scripts home with you."

"That's insane," Sophie said. "People can't memorize their lines under those conditions."

"She thinks people seeing it is important."

"Why?"

Rose froze. *I don't know what to say. That Mrs. Stein is a crazy idealist who thinks a play can change the country?* "It makes a statement."

"The play 'makes a statement'?" Sophie asked. "What 'statement'? 'I want to get arrested'?"

Rose said, "She wants me in it."

"You can't."

"I know. I think—"

"Rose, you can't." Sophie clutched her arm.

"I know."

"Tell me you won't. I can't lose you, too."

"I—" Rose calmed herself. Sophie was getting panicky, and that made Rose emotional. "This isn't about me. It's about S.T. We have to—" Even though the cafeteria was noisy, and they shielded their mouths as they spoke, she dropped beneath a whisper, and required Sophie to read lips. *I'm going to talk her out of it.*

Please don't.

Tears formed in Sophie's eyes, but she inhaled, held her breath, and steeled herself. When she spoke, she was all business. *When no one goes out for it, she'll realize she has to cancel it.*

Abruptly, Rose and Sophie saw the three observers step into the cafeteria. As the blonde woman strode through the center of the circular room, the volume cut in half. A lot of freshmen and sophomores kept talking, and laughter erupted, but most of the juniors and seniors, Rose saw, froze in place.

The blonde woman stopped dead center. She gestured toward the prayers written high on the walls of St. Max's cafeteria. One of her assistant's eyes went wide. Rose began reading their lips.

Superstitious bullshit, a young, precise blond man said.

Don't knock it, their leader said. *I was raised with religion.*

Yes, ma'am, the same man said.

Look how docile they are, the leader said. *Religion is an instrument of social control.*

The younger man's eyes widened.

You call it superstition, the woman said. *I call it the perfect means of forming ideal citizens. That's why societies have used it for thousands of years. That's why it persists.*

She waited. The younger man looked deep in thought. *Why?* he asked.

Rose felt like they had a master-apprentice relationship, and that she frequently asked the younger man questions to see if he could supply the right answers.

You call it superstition, the woman repeated. *Think about every strategy and method that we borrow from them. Think about how most of their parents have to borrow money, and work two jobs, and beg their own parents to sacrifice their resources to send them here. Think about how cohesive all of their sacrifices make them.*

They stick together, the man said.

They're parasites. The second man's face was a sneer.

If we could only get them to do this for the nation, the first man said.

The leader gave a relaxed laugh, almost a cackle. *Why do you think we're here? To study them. C'mon,* she said. She turned her back to Rose and lead her assistants to the lunch line.

"I'm going to see her now."

"If she's still here," Sophie said mournfully.

Rose froze. Sophie was right. Dismayed, she realized her hand was drifting toward her pocket, and what it contained.

Sophie rose. "What are you doing?" Rose asked.

"Coming with you."

"Don't," Rose said.

"If anyone asks, we can say we had a question about our assignment," Sophie said.

"You should drop the class," Rose blurted.

Sophie looked at her, startled.

"Don't take risks, Sophie." She was shielding her mouth from the cameras and talking below the crowd's noise. "You don't need the class. I can—I can tell you everything we learn for the rest of the year."

Sophie touched Rose's elbow, and strolled ahead of her.

Rose kept her face controlled. *We all take too many risks,* she communicated.

In the hall, they began chattering about things they didn't care about, just like Rachel and Suzanne in the restroom, but they both knew they were creating a cover story for the cameras, for any listening devices, for that new boy, Harry Dent, or any other potential informants who happened to be nearby. *You have to assume,* her mom constantly reminded her, until she was long past sick of hearing it, *that some your closest friends are compromised.*

Rose's whole body felt cold. She'd felt safe here, as a freshman. Now she didn't feel safe anywhere in the city—not even at home.

They shot down the hall, unnaturally fast.

"Honestly, I've seen the way Mark Wingfield looks at

you." Sophie-the-actress was smiling. *"Rose!"*

"Maybe," Rose stuttered. "Mark—What if—What—"

Sophie gave her a dire look that told her to get it together.

What if she's not there? Rose thought.

"Why do you think that? About Mark?" Rose blurted, but she didn't listen to Sophie's answer, because as they rounded a corner, and tread toward Mrs. Stein's room, Sophie's fingers were drilling into her forearm.

What if they take her? No teacher had disappeared before—not at this school—and all of the rumors about classmates who had vanished also came with plausible stories like, "They moved away," but Mrs. Stein was different. She was always their advocate, and funny, yes, but she also told them the truth about things. Mrs. Stein showed them how propaganda worked. Her classes unmasked the labor camps from the past. The plays she selected showed them what really happened before the Fracturing. There was nothing comforting about what Mrs. Stein taught.   As Rose and Sophie approached Mrs. Stein's door, they saw her at her desk. She had her back to them.

Rose turned on her phone's signal jammer. When she knocked, Mrs. Stein startled. She jammed whatever she was looking at beneath a book. Seeing Rose, she motioned for the seniors to enter.

"Thank God," Rose said.

"Do you want to hear some music?" Mrs. Stein turned up the volume on her computer, and Mozart permeated the room. They would speak under the music.

"Mrs. Stein, thank God," Rose said. "We were worried about—" She looked at Sophie. *Do we dare?* "About—"

"About the project."

"Already?" Mrs. Stein was searing their faces. "It isn't due for three weeks."

"No," Rose said. "Not the assignment." Despite the music, she dropped her voice further. She was paranoid about whether the observers, or the new boy, Harry Dent, whose notebook was filled with hieroglyphics, had left a listening device in the classroom. She wanted to look over his desk. "About you. Thank God you're here."

Mrs. Stein grew very still. "We shouldn't be having this conversation."

But it all spilled out of Rose. The multiple deaths at Shenanigans. How Mosley straight-up told them falsehoods—but maybe he didn't know they were false. How the three inspectors were bound to find out about the play.

"Come here," Mrs. Stein embraced both seniors. "It's…" she started.

"*It's going to be fine,*" Rose finished for her. Except Mrs. Stein didn't lie to them.

"I'm okay for now," Mrs. Stein finished.

"We were so worried they'd take you," Sophie said.

Mrs. Stein's gazed toward the door, which Rose had closed behind them. "They can't."

"Why not?" Sophie asked.

"Because I'll scream," Mrs. Stein said. "I will make the biggest, most hysterical protest they've ever seen."

And because her record was spotless, Rose thought. Three years ago, she was teacher of the year. Her plays won awards and media coverage.

That was long ago. "They'll make up charges," Rose said. "They'll plant evidence. They'll take you out in handcuffs."

"I know." Mrs. Stein was putting on a brave face for

them, but Rose was an actress, too: she could see beneath the surface.

"None of this is worth it," Rose suddenly exclaimed. "The play. The class. I mean, they're great, but why don't you just live your life? You have a five-year-old son. You're married." She covered her mouth. *I didn't mean to say all of that.*

"You know it's worth it," Mrs. Stein said.

"Even if they never see you again?"

"It might not go that far," Mrs. Stein said.

Sophie said, "We have to go."

The three women nodded. They had three minutes until their next class.

"We shouldn't stay here," Rose said.

"At St. Max's?" Sophie whispered.

"In this country!" Rose whispered.

"Go." Mrs. Stein was looked pale. Rose knew she shouldn't have said that. Nobody could leave. Even talking about it was a felony. Besides, where would they try to escape to? No one would take them.

The Island. The thought came to Rose unbidden.

But why the Island? she wondered. Because everyone knew the Island had modern slavery.

Maybe it's all lies, Rose thought. *Like everything else.*

Rose hugged Mrs. Stein one last time, and the two friends shot down the hall.

"I thought for sure, with the inspectors, and the fake new boy, she—"

"Me too," said Sophie.

"Maybe she's right. Maybe they don't dare."

"Yet."

"Yet." Rose shivered. They passed a line of students who looked like mourners at a funeral. As the day staggered along, and the photos spread, people's fear was increasing. The whole school felt like a morgue to Rose.

"Hey." Sophie nudged her. "She's okay."

Rose forced a smile.

"We'll think of something," Sophie said.

How? Rose thought. All of these problems had only worsened over the last three years, ever since—since—

Since—

Abruptly, from the traffic going the opposite way, Rachel Rosendahl darted into their lane, did a U-turn, hooked Rose's arm, and walking with her and Sophie. Rachel looked on the verge of tears.

"They've taken him," Rachel said.

Panic flooded Rose. "Who?" Sophie asked furtively. Their heads were down. Their voices were under the hallway noise, as little of it as there was today.

Because Rachel was crying, Rose immediately realized. *Dasch*—

G.J., Rachel finished.

"You're mistaken," Sophie said. But Rose felt the fear that Sophie radiated.

"I saw it," she said. "He and I were…talking…in the band room…in one of the soundproof practice chambers…when two men came in. They were clearly looking for someone. He made me hide."

Behind a piano in the practice room, Rose thought. There was a nook. It had led somewhere, once, before they walled it off a long time ago. Students used it when they wanted to talk, among other things.

"He stepped out to meet them."

"To *meet* them?" Sophie asked.

"Distract them. He's not stupid. They asked him, 'What are you doing here'?

"'Practicing,' he said. Then they asked him a few questions I couldn't hear, and then I heard the outside door click shut."

The band room had steel doors that led outside. Rose scrambled to think, but even as her mind raced, no words came.

"It's a misunderstanding," Rachel blurted. "He didn't mean it. He didn't mean it!"

"Didn't mean *what?*" Sophie asked.

But as Rachel shielded her eyes from the cameras, tears poured down her cheeks. Rose quickly pulled her to the left of both of them. People would notice, of course, but they could say she was crying over something else. *Like the photos,* Rose thought. *The corpses at Shenanigans.*

Which Mr. Mosley and Mrs. Brennanlicht told us weren't real.

"You get it together."

"They stole him. They stole him! Because of what he can do. Because of what he knows. Because he digs in places and sees what they do—"

Rose dug her fingernails into Rachel's arm. Just as Rachel started to cry out, Sophie elbowed Rachel hard enough to bruise a rib.

"Shhh," Rose said. "This is what you have to do." She felt harsh, but she'd seen Dad do this, and it was necessary. "You'll sit with me, pay attention in class, and keep yourself together. You'll be invisible. You got that?"

Rachel nodded. When they turned a corner, everyone knew there was a gap in the camera coverage, and Rachel hastily dabbed her eyes dry.

We'll get him back, Rose wanted to say. But try as she might, she couldn't bring herself to lie.

Peter Müller, she thought. *Klara Fogarty. Thomas Berger.*

No one comes back.

G.J. Dasch.

But as tears threatened to well in her own eyes, she summoned every bit of her acting ability. *I am just another St. Max student,* she thought. *Someone who lives six miles from Shenanigans. I'm just another anxious young woman preoccupied with keeping herself safe. I'm a prep school young adult with too much homework to do.*

But once she was in English class, and trying to concentrate on the new, approved texts required by the state, she wondered: *How long before they come for us?*

CHAPTER TWO
Shenanigans

Hours earlier, 6:31 a.m.

With dismay, Mark looked at the stack of bills neatly arranged on the counter. Mom had a system: who had to be paid now, who could put off past the due date, and who would get paid if they won the lottery.

"Jason," Mom's voice rose from the hallway to the bedrooms. "Hurry up!"

Mark glanced at the clock. The kid wasn't late—yet. But it was only a matter of time.

From the not-to-pay-ever pile, he lifted the bill from his school, St. Maximillian Kolbe's. The envelope had a picture of him on it; he was on the basketball court, dunking the ball. But as much as Mark loved basketball, he didn't want to put himself in the public eye ever again.

He cast the bill aside. "Jason!" Mark yelled. "Hurry up!"

"I'm *coming!*"

Mark sighed, and scuffed his foot against their torn linoleum kitchen floor. It was a two-bedroom ranch-style house; he and Jason shared a room, while their older sister, Maria, stayed in the unfinished basement. When Mom shouted again, Mark sighed. He clicked on the news so he wouldn't have to listen.

"…Vice President Thompson," a talking head was saying. "Look, I get that President Holder was trying to create national unity when he put an opponent in his administration. But a no-compromise, bull-in-a-china-shop hardliner like *Thompson?*"

Frowning, Mark changed the channel. Mom watched these opinion networks rehash the same points, but he wanted real news.

"…increasing signs that the unity government is coming apart," said the anchor. "Meanwhile, in the streets of Hanover last night, more fallout from the street battle. The death toll from the clash between rival paramilitaries—"

Since they didn't say who the paramilitaries were, you knew it was the Blues and the Yellows.

"—has risen to six, with twenty wounded."

Mark already knew all of that. Further, the illegal YouTube channels insisted the government was downplaying the figures. He leafed through their bills on the counter without opening them. Mom yelled if he read them; she didn't want him, Jason, or even their adult sister, Maria, to see them—although, several times, he had stolen those from the utility companies, paid them, and discreetly filed them in her system.

I don't want you worrying about bills, she'd said.

I live here, too, he'd said.

You're a junior in high school, she'd said, last year. After that, she refused to discuss money anymore. *Just score twenty points per game. That pays the biggest two bills.*

And let the family go without heat? he'd asked.

I'm getting a raise, Maria said, last year.

How much? Mark asked.

Mark! Mom said.

Fifteen percent, Maria said, modestly. *And a bonus.* She took a hundred dollars from her pocket and handed it to Mom.

That's great, Mark said, *but it's not enough.*

I know, Maria said. *I need to buy a gun.*

We make enough, Mom insisted. When Mark startled

rattling off amounts, and compared that to the income of Mom's two jobs, and Maria's raise, Mom cut him off.

Your father sent us a check.

Mark raised both eyebrows. *You heard from Dad?*

Yes and no, Mom replied—but it was clear she didn't want to talk about it. Even a day later, when Mark picked a moment when they were alone and she was in a good mood, she still wouldn't say. It was possible, he realized, that Dad had set up some sort of periodic, automated system for paying her. So, she hadn't really *heard* from him; she'd just received a check.

Or she was lying.

Either way, Mark had asked, *how do we cash it? Legally, isn't he a missing person?*

A dozen years ago, he'd said he was leaving the nation, for Saxet. But—caught on camera, long before he was president—Holder had said, "Saxet must return to our governance." Saxet was a breakaway state whose independence their nation did not recognize.

I can cash it.

You'd have to go through the black market—

No, I wouldn't, Mom had told him, standing on a threadbare carpet in their TV room. *There are banks that—*

"Jason!" Mom yelled.

Mark sighed, but his eye caught a glint of fake gold on the floor, underneath the wastebasket.

Nervous, with very controlled motions, he bent at the knees to pick up the epaulet.

Maria, he thought. His heart filled with dread.

Glancing toward the basement where she slept, he observed the lights were still out. She worked late. He would confront her later.

He slipped the golden pickaxe in his pocket. Wracked

with worry, he closed his eyes.

"—and threatened essential government serves for the elderly in Cottbus," the reporter said. "A new militia claimed responsibility."

The screen shifted to a military officer standing next to chief of police. The officer said, "They call themselves the Redeemers. They published an online manifesto. We've taken it down to prevent copycat crimes, but released key passages. They demand that the middle-class hoarders—"

Mark turned down the sound. He could tell from the nervous look on the chief of police's face that he knew the military man was lying. The chief of police looked like he was standing by the colonel because he had to, not because he wanted to.

When the camera started rolling stock footage of empty buildings, Mark hefted the golden pickaxe in his hand. He closed his eyes.

Maria, he thought. He massaged his eyelids. *How can anyone that smart be this stupid?*

"I'm ready," Jason said.

Mark's eyes snapped open, he clicked off the TV, and glanced at his hassled mom. "I knew you could do it." He patted his younger brother's back, and winked at Mom. "Let's go."

"Are you…" Mom asked, sotto voce.

As Jason put on his shoes, and wasn't watching, Mark patted the .44 in his pocket, and nodded.

"Packing heat?" Jason asked, like the immature kid that he was.

"Yes!" Mark rushed his brother, blocked him like a football player, and messed up his hair. Playfully, Jason pushed back.

"You don't miss a trick. Do you. *Do you?*" Mark

gripped his brother in a wrestling hold and dragged him to the floor.

"Hey," Jason protested. He laughed and maneuvered.

"Boys," Mom said. Now that he had him, Mark let Jason go free.

"C'mon," Mark said. He opened the door.

"Mom," Jason said, chewing gum, "make Mark go out for basketball."

Mom looked hassled, put on the spot. "Honey, that's his decision—"

"It's millions of dollars," Jason said.

"That's not guaranteed," Mom said.

"You don't even mean what you say. You're just saying it's his choice because that's what you think you're supposed to say."

"C'mon," Mark strong-armed Jason and pulled him toward the door.

"He's the best athlete they've ever had," Jason said. Mark put him in a headlock and pulled him outside. Only when Mark kicked the door shut harder than he intended did Mark release him. "Sheesh."

"Get on," Mark said, pointing to their ride.

"You keep pushing school as the way out of this neighborhood," Jason said, "but look at Maria."

That stopped Mark. "What about Maria?"

"She made straight A's. Always reading a book. Look where it got her."

Mark whirled his hand for Jason to get to the point.

"It got her nowhere," Jason said. "She's a grocery store stocker. No chance for advancement. They cut her pay last week."

"You can't blame Maria or the store for that," Mark said. "There were cuts all across the city."

"Exactly," Jason said. "*She's* doing everything she can. *You* could get us out of this." His arm swept across the horizon.

"Is Maria in trouble?" Mark asked, thinking about the golden pickaxe on the floor. Maybe she just found it in the street.

"No," Jason said reflexively. Mark could tell he hadn't even thought about it, yet. "Is she?"

Mark felt uneasy. Anything was better than Maria using her extraordinary beauty to latch onto a paramilitary. "If she is, not for long," Mark said. *Because I'll pull her out of it.*

"Because you'll get us out of this," Jason said.

Mark sighed. "Let's go."

Outside, a patrol car crept through the modest neighborhood, which was a mile east of Eastgate, the city's premier shopping and nighttime district. Like his neighborhood, Eastgate was protected by two rings of an electrified, barbwire fence with a no-man's land in-between. But Eastgate had more: in the no-man's land between the fences roamed any number of snarling Rottweilers who were never given enough to eat. The fence kept out thieves, as did the constant police patrols.

Mark waved at Officer Darré, whose patrol car crept by. Darré gestured back. The man had grown less honest the longer he stayed on this beat.

Mark and Jason got on their motorized bicycle. Mark had built and added the motor himself from spare parts. He could either pedal the bicycle or let the gas-powered engine propel them. Every school morning, they rode to the streetcar station, take the metro six miles to Jason's grade school, and then Mark would take the last mile to the stop near St. Max's.

"Cutting it pretty close," Mark said to Jason. As he pedaled, he took it up to twenty mph, which felt like sixty in a car. The wind hit his face.

"What are you talking about?" Jason asked. "I was ready by six-thirty." That was earlier than all week.

"I know you think school is pointless," Mark said. They shot past boarded-up houses. "But I'd like us to move out of this neighborhood."

"You and what magic wand?" Jason asked.

"Just try, okay?"

"You're playing basketball, right?" Jason asked. "Because that's the magic wand."

"Man, you just don't quit, do you?" Mark interrupted.

"We also talked about my grades. What were they again last quarter?" Jason reminded him.

Mark let it go. The kid did well.

They zipped past a Dutch-style house, now split into four apartments, not counting the attic. Mark couldn't prove it, but he was convinced that more than just Mr. and Mrs. van Pels lived there. The van Pels were careful; their house didn't stand out. Like most of the neighborhood, it needed paint and repairs, but the shabby look didn't actually mean it leaked or was drafty. *As if they're trying to be invisible,* Mark thought, as he half-listened to Jason explain how he'd brought up his grades in the last week. *Because they're hiding subversives.*

Maybe they know someone who can get us out, Mark thought.

They reached the checkpoint. The electrified fence stretched both east and south for a mile. A security camera stared down on them. When Mark reached into his pocket for his bribe, the guard, old Jay Bowen, flipped a switch.

Mark placed his back to the camera and asked, *Is it*

off?

Bowen pocketed Mark's cash and nodded.

Mark frowned. He disliked trusting Bowen. Bowen was neighborhood security; half of his salary was paid for by the neighborhood association, and the rest by the city police. And even with all that, they still couldn't afford someone younger, better with a gun, or who actually cared about the residents.

"Ten dollars next week," Bowen whispered.

"It was eight last week," Jason whispered back.

"I can't help that," Bowen said.

"We know. Be careful," Mark said to the older man.

"Ten is ridiculous," said Jason.

"Can't be helped," Bowen said too quickly.

"Thank you," Mark said, and yanked Jason along the cracked street toward the train platform.

"The old cheat," Jason murmured.

"What do you expect?" Mark asked. On the platform, they could hear the train rumble from a half of a mile away. Mark scanned the nearby people for anything that looked unusual. He saw an older woman…a sullen young man in dirty jeans going to a construction site…a few private school kids like themselves. Unbidden, Mark remembered school uniforms from grade school, but the school abolished those. The stated reason was that this was a new era, but Mark knew that wasn't the real reason. The real reason was—

"I'm tired of getting ripped off," Jason whispered.

Mark sharply elbowed his brother. He brushed his waistband with his elbow to remind Jason that Bowen was letting them bring Dad's .44 into a train station.

He'll sell us out soon as he gets a chance for a bigger payout. Jason shielded his lips as he spoke so only Mark could see.

Let's discuss this later, Mark said.

But as the train arrived and they boarded, the cracked glass door sliding shut, Mark realized that Jason was right.

Because right now, they were counting on Bowen not saying anything because, if he ratted them out, Mark could tell the authorities about all of the bribes Bowen took. *He'd have to strike some kind of immunity from prosecution—*

Less than a minute later, the train lurched to a stop. "What the hell," the ticket collector muttered.

Mark tensed. They were not inside Eastgate yet. They were in three square blocks of dead housing—abandoned properties occupied by no one, not even gangs or addicts, because some of the paramilitaries obsessed with purifying the city would randomly sweep in and assault anyone they found, calling them traitors.

With a pneumatic hiss, the train doors slid open. "Mark." Jason's fingernails dug into Mark's arm.

Through a broken picture window, they saw people in black uniforms with golden pickaxes run toward the train.

A woman shrieked—a chilling cry of terror. Jason burrowed into Mark, and Mark's hand went to his .44.

A man of uncertain race, his chest bulky with bulletproof armor, stepped aboard, and the train was flooded with a dozen new people, all armed, all wearing golden pickaxes.

The woman who shrieked struggled to stifle herself. What came out were horrible whimpers, like an animal in pain. "Be quiet," yelled the first man to board. "Get on the floor."

Rigid with shock, no one moved.

"Now!" the man shouted, swinging his gun at a middle-aged man's face.

"Don't shoot!" the man shouted.

All around them, people scrambled, stumbling as they lay down on the dirty tile. Mark kept one hand around Jason, and another near his hidden gun. "If you stay down, you will have proven your loyalty, and be rewarded by the National Solidarity Democratic Action Party. The liberation of the city in the name of President Holder has begun!"

The door slid shut and everyone slid on the linoleum as the train accelerated. *They must have had an insider,* Mark realized. Because the paramilitary couldn't block the tracks, or otherwise stop the train. There were cameras every fifty yards, the train's windows were made bulletproof glass, and the metro had armed security.

It's an insider, Mark was sure. *Because people are choosing sides.*

What are we going to do? Jason whispered. They lay close together in the center aisle.

What they say, Mark said. He hit his brother to shut up.

In less than a minute, they pulled into Eastgate Station. "Get out," the leader barked.

No one moved.

"I said *get out!*" he shouted. He jammed his gun in a woman's face. As she whimpered, he reached down and pulled her to her feet. Looking disoriented, people stumbled up from the floor. "Out!" the leader shouted.

Uncertainly, people stepped toward the platforms. As Mark helped Jason up, two hands from a woman seized his arm and yanked hard. She had a knife scar that ran across her throat from ear to ear. "Move!" she said. In her other hand, she held a .22.

"Yes ma'am," Mark said, and pulled Jason to his feet.

He pictured shoving her backward, into the seats, making her lose her balance and drop her pistol. After that,

Mark would whip out his .44—

—and ten Yellows would shoot him. He lifted his hands, where she could see them, pulling up one of Jason's as he did so.

Dread flooded him as she forced him and Jason off the train. As she stepped off behind him, ramming his back with her gun, people on the platform screamed.

The dozen Yellows, in their black bodysuits, stepped off, behind the former passengers. *They're using us as human shields.*

They were on the corner of 73rd and Main, near a cluster of popular nightclubs. An older security officer stepped forward. He was dressed like a police officer. He'd drawn his gun—when abruptly, Mark heard a *rata-tat-tat*, and the older security officer was lifted off his feet. Soon on the ground, somehow amidst all of the wailing, and people frozen, and other people fleeing, Mark heard him give a ghastly moan.

He's still alive, Mark realized. The man lay contorted, slick with blood, his fingers searching for his gun, which he'd lost his grip on when he'd been shot.

"Mark!" Jason hissed. But the woman's pistol jabbed his spine, and Mark struggled forward.

How do we escape? He asked himself. *What do they want?*

They appeared to be heading straight for Shenanigans, Eastgate's most famous bar. Too many thoughts collided in Mark's head. He could abruptly yank Jason into an alley, try to pull him behind a dumpster, and draw his .44. He was a dead shot, but there were a dozen of them, and a dozen more hostages. There were cameras on the street.

What about the alleys?

"What do you want?" Jason blurted.

"Hell's bells, I said *shut up!*" the woman snarled. "Keep moving."

Ahead, they saw a flash of green light and heard a sudden boom, like a cannon. Mark had never seen anything like it; he wasn't sure what he had witnessed. Two seconds after, the lights in every shop nearby died out. Mark's gaze flashed to a street camera. Its telltale red light that indicated it was always watching and recording winked out.

The Yellows behind them cheered. The scarred woman laughed.

"And that's the power grid!" a yellow shouted, to many cheers.

"Ma'am," Mark said, "just take me and please let my brother go. He's only fourteen—"

"Keep moving or I'll kill your brother." The woman jabbed the pistol into Mark's back. He winced; she'd rammed his sciatic nerve like she knew where it was.

Behind the weeping former passengers, who marched down the street prodded by the paramilitary, someone's walkie-talkie behind them burst with static.

Click. "I'm here," the device said.

Click. And then garbled words from the walkie-talkie. Mark struggled to understand what the words were. It all sounded like gibberish and hisses to him until, "—Blueshirts are at sixtieth street."

Mark, Jason communicated, his lips moving. To Mark, his little brother looked on the verge of panic.

Mark raised his eyebrows to show he understood. The Blueshirts were thirteen blocks away. The Blues mirrored the Yellows, and were their worst enemy, although Mark couldn't tell their demands apart.

We're on the front lines. We're human bullet blockers.

All around them, shopkeepers were boarding up their diners and boutiques. Pedestrians saw the proud paramilitary, marching down Main Street in uniform with rifles pointed forward, and they fled.

If I don't do something, we are going to die, Mark realized. But the woman's pistol barrel never left his back. He couldn't think. He wiped away sweat. In other cities, Blues and Yellows shot each other in the street. Both wanted control of the government. Both preached "a revolution within the revolution," and each had a long list of enemies, but their top targets were each other. Mark couldn't tell their demands apart. *"Free the workers from exploitation—"*

But Eastgate was the showcase neighborhood of the city and the suburbs, and it was supposed to be heavily fortified. How did the Blues and the Yellows get in?

A block ahead, two pedestrians pounded on the door of a shop and begged to be let in. But the door didn't open. As the paramilitaries' boots slapped in synchronicity against the street, the woman behind Mark laughed at their misfortune, her voice a rheumy cackle.

And then Mark acted on instinct.

To the right, an alley created a gap between a boutique and Shenanigans. Mark shoved Jason hard into the alley, whirled, and knocked the woman's arm down. As her gun clattered against the concrete, he ran after Jason, who stood frozen in the alley.

"Run!" Mark shouted.

They made it ten yards before Mark seized his brother's arm and pulled him behind a recycling dumpster.

Pop pop pop. A series of gunshots. The metal of the dumpster pinged; concrete from nearby bricks exploded, and clouds of cement dust rained down.

"What the hell," Jsaon said.

"Don't cuss," Mark said.

Pop pop pop. Click. Click.

"Kill them!" the scarred woman shrieked.

As hostages cried out, Mark seized Jason's hand, yelled, "Keep down," and led him, crouched, with the dumpster hopefully shielding them, to the end of the alley.

Shouts from the street. Gunfire. Someone screamed, and wouldn't stop screaming, a horrifying wailing—

Mark pulled Jason around a corner, into an alley that smelled of rotting vegetation and human feces—

—when they heard a harsh, deep voice shouting back at the screaming hostage, who wouldn't stop. And then a gunshot.

Quiet.

"Do what you're told!" Mark heard the harsh, deep voice say.

Fearing that the Yellows would come after them, Mark found what he was looking for. At ground level, he found a dusty window to a basement. When he started kicking in the glass, Jason joined him. They heard boots slapping closer. Guiding his brother, Jason's legs went in first, and Mark lowered him to the basement floor. As two Yellows with Kalashnikovs rounded the corner, one yelled, "Stop!"

Mark dropped to his tail, shot his legs inside the basement, and propelled himself with his hands along the dirty alley.

Gunfire.

And he flung himself into darkness, hoping he wouldn't drop himself atop his brother.

His feet landed on concrete. In the gray room, he saw Jason's silhouette standing a dozen feet away, by a staircase.

"Mark, this way!" Jason said, quiet and intense.

Mark touched his elbow, which stung. He'd gashed it embedded a shard when he shot through the window frame. He plucked it out, withdrew his .44, and they climbed the stairs.

"Here," Jason said, handing him a handkerchief to bandage it.

"Thanks," Mark whispered.

Abruptly, six gunshots exploded around them. Glass shattered; bottles crashed to the floor. Their two pursuers were shouting.

At the top of the stairs, against a wooden door, Mark held Jason absolutely still. He jammed the cloth into his pocket. The cut wasn't severe; he'd fix it later.

Play dead, Mark whispered, and Jason nodded. Both were slick with sweat.

"Listen," one of the men said.

After a pause: "Did we get them?"

"It doesn't matter," said the first. "We have to rejoin the others."

Jason smiled brightly, and nearly took a step, but Mark held him in place. *Wait*, he said.

They heard boots running, the sound soon fading to nothing.

"What the hell?" Jason asked.

"It's a paramilitary," Mark whispered.

"No shinola, Sherlock," Jason said. "How'd they get on the train?"

"Take a guess, Watson," Mark said. "C'mon." His hand was on the doorknob.

"Wait." In the near darkness, Mark smelled his brother's fear. "Do we want to go in there?"

"Do we want to stay trapped in a basement with no way out?" Mark asked. "Wherever the paramilitary is going, we need to go the opposite way."

Jason nodded and jostled Mark to hurry up. His .44 drawn, Mark silently turned the knob.

The bar was as bright as a searchlight. They blinked—

—and flinched. From outside, they heard a burst of gunfire. Looking through the picture window, they saw dozens of Blues running past. A man with medals, stripes, and a beret was screaming at them, his arm whirling, and he urged his people to keep running north.

Two bloody civilians lay in the street, their limbs bent unnaturally, their breath rheumy. Jason gasped.

"Hands up!" a bass voice yelled at Mark and Jason.

Jason gasped. "Do what he says," Mark blurted hastily. He turned.

The bartender had two .38s pointed at both of them.

Seven patrons hid behind overturned metal tables. Mark said, "I'm placing this on the floor."

Jason was breathing hard, on the verge of hyperventilating.

"Drop it!" the bartender shouted.

Beginning to crouch, Mark dropped his gun the final two feet. "Jason, he said, "don't move." Because he could feel it…the kid wanted to flee…

"We're not with them," Mark said. "We're students. We're running from them."

"Kick it over to me!" the bartender yelled.

Mark could tell the man was jittery, dripping with sweat, on the verge of panic. His eyes were so skittish that Mark wondered if the bartender was high on amphetamines. Mark didn't want to rattle the man—

—when a horrific, epic explosion took place: the picture window that read *Shenanigans* shattered, glass bursting toward them. As patrons cried out, the bartender's body arched and froze as though he'd gripped a live wire. His chest blossomed red, and he stood balanced on his tiptoes like a dangling puppet before he plunged backward.

Mark yanked Jason to the floor one second later. Kalashnikov fire sprayed above them. Flat on the tile, Mark seized his .44.

The cacophony of cries, commands, and hysteria was overwhelming. When the man who had sprayed Shenanigans with bullets himself was shot—who knew what was going on outside?—Mark yelled, "C'mon!"

From childhood, long ago with Dad, he recalled the layout of the bar. Now, he yanked Jason upward and propelled them for a hallway that led to the stairs. Along the way, he picked up one of the bartender's guns.

"Open it!" someone shouted behind him. From the streets: more gunfire and shouts. Inside: five people were clustered behind him. Mark rammed the door with his shoulder. Nothing.

With people shouting at him, he took aim at the lock and squeezed the trigger. Jason flinched; the door flung backwards and bashed the wall; Mark grabbed Jason, and they sprinted upstairs, four people following him.

"Damned Yellows," someone said. "Eastgate is supposed to have airtight security."

"Well, not when the Mayor is kissing their—"

A burst of machinegun fire from the streets interrupted the waiters. Crouching, Mark pulled Jason toward the ledge of the nightclub's deck, between the high-top tables and umbrellas, to see the street.

Carnage lay below. Yellows, in their black body suits, toting Kalashnikovs, crouched behind cars, some burning, and others perforated with bullet holes, and the Yellows fired at the other paramilitary, most of whom were a block away.

A block north, crouched behind a truck that had ran off the road and was smoldering inside the wrecked façade of a grocery store, several Blues shot back.

"We are going to die!" a woman behind Mark murmured, her voice shaking. He glanced at her. He had never seen anyone that terrified in his life.

Below, in the street, a Yellows behind a lamppost suddenly twisted where he stood, crumpled, and collapsed. And then a second man did the same.

Snipers, Mark realized. *The Blues have someone up high.*

A third Yellow met his end. "Get inside!" screamed a harsh, deep voice, whom Mark recognized from earlier. *Their leader from the metro*, Mark thought.

And then fear surged within him. *The Yellows on the street were now running inside of Shenanigans.*

"Crap. Oh crap. *Crap!*" The woman behind him was babbling.

The woman near Mark was shrieking. They could hear that, downstairs, people were rattling about. Sounds of furniture getting moved; the leader yelled commands.

Mark seized Jason's arm. "They're going to seek higher ground. We can't stay here," he said.

Jason's eyes darted to the nearby rooftops, and then looked at Mark like his older brother was out of his mind.

"No choice," Mark said.

"Fire escape," Jason said.

Mark shook his head. The Yellows who weren't running for Shenanigans had bolted into the alley. They could hear the fire escape rattling.

"They're climbing it," Mark said.

"What are you going to do?" a man demanded. He looked about thirty. He looked a little tipsy.

"Follow us if you'd like," Mark said. "Jason, you can do this. You've *done* this in track."

Jason shook his head.

"Go." Mark prodded Jason. "You can jump a whole five feet farther than me."

"You go first."

Mark wanted to argue, but he heard boots slapping up the steps, and in his peripheral vision, he saw a beret stick up the from the fire escape.

"Oh no," someone gasped.

The man who had taken the bartender's other .38 suddenly fired it toward the fire escape. "Stand back!" he shouted. In a panic, he shot three times.

Mark gripped Jason's shoulders, locked eyes with his brother, and said, "Together."

Bang, bang, bang. More gunshots as the freaked out, tipsy man with the .38 missed the Yellow with his sixth and final shot.

"Three, two, one, go!" Mark yelled, and he and Jason sprinted for the edge—

—leapt—

—saw the concrete twenty feet below them—

—and landed on the new rooftop.

Abruptly, surprisingly, a man and woman landed behind them.

The man cried out, and a sickened look took over his face.

"Matt." The woman went to him, and tugged at his arm.

"I'm fine," he said.

Abruptly, a shot exploded, and someone cried out. Yellows were storming the rooftops of Shenanigans.

Mark, Jason, the woman, and the man ran for the

roof's trapdoor. The streets below now saw the Blues surging into the territory the Yellows had abandoned as they flooded inside Shenanigans.

"Hurry!" the woman shouted at Mark, who pulled at the trapdoor. "They're shooting people."

Pop pop pop. Nearby. The rooftop of another nightclub, Cabaret. Mark didn't dare look back. He focused on the trapdoor. Because it was locked, he took careful aim and blew the mechanism apart.

"Faster!" the woman exclaimed. He opened the door, which led to rotting wooden steps, and a gloomy attic. He surged down the steps, three at a time. Jason and the woman followed.

A gunshot—

—the man froze—

—the woman shrieked, and Mark feared the worst—

—but the man restarted running down the stairs.

"Your shoulder," the woman exclaimed.

"I'm alive," he said. To Mark: "I'm Matt. This is Shannon. You saved our lives."

"I'm Mark."

"Jason."

"What do we do?"

"You drop your damn guns!" a voice yelled at them.

Matt, Shannon, and Jason cried out in fright. A lone Blue, with a submachine gun, crouched behind a dusty box of flags from before the Fracturing. Pointlessly, Mark remembered that this bar once was nicknamed Patriots' Pub because of all of its décor: flags, portraits of monuments, paintings of the original nation's Founders. All of that décor was now in these boxes.

Just one man, Mark realized. *About twenty years old. Physically smaller and weaker than me; maybe second string in JV basketball in high school, if he graduated.*

"Okay," Mark said. The couple behind each other was frozen together. *Thank God,* Mark thought. "We are all calm. We're doing what you say. I am laying both guns on the floor."

The boy was slick with sweat. They heard shots, and shouts. The boy glanced out the windowpane. Foul dust floated in the sunlight. Blood trickled down his neck.

Flustered, the boy focused back on Mark who set his guns on the floor.

"I'm slowly standing up," Mark said. "No sudden movements."

The boy inhaled sharply, a panicked reaction. His gaze darted back to the street.

"Not what you signed up for?" Jason asked.

"What?" the boy exclaimed, and thrust his pistol at Jason.

"What he means is, we were just trying to get away from the Yellows," Mark said, elbowing Jason. "We didn't sign up for this."

The boy's breath came in hard pants. He looked green.

"Just let us leave you alone," Mark said. He saw the stairs, and had a plan: get to the first floor, find the back alley, and run away from this eye of the hurricane before the cops or the military arrived. *We can't be caught up in this.*

"No," the boy blurted. He coughed suddenly, drops of blood flying out of his mouth. He was shaking; his eyes looked ready to dilate.

He's having a panic attack, Mark thought. *We can't risk what he'll do—*

Mark blitzed him.

Startled, the boy squeezed the trigger as Mark's

plowed into him, seized the boy's spindly arm, and wrenched his elbow toward the ceiling. Bits of wood rained down as Mark knocked the boy to the floor and landed on top of him. The boy cried out as Mark twisted his wrist unnaturally. His fingers loosened and his gun hit the floor.

The boy tried to fight, but Mark pinned him in a classic jujitsu hold. "Get the guns, Jason," he said. As he heard his brother hustle from behind him, he restricted the blood flow to the boy's carotid artery, and the Blue passed out.

The man and woman were petrified. Mark took two guns from Jason and left his brother with one. He tucked one into his waistband and pointed the other at the floor.

"Down," he said to Jason. His little brother blushed, and pointed the barrel down.

"Sorry," Jason said.

The woman opened her mouth to speak, but was distracted: now there were sirens in the distance. Mark said, "My brother and I can't be caught up in this. We are going down those stairs, going to an alley, and running."

"We'll come with you," the man said.

"We want a gun," the woman said.

"No," said Jason.

"Not yet," Mark said. "C'mon."

They stepped over the unconscious boy. Mark stereotyped him as unemployed and disconnected from his family. The boy probably experimented with alcohol and drugs; knew school was worthless, and dropped out right around the Crash like thousands of people. Soon, the Blues came along, asked him how damn frustrated he was and if he'd like to crack some of the skulls of those in high society who had ruined his life before he even knew what they had done to him.

Do I get a gun? he'd probably asked.

You'll get more than that! they'd most likely told him. *Women, respect, money—you'll get everything you deserve.*

They tiptoed down the concrete stairs into the main floor of Cabaret, the nightclub next to Shenanigans. The stage for performers, the bar, and the white-clothed tables were all deserted; the place looked immaculate. The front door hung open the way the boy must have left it.

Abruptly, a titanic explosion rattled the windows and shook the floor. "That's a block away," Mark said.

"Ahhh," the woman murmured.

"That's a rocket," Mark said. He recognized the sound from the news—the real news—the dark web channels that the authorities hated and shut down as soon as they discovered them. The noise terrified Mark. *They used rockets in Hanover,* Mark thought. *And other coastal cities. Not here.*

"What do we do?" the man asked.

Jason, too, looked at Mark. "We're going in the opposite direction," Mark said.

"Which way is opposite?" the woman asked, but Mark was already bolting for the kitchen. They ran past skewers and cleavers. A family picture hung crookedly on a wall.

A family business, Mark thought, distracted for just one second by the happy parents and their four children. He had no time to think about family, now, but he was abruptly flooded with memories—his mother, who tried so hard to keep them safe and together. She worked two jobs, bought Mark a gun, and signed him, Maria, and Jason up for jujitsu and krav maga.

Mom tries so hard. If only Dad were here.

"Mark." Jason jostled his arm.

Mark nodded, continued past the meat lockers to the backdoor, and unlocked it.

In the filthy alley, with its needles and the rotting smell of dead rats and human feces, a drug addict looked up at them blearily from behind a dumpster. He looked both drunk and narcoticized.

"It's the end of the world," the man in rags said.

"True," Mark whispered. When the man began to reply, Mark put a finger to his lips. Everyone listened to the street.

From the east: Occasional shouts. Sporadic gunfire.

Mark pointed west. Jason, Matt, and Shannon agreed.

Weaving between trash, the little band fled the scene of the battle of the nation's two largest paramilitaries, who until this morning, Mark believed, from the approved news, had few troops in their city. But now he realized that this full-on battle hinted at many more.

The sirens hurt their eardrums, now. But despite the police flooding the scene, there was still the distinctive sound of Kalashnikovs from the Yellows, and the Blues launching rockets in retaliation. Mark had to lead the others out of here before the police, and probably the military, entered the melee.

CHAPTER THREE
The Fishbowl

Don't cry, Rose told herself.

As Rose and Sophie walked to English class, Rose didn't look at Sophie, and they didn't speak, because both of them would have burst into tears.

There are cameras everywhere.

As they passed hundreds of kids, she made her face a mask, but she wanted to scream. A delicate 14-year-old blonde strolled by, chatting with her friends about boys, and Rose felt pierced, as if by a sword.

That's Lindsay Rosendahl, Rachel's younger sister.

Rose wanted to look at Sophie for reassurance. She wanted to seek out Peter Bourman or Aiden King, friends since kindergarten, who—if circumstances were right— maybe she could see in a different way. She longed for strong, manly arms wrapping around her, holding her, comforting her, making her feel safe.

Because G.J. disappeared.

When they reached the stairwell, a camera blind spot, Rose restrained Sophie on the seventh step, just behind a boy and girl who were kissing. Others pretended not to notice and moved around them.

We have to get him back, she whispered.

Sophie's gaze darted fearfully. She was shaking.

Calm yourself, Rose communicated.

We can't discuss this, Sophie said.

I know we can't discuss this here, Rose replied. She and Sophie both had their lips shielded from kids who, frustrated, had to side step them, the kissing couple, and a cluster of girls furtively showing each other more forbidden photos from Shenanigans.

No, Sophie said, *we can't discuss this.* Sophie searched Rose's face, imploring her.

If she really thought it was hopeless, she'd desert me, Rose thought. *Because we can't live without hope.*

We're getting him back, Rose said.

Sophie's eyes grew even wider, more fearful—but she gave Rose that look that asked, *What are you thinking?*

C'mon. Rose led Sophie around the couple, who also decided they needed to get to class.

Miss Anne Carpenter's room was wallpapered with posters. She didn't have desks; students made themselves comfortable in a circle of beanbags, blankets, and pillows. Miss Carpenter, a frail twenty-five-year old who fasted frequently, who was pretty but rail thin, smiled but looked unhappy.

From the shelf, Rose, Sophie, and twenty others found their playbooks. "An instant classic!" the back cover read. Rose hopped down on the floor, and leafed through the play, as the others found their places. *Do you think she'll discuss the photos?* Sophie's eyes asked her.

No, Rose said soundlessly. Lowering herself, she read a blurb on the cover: "A re-imagining of a second-rate play into a first-rate masterpiece!"

"Welcome, everyone." Miss Carpenter frowned. "We are now on page thirteen of a just-released play. The Department of Education just delivered the copies today."

Sophie raised her eyebrows at Rose. Rose found the page. One of the readers, she waited for Miss Carpenter's signal. After the kissing couple took their assigned beanbags—separated across the room by Miss Carpenter—Miss Carpenter nodded.

Rose and two others read their lines:

SONJA: I wish you'd grow up.
ROSE, as LISA: Anna!
JONAS: I mean it. I don't think you understand what we're up against.
LISA: I understand.
JONAS: No, you don't. I know what they're saying sounds attractive.
SONJA: Jonas, I'll handle this.
JONAS: (Bitterly.) 'Freedom.' 'Individuality.' 'The right to pursue your own destiny.'
SONJA: Jonas.
JONAS: No. She doesn't understand what we've gone through. What they've done to us. Because they *hate* us. Because they're fanatics.
LISA: I keep telling you, I understand—
JONAS: Because you can't understand. Growing up as you did.
LISA: I understand!
JONAS: Entitled. You, with your false consciousness. Fine.
SONJA: I'll handle this! (Pause. To Lisa.) Lisa, they're out to destroy everything about our community. Our new society in which we are remaking humankind. The new, ideal person is now here. No more greed. No more selfishness. Just love and community in which all are one. Don't you see?
LISA: But what about—
JONAS: (A sneer.) 'Freedom.'
SONJA: 'Freedom' was just a word that the hoarders used to justify their exploitation.
LISA: Can you just stop?
SONJA: You think we're lecturing you, but we're not.

JONAS: Do you want to be fulfilled? Do you want to be perfectly happy? You can be. All you have to do is surrender the worst parts of yourself, Lisa. You'll be perfectly fulfilled when you seek the greater good, and when you join the people's community!

SONJA: At first, it may feel like a sacrifice.

JONAS: But that's just the old selfishness dying in you.

LISA: (Meekly.) I'm not selfish. I just want—

JONAS: '*I* want.' '*I* want.' Listen to yourself!

SONJA: We're not blaming you. All of us were forced to be selfish under the old regime. We had no choice!

LISA: (Meekly.) But that's been swept away.

JONAS: That's right. The old regime's indoctrination is no more.

SONJA: The unenlightened don't understand how lopsided things have always been. Tell me you're not one of them.

JONAS: Not one of the unenlightened! The pampered. The indulged.

SONJA: They got richer, while the rest of us tried to warn the community—

"They wrecked the story," said Davis, "worse than usual."

"Thank you, readers," said Miss Carpenter, not looking at Davis. "I need to give you a little background because of what happened the year you were born." She composed herself. All eyes were on the underweight woman. "For ten long years, since the catastrophe, the old nation was hopelessly divided. One party would win the parliament, but another would win the presidency. And because of how our system worked—didn't work, actually—the side with less votes would actually be put in charge."

"Or the side that didn't deserve to win would get a

majority, and seize power," Lane Chambers blurted. Rose looked at him, surprised, because Lane seldom said anything in English. His face quickly became blank again; it was as if Lane never had any emotions.

"That's crazy," someone muttered.

Davis's hand shot up. *I hope he doesn't endanger himself,* Rose thought. Because Davis was a loose cannon.

Reluctantly, Miss Carpenter said to Davis, "Make it brief."

"It wasn't called a parliament, then. It was a—"

"Thank you, Davis," Miss Carpenter said. She cleared her throat. "So, no one could get a clear majority. Meanwhile, half of the so-called leaders were fighting for their version of justice, but the other half were enriching themselves. And the people didn't get enough to eat. They were dying because they couldn't afford to live. So, in this re-envisioning of what was really a forgettable but strangely popular play—into this new masterpiece—the characters Sonja and Jonas are trying to convince their friend that not everyone grew up with everything. Lisa is taking luxury vacations while other people have always been cheated by bias. The few receive everything—"

Abruptly, Rose had an idea. She startled in her seat.

Miss Carpenter and several others looked at her, including the new boy, Harry Dent. Fortunately, moments ago, she'd made her expression as blank and boring as possible, as though she'd been spacing off. She projected for others: *I am the most forgettable person here.*

"So, on the surface, it looks like the old nation agrees to go its separate ways," Miss Carpenter said. "But the citizens are unhappy about the split, because we know that some of the new nations will increase their exploitation. Even so, for the first few years, citizens are allowed to move almost anywhere."

"That period was four years long," said Davis.

"But the other nations wouldn't accept people moving about," Harry Dent said bitterly.

"That's not accurate," Davis interjected.

"I'm getting to that," said Miss Carpenter said to Harry Dent, ignoring Davis.

"The rich don't like the separation," said another boy. "No more poor people to steal from."

"Right," Miss Carpenter said. "Officially, no one says you can't come—"

"—except the Island," said the second boy.

"The Island is a myth," the new boy, Harry Dent said. "It doesn't exist."

"Oh, man." Davis started laughing. "Haven't you ever seen a map before? 'The Island doesn't exist.' Do you believe every bit of garbage you see on TV?"

"No, at the time, the Island let people migrate," said someone else.

"They were rich," a second boy said. "They could take as many as they liked. But they wouldn't."

"What I mean is," Harry Dent said heatedly, "that anything good you hear about the Island is a myth."

"Nice backtrack, new kid," said Davis. "And further, I never said the Island is good. But accuracy is important. You can't say, 'The Island is a myth' just because every talking head on TV says that. Do you know that on some maps, they don't even show the Island anymore? All they show is water."

Because nearly everyone was caught up in the conversation, parroting what they'd been told in their other classes and heard on the news, Rose used the opportunity to write a coded note on a sheet of paper. Discreetly, she passed it to her right.

Miss Carpenter shrugged as if to say, *I can't disagree,* and yet also, *Shut up and let me talk, Davis.*

"They *were* rich,' Miss Carpenter said. "And, on the surface, they issued an open invitation. Millions of people did migrate."

"Suck-ers," Harry Dent said. "They probably didn't realize they weren't going to get the right to vote."

"They vote, Brainiac," Davis said. "I understand that they taught you nothing at your former school. But can't you at least read an actual book on your own?"

"Davis, that was uncalled for," said Miss Carpenter. "And let's not talk about the Island. It's a very ugly topic, and you all know what happens there."

Various people nodded, but several looked to Davis, and hoped he'd blurt out stories about the atrocities.

Abruptly, Rose grew alarmed. *Davis sees the note,* she thought. She'd hoped others would keep it hidden from him. Davis was unpredictable. He was provocative. He loved to undermine authority, but Rose never knew whose side he was going to take. *It's a wonder he's still here,* she thought, but that train of thought made her sad.

"See, it was a double game they were playing," Miss Carpenter said. "A lot of the former regions, the new nations, were two-faced. They would promise the people everything, and then make them worse off than they ever were before."

"Shocker." Davis smiled. He looked delighted. "You have two or three parties, and they all promise the same things while pretending to be different from each other. In our case, we have Holder, Thompson, the Yellows, the Blues, and other paramilitaries. They promise to steal from the rich and give to the poor, but it's all just propaganda. What you end up with is leaders with mansions, mistresses, and a disintegrating economy. And every new restriction is 'for our safety.'"

"You lump Holder in with Thompson?" Harry Dent asked.

"They put themselves together on a 'unity ticket,'" Davis replied, "when, supposedly, their parties are opposites. But they're partners, now."

"The Island has slave labor camps," Dent blurted.

"Perhaps," Miss Carpenter said to Dent. She tried to sound measured, but Rose thought Miss Carpenter looked lightheaded, like felt the discussion had plunged into dangerous waters. And she was ignoring Davis completely. *Is she pretending she didn't hear in case she gets questioned?* Rose thought.

"No, it's proven. They take the immigrants and make them do dangerous work that actually hurts the world community, and the only feed them three hundred calories a day," said Harry Dent. "If you speak up, they ship you off to a secret prison where it's worse. Do you know what the death rate is for working on one of their rigs is? One in six."

"That's an internet rumor," Miss Carpenter said. When people looked at her, she added, "I'm not defending the Island."

"Obviously not. Why-would-*anyone*-defend-the-Island?" Davis asked in a mocking singsong. The room froze. Davis was saying things that everyone—Holder, Thompson, the media, every paramilitary—had forbidden. "Especially when it's so much easier to repeat something you hear all day, every day, from every approved-of source."

How do you get away with it? Rose thought. Davis was so contrary that no one ever asked him questions about what he thought. Instead, everyone around him always changed the subject away from whatever he was talking about—or they came up with a reason to leave the room.

"Miss Carpenter is right, new kid," Davis was saying. A few people laughed at Davis calling Harry Dent, "new kid." "The-Island-is-a-terrible-place. Not-much-is-known-about-it," Davis bobbled his head in syncopation with his singsong mockery. But now he looked determined. "Some people who are addicted to lying would prefer that you not even realize it's an actual country. They airbrush it out of existence. What's next? Saxet? Are we going to just take Saxet off the maps, too? They've already removed a third of the books from the library and cleaned out YouTube."

"What are you saying?" Dent looked disgusted.

"I'm saying, you can't just assert, 'The Island doesn't exist,' and then flip on a dime and tell horror stories because you saw some fake documentary at three a.m. because you don't care about school enough to get decent sleep."

"Whatever," said Harry Dent.

The note made it three-fourths of the way around the room. Before it could reach Harry Dent, Rachel Rosendahl discreetly retrieved a black marker, and was now blotting it out.

"That's enough, Davis," Miss Carpenter said.

"It's true," he said.

"I'm not saying it isn't."

"You're not saying it is."

Miss Carpenter's chest rose, and she forgot to exhale. All Davis did all during school was read forbidden documents on his laptop that he could delete in an instant, and all he did after school was read books. Rose wondered how many of them were forbidden; if he weren't careful, they'd raid his house. Even so, he apparently knew everything; she'd heard all of the same things at home, from her parents. At least, in Davis's defense, he'd respectfully taped the official portrait of President Holder on his locker.

That's his cover story, Rose thought. Because, in person, Davis referred to the president as the world's greatest double-speaker since the 1930s.

Silently, behind her notebook, Rose watched Rachel now shred the note she had just blotted out. Discreetly, she handed half of the pieces to her left, and half to her right.

"Davis, I said that's enough," Miss Carpenter said.

"All right, all right." Davis raised his hands. Already, behind their notebooks, Rose saw several kids text the coded message to other students across the school. They were using the illegal *Dolls with Layers* app, which lay hidden behind a locked, second screen, even though it was illegal to have hidden screens. "I'm just saying as bad as this play makes them out to be, it doesn't get to the bottom of how the Island tortures and brainwashes people. And the new kid, here, isn't doing anyone any favors by reciting contested facts."

"What are you even talking about," said Harry Dent again, but he wore a strange smile.

"Because when you say things that are false, you don't help your case."

"Davis!" Miss Carpenter chastised. Davis put up both hands. Except for Mrs. Stein, Rose's teachers danced around difficult topics.

Davis was helping Rose, now; she was sure of it. He'd taken over the conversation, which would provide cover for what she wanted to do. She would have to thank him, later.

Four minutes? Sophie asked her.

Subtly, Rose shook her head.

Sophie looked back at her, confused.

You can't come, Rose communicated.

Sophie looked hurt.

I need you to keep people safe, Rose said.

"If I may shift gears and say what most commentators think," Davis began, "our problem today is the saboteurs from within. There's always a certain percentage of misfits who get greedy. They go against what our school teaches us, and what President Holder wants, which is for all of us to lift each other up in a spirit of shared sacrifice. All the misfits think about is 'me, me, me.' Things were great for them back in what they call, 'The Golden Era,'"—which was only four years ago, between the hyperinflation and the Crash— "and they wonder why they can't have it like that for themselves all the time."

"That's right," Harry Dent said.

"Amen," said Miss Carpenter, but she looked afraid to Rose. Because despite the poverty and crime most of them lived with, they were all still in a private school. Their parents had sold most of their possessions, and they'd borrowed to the hilt, but they were all in a safe institution. Rose had overheard Miss Carpenter privately tell another teacher that she felt guilty for teaching at St. Max's.

Rose raised her hand, and put that female look on her face. With relief, Miss Carpenter called on her. "May I?" she asked. Her face said: *female emergency.*

Miss Carpenter nodded, and Rose did the fast, furtive walk for the hallway.

Three...two...one...

Abruptly, the fire alarm blared, and the lights pulsed blood red. Rose jumped, and thought: *Even though I caused it.* Because that was the note she had passed asked her friends to do: use Dolls with Layers to get someone to light a match on her behalf.

As classroom doors sprang open, Rose ran past the restroom and for the stairwell, which she sprinted down in seconds.

By the time she reached the first floor, hundreds of kids were already in the halls.

"What if there are shooters outside?" someone muttered.

"Shut up about that," a senior said. He was a basketball player—one of Mark Wingfield's friends. "I saw out the window. No one's out there."

"What if—"

"Shut up!" the basketball player said, and gave the panicked boy a shove. "I'll go first and prove it to you."

Rose kept her head low, and smiled. *It's working.*

In the strobing, scarlet light, she weaved past a cluster of nervous sophomore girls—but the seniors were doing what she asked. They were shepherding the younger kids and keeping them calm.

The principal and the disciplinarian were guiding the three observers toward an exit. "Be orderly!" a voice shouted. "Single file!" But Rose saw what he was really doing: clearing a middle aisle so the old, blonde woman and her two aides could get to safety first.

Each man had a hand inside of his coat. In the infrared light, she saw their .38s glint. *With their bulletproof vests, they're ready for killers,* Rose thought.

When she approached the corner where the chapel entrance was, she shouted, "Hey!" as if she were greeting someone, and ducked around the corner.

That's my alibi, she thought. *If anyone asks, I was doing what you're not supposed to do: joining a friend, and making sure she is safe.*

Not that she believed, in their anxiety verging on

panic, that anyone was paying any attention to her.

Within thirty seconds, the first-floor hallway was clear. Then, underneath the cameras, she ran inside the empty front office, and straight to Mrs. Melnitz's desk.

Hastily, she knelt on the floor before Mrs. Melnitz's computer. Not that crouching to hide would help: Mrs. Melnitz's desk was in the center of the fishbowl, as students called the front office. Mrs. Melnitz sat behind a four-foot ledge, with open space surrounding her on every side, and her desk was in the center of a vast, open office.

Retrieving her flash drive, Rose inserted it in Mrs. Melnitz's computer. *Please, God,* she thought.

Because everyone knew Mrs. Melnitz's monitors—she had four—could display every camera at St. Max's. She hoped this system would be like Dad's, at the police station. He wasn't supposed to teach her how it worked, but he taught her a lot of things that he wasn't supposed to. He and the other SEALS, like Gretton.

Abruptly, Rose's phone pulsed. *Mom!* she thought.

Her mind made fast connections: they had a police board at home, and Mom monitored it to get real-time information about threats. She knew about every bombing and arson before half of the authorities did.

Where are you? Mom would ask, anxiously. On the board, St. Max's would pulse an terrifying red: fire.

Safe, Rose thought, but did not pick up.

Rose, pick up! Mom would be frantic.

I can't concentrate, Rose thought, and turned her phone upside down, and tried to focus—

Are you tampering *with Mrs. Melnitz's system?*

Mom, go away.

You'll be caught! You'll go to jail!

Mom! Rose yelled. She tried to stare at the screen,

tried to refocus.

We'll vanish! Think about what will happen to your little sister!

Rose closed her eyes. *What about G.J.?*

The mom in her mind's eye fell. *Nothing can be done for G.J.*

Rose pushed the thoughts away. *Precious seconds,* she thought. She felt frenzied. *Thrown away.*

She forced herself to concentrate. The flash drive finally popped up on the screen. *Thank God,* she thought, and hastily worked to display on all twelve outside cameras. From there, she rewound the recordings to an hour ago—

—and saw it.

Two very fit-looking agents, a man and a woman, each professionally dressed, were escorting G.J. Dasch out of the fire escape door near Mrs. Stein's classroom.

The man gripped G.J.'s shoulder. The woman's right hand was inside her jacket. *She has a gun,* Rose thought.

She could see only their backs. However, she had never seen G.J. so hunched into himself. Rose found herself shrinking in fear. The male agent dwarfed G.J., who was 5'10" but rail-thin. Even the female agent looked like an Olympic champion: either one could easily subdue her friend. The male agent's grip looked painful—

—and then G.J. did the impossible. He wrenched himself free, and started sprinting for the parking lot.

The woman drew her pistol. In horror, Rose's hand covered her mouth. *Don't kill him—*

But the man sprinted across the grass like a track champion, and he seized G.J.'s shoulder. With a violent twist, he hurled G.J. to the ground. Before G.J. could get up, the woman had caught up and pointed the gun between G.J.'s eyes.

Hastily, Rose dragged these recordings to her flash drive. She glanced at the clock. It was already minutes since someone pulled the fire alarm for her. She realized she really didn't know how soon someone would come back inside—or if anyone had stayed inside St. Max's.

Hurry, she whispered.

As the bar across the screen showed how fast the computer was copying the data, she watched the man yank G.J. up by his arm. G.J. winced as though the man had wrenched his arm out of his socket. Crying, G.J. raised his hands in surrender. The woman slapped him hard anyway. Rose gasped.

The computer chimed. The flash drive finished. Rose ejected it, and then entered a special code that even her father was not supposed to know.

Her fingers trembled. She hit the wrong keys, and had to delete and start over. Because she was terrified. Because if this were traced back to Dad, she knew she wasn't just risking her own life; she'd destroy her whole family. Whatever they were going to do to G.J.—wherever they were going to send him—would be far better than what they would do to Dad, and probably Mom her brothers and her sister.

They'll send us to re-education.

But if she didn't do this, she would get caught for sure. Because she'd ran right underneath the main hallway camera, and straight to Mrs. Melnitz's desk in the fishbowl's epicenter.

She pressed the keys slowly, deliberately, to avoid mistakes. When all of the screens winked out, and were replaced by code, with only a single prompt at the bottom, she read what it said, in green and black:

> Are you sure?

>

She typed "Y" and hit return.

Suddenly, Mrs. Melnitz's screen went black—as did every other computer in the fishbowl. Rose held her breath.

One, two, three…

And they all rebooted. A dozen screens rang around her, a jangle of sounds. Hastily, she sprayed Mrs. Melnitz's keyboard with the cleaner sitting nearby and wiped away her fingerprints. Then she cleaned the bottle, stuffed the rag into her pocket, and exited the front office. Soundlessly, she dashed to the chapel.

Overhead, she saw that the camera's red light was dead. Because not only had she just erased all of the video taken that day, she had disabled every camera in the school.

Inside the chapel, despite the air-conditioning, she realized she was sweating. Getting on her knees, she dabbed at her forehead. *My makeup is going to run and I'm going to look like I'm ready for Hallowe'en.*

Her eyes gravitated toward the crucifix. At first, she gazed upon the realistic, life-like worn-out Christ hanging on it, his hands and feet mutilated; blood dripping from the thorns embedded in his skin and hair. But she found herself focused on an image in the frosted walls of the chapel: that of a priest who stood between the barbed wire passageway that led into Auschwitz. *Father Maximillian Kolbe,* she knew. He offered his life in place of another whom the perpetrators had slated to die.

Within minutes, people were re-entering the school. When Rose could hear enough noise, she slipped the flash drive behind a hymnal book; she had to hide it in case anyone had seen her; in case anyone questioned her; had her frisked. Staying inside was a serious offense.

Discreetly, Rose drifted into the flow of students as they returned to their classes. No one even spared her a look; perhaps she'd reentered the school first, they thought, and went straight to the chapel. Who wouldn't want to thank God that the false fire alarm wasn't meant to lure them outside, so that a paramilitary could do to the student population what it had done to Shenanigans?

Corpses in the streets—

"No, that wasn't scheduled," the principal murmured to the old, blonde woman. In her peripheral vision, Rose saw him anxiously fidget with his tie. *A noose*, she thought.

"Um, let me check the calendar," the disciplinarian said.

"Slipshod," the blonde observer said. Rose didn't dare look at her. "Of all the days that this could happen."

"I sincerely apologize." The principal couldn't keep the worry out of his voice. "We'll review the tapes."

As Rose distanced herself and his voice faded, she felt sorry for the principal. She liked him. She hoped he could explain away the erased recordings as some kind of glitch—

—but with horror, she realized that the blonde woman might use that as an excuse for the authorities to install their own cameras.

She met Sophie on the second floor. "How did it go?" Sophie whispered to her.

Rose nodded affirmatively. *I can identify* them, she said, her lips moving without sound. *If Dad is willing to help us, maybe we can...*

She stopped, and swirled her hand in the air. Even though the cameras would be out for the rest of the day, she didn't want anyone to overhear her. Anyone could be interrogated; anyone could rat her or Sophie out. So, she let

Sophie piece together what she would have said:

Dad could help us figure out who they are, and what agency they work for. If he's willing to take the risk, he can use the city cameras to trace where they went.

"Good." Sophie broke into a wide grin. She stuck her tongue at the camera overhead, with its dead red light.

Is this what it's like in those parts of the city with no cameras? Rose thought. She felt free. She tried to keep her face blank, but a grin escaped her.

But she wiped it off her face when she saw the new boy, Harry Dent, leaning against a portrait of St. Philomena.

He was staring right at her.

CHAPTER FOUR
Secret Lives

His .44 and the bartender's .38 hidden beneath his shirt, Mark jogged the final mile to St. Max's through the runner's path. The cross-country team once used this dirt road, which twisted through a forest, which was now bright with Hallowe'en colors. They'd always stationed guards along the way, but with the rise in drug addicts camping in tents in the woods, and the night-time surge in rape and robberies, they didn't use it anymore; they ran along the road, always in packs, with no sprinters surging ahead or stragglers struggling behind.

As Mark reached the edge of the trees, Mark witnessed something he wished he hadn't:

A man and a woman in suits—looking like national security—marched G.J. Dasch to the parking lot.

Mark hid behind an oak, his hand resting on a lovers' heart carved in the trunk. Fifty-four dots made the heart, with five more as a tail, leading to a cross. In the center of the heart, the lovers had carved their initials: *W & S*. Mark had always wondered what happened to the lovers.

Please, God, make those authorities realize they've made a mistake, Mark thought, aghast. He respected G.J. a lot.

Abruptly, G.J. writhed like a wildcat, and wrenched himself free from the powerful man's grip. He tried to sprint—

—the woman's arm flashed upward, and she aimed at his back—

"No," Mark whispered to God.

The woman's arm tensed as if she were squeezing the

trigger—

—when the male agent, his muscles rippling beneath his suit, dashed with Olympic speed, a hand reaching for and soon gripping G.J.'s shoulder. The man yanked the much smaller G.J. backward, and the younger man tumbled to the ground.

The woman shoved her pistol barrel against G.J.'s forehead. "Okay," G.J. said, his hands up. From over hundred yards away, his voice was faint.

"Boy, we are doing you a favor," the woman snarled. "If you defy us, we have the discretion to put you down."

"Yes, ma'am," G.J. said.

"Elizabeth," the man said.

Elizabeth looked at the male agent resentfully, all the while grinding the pistol barrel into G.J.'s forehead.

"Get up," the male agent said, and pulled G.J. to his feet.

Resentfully, Elizabeth lowered her weapon. And then, her hand shot forward, and her fingers stabbed below G.J.'s breastbone.

G.J. sucked for air and lurched over. As his gasps turned to wrenching coughs, the man pulled him along.

"You're lucky Philip's here," the Elizabeth said. "I don't like traitors running from me."

Philip pressed a key fob, and the doors of a sleek red and gold sports car opened up. By far, it was the most expensive car that Mark had ever seen. They shoved G.J. inside the back, and a sheet of glass slid up, separating the front and the backseats. The man said something too softly for Mark to hear. Abruptly, the woman laughed hard, they climbed in, and closed the door.

Mark watched the two agents reach the end of St. Max's parking lot, exit, and drive away.

Tinted windows, he thought. *No road camera can see who is inside.* But when he looked at the cameras themselves, the telltale red lights indicating that the cameras were recording and transmitting were also shut off.

What the hell, he thought. Did the agents disable them? Of course, they wouldn't want a private institution to know who had taken G.J., but what explained why the road cameras were also deactivated?

Mark closed his eyes and pressed his forehead against the lovers' heart carved in the tree.

G.J., Mark thought with dread. They had been friends since kindergarten. They always ended up in three or four AP classes together, and they always had easy conversations. G.J. was discreet about it, but he'd given Mark plenty of tips about the flaws in the surveillance and security systems. Mark had exploited those tips all over the city.

People who go away never come back. The thought came unbidden, and it filled his heart with dread.

Please, God, let this be a mistake.

He felt stupid, with his eyes closed, his forehead pressed against a tree. Idiotically, he wondered if the couple who carved the lovers' heart were still alive.

"Go to class," he said aloud. Hastily, he hid both guns where he always did—underneath a mossy rock that sat seven steps into the woods. He carefully left the ground undisturbed. He wished he had a plastic gun that he could get past the metal detectors. He felt it was inevitable that, one day, a paramilitary would target St. Max's. *And I'll be unable to defend anyone.*

Shaking it off, Mark forced himself to jog—

—but his phone pulsed. He glanced at it, stopped, and returned to the trees. "Hi, Mom," he said.

"Mark! Thank God!"

He scanned the woods for eavesdroppers, for the hundredth time.

"So, you heard," he said, referring to what happened in Eastgate. "I'm okay. Jason's okay. He's at school."

"The news is all over the neighborhood." She hesitated, unsure of how much she should say in a call that was being recorded and stored in a database. "People are…worried."

"Yeah, well, I heard about it, too," Mark said. In that moment, he thought of something true to say that would be misleading. "But we actually took the long route."

"You took the long route?" Mom blinked. The long route didn't make sense.

"Yeah," Mark said. "There were delays. No one told us why."

When Mom furrowed her brow, her face grew wrinkles; her expression was locked in a rictus of tension. He could tell she was now wondering just how late to school both of them were…or if they had actually taken a longer route…or if they had somehow passed through Eastgate and yet remained unscathed.

"I guess a train stopped…" Mom dangled the phrase, fishing for information.

"Huh," Mark said, feigning disinterest. "Hey, can I call you later? I have class." Once more, his gaze probed the trees, looking for anyone who might be hiding.

"What are you going to do?" Mom blurted. Her urgency suddenly shifted.

He sighed. He knew what she was getting at: basketball. "Study for calculus," he said.

"What I mean is, have you decided?"

I've decided to stay out of the public eye, he thought.

"Mom, I have to go."

"Because it's your choice," she said.

He felt like smashing his phone against a tree. "You say that, but I know what you want."

"I'm not pressuring you, Mark."

"No, you just get Jason and Maria to do that for you."

"I can't control their opinions!" Mom said. "They *are* giving you a free ride to a prestigious college." She didn't add: *And that's the worst-case scenario.* The truth was—with his stats—he'd actually skip college ball and go straight to the NBA. He would either play next year, or they would develop him in Division I, and he would go pro within eighteen months.

"It isn't *free,* Mom," Mark said. But she couldn't see what little freedom they had would soon curl up and burn like paper in a fire. All she saw was an end to their immediate problems. "If you kept a closer eye on Maria and Jason, we wouldn't be in this situation."

"*Excuse* me?"

Mark regretted bringing it up, but now that he started, he couldn't stop himself. "They're both lazy."

"Maria's not lazy."

"Okay, she's not lazy, but she's going nowhere."

"Your sister works very hard."

At collecting golden pickaxes from the damned Yellows, Mark thought. He hoped to God that what he found meant nothing. Maria was too sacrificial for her own good; he could see her doing anything to save the family. Because their family couldn't even stay current on the rent for a two-bedroom ranch house located inside a flimsy fence with aging, crooked security guards in a neighborhood overdue for a government raid—

The Van Pels, hiding in that attic, for two years,

now—

"I know she does. That's not the point," Mark snapped.

"Then what is the point?"

"She works hard at the wrong things. She made straight A's in every AP and STEM class there is. Why doesn't she get a real job?"

"Because there are no 'real jobs'!" Mom said. "She applies for ten per week, and they all say, 'No one is hiring.' What do you want from her, Mark?"

"Step it up," Mark said. "I'm working. You have two jobs. She has time to apply for twenty."

"For goodness sake, Mark, there's nothing available. Stop picking on your sister."

She was right, and it frustrated him, because he couldn't say over the phone: *I found a golden pickaxe on the floor this morning, and I'm worried about her.* Not over a recorded conversation. Certain words would trigger the software, and then a human listener would review their conversation. Associating with a paramilitary was a felony.

"Fine. I'll call out Jason," Mark said. "You let him play videogames instead of study."

"Mark." Her expression was firm; Mom had composed herself. Apparently, she'd decided he was in an unreasonable mood, and she was going to be the calm one. "Your brother makes top grades."

"Taking lazy classes," Mark said. "And we still have to hound him."

"He's fourteen," Mom said. "Be grateful."

"He said that Maria is proof that school gets you a dead-end job."

She gave him that look that said, *Cool it.*

He controlled himself. She was right. He'd wasted

five minutes in the woods when he was already late, which would draw even more attention to himself.

He wished he hadn't been so foolish, long ago, playing basketball. He'd been just a naïve kid. He had no idea what trap he'd walked into.

"I have to go." He looked at St. Max's, and the nation's month-old flag, which was changed to that of Holder's party on the day after the election, as it fluttered above them all.

"Give Maria and Jason a break," Mom said.

"I will."

"I love you." But now her face grew larger; she was leaning toward the screen. *She expects me to say I'll go out. To provide for the family.* Did she really have no idea how dangerous that was? Or did she just think they could make it through all of that intact?

"I love you," he said, and clicked off.

And for no reason at all, he thought about his father. As he began running, his limbs feeling loose and fluid, his breathing easy, he nonetheless couldn't shake his dread. *If only you were here, Dad…*

Angry at himself for wasting time and getting into a pointless argument, he started jogging again, but not directly to the school. He wanted to be on the street in case the cameras came back on; he didn't want a record of himself emerging from the woods. He'd run a mile along the road to the main driveway, go to the front door, and stick with his original plan.

He began rehearsing what he would say. *I'm sorry I'm late. There was a problem with the public transportation. Jason and I took a different route than usual* —he would never admit they'd been in Eastgate that morning— *and it didn't work out.* Mrs. Clough, the attendance lady, knew he had to get his little brother to school. Mark and Jason had to ride their motorized bicycle, take the train, and transfer to a bus. The news said breakdowns were supposedly getting better, but everyone knew the truth. In any case, because he was the best basketball player and he helped around the school, Mrs. Clough gave him a lot of leeway. As he approached the road, though, he saw those cameras were dead, also. *They want what they do off the books,* his Dad's voice popped in his head.

Mark shook his head, struggling to clear it. *Maybe if I just listen to my feet slap the pavement.* But he felt shaky. His thoughts were shards and fragments, a bag of broken glass.

I'll get you, Maria, Jason, and Mom out of the country, Dad's voice said. Dad was kneeling in their kitchen, his hands resting on five-year-old Mark's shoulders. As he ran, Mark could remember how comforting his father's strong hands felt.

You left us, Mark thought, now.

The divorce wasn't my choice, Dad replied.

Honestly? Mark asked. Mom had told him stories— but more frequently, she had ducked all of Mark's questions. She didn't even tell Maria, and the two of them were very close.

Mark ran along the driveway. For just an instant, he closed his eyes, and ran blind. *I don't know what to do,* he thought. When he opened them, he ran past a stone stenciled with a Bible verse.

Things are getting worse, Dad had said, thirteen years ago. *I have to make a new home for us.*

Mark couldn't think straight.

You saw sixteen dead people yourself, Mark, a voice in his head asked. The voice sounded like his father. *You know it was an inside job.*

Mark reached the long driveway.

Sometimes, he tried to imagine what his father would tell him. It was confusing, because he seemed to remember how his dad talked from when he was little. And on their computer at home, he had endlessly watched old family videos. He'd heard his father say thousands of words.

Disappearances are up, Dad might say, *and they lie about it. On TV, the president from the so-called "liberal" party picks a so-called "moderate" from the "conservative" party to create a unity government—and despite all of their speeches about how crime is dropping, the economy is improving, and people feel a new sense of community—well, take a look around you. Is that what's really going on?*

Our country, President Holder had said on TV this week, *is the safest, most unified nation to come out of the Fracturing.*

"Mark!"

He startled—and chastised himself. He'd let himself get lost in his thoughts. He'd lost track of his surroundings.

Pretty Delilah Samson waved at him. She and Daisy Ginevra were at Delilah's red Ferrari. They had the door open. With their backs to the dead cameras, they were passing a joint.

"Delilah, Daisy," Mark said.

Delilah waved for him to come over. Reluctantly, he jogged into the lot.

"Living dangerously?" he asked.

"You know it." Delilah gestured to the joint: *You want some?*

Mark shook his head. "Basketball drug tests."

"I play, too," Delilah said, and laughed. "Drink a lot of water."

"The cameras can't see the smoke," Daisy said.

Easy for both of you to say, Mark thought. *Your parents are big donors.* And he was sure that the women also knew the red lights were out.

"Why are you so late?" Delilah asked. She had glided close; somehow, she was eight inches from him. She gazed up at him, looking intrigued. She brushed dust from Shenanigans off his shoulder; her hand lingered.

"Jason," he said.

"Did you hear?" Daisy asked. With her long, blonde curls and perfect runner's body, she was just as gorgeous as Delilah. In junior high, Mark even went out with her, but that was a long time ago, and now she was dating the team's second-best player. "There was a shooting."

"Where?"

"Eastgate." Delilah retrieved her phone. She displayed a bloody woman lying dead in the street.

Mark shuddered. The deceased was the woman who had the scar running from ear to ear. *The one with the pistol in my back.*

"It's gross," Daisy said, reacting to Mark's dismay.

A second photo: five dead Yellows, their limbs contorted unnaturally as they lay in the road, their eyes closed against Heaven.

"Horrible," Mark said.

"Society is going to Hell." Daisy took a long drag on the joint. She coughed.

"Whoa," Delilah said.

"I should get to class," Mark said.

"And miss Pottery?" Delilah playfully hit Mark's arm. Her eyes looked like frosted glass. "Mark, you are playing basketball this year, right?"

"You have to!" said Daisy.

I am getting Mom, Maria, and Jason out of this rotten

country, he thought. Mark really wanted to be on the other side of the world, but he couldn't tell Delilah or Daisy that. He hadn't even told Maria or Jason. In fact, he'd only told Mom this ambition once, and that was the one and only night that they drank the last bottle of wine in the house. Neither drank much; they hadn't had a drink since.

People who escape just end up getting robbed or enslaved. Or killed. He thought about his twenty-one-year-old sister, who was too beautiful for her own safety. *If they're lucky.*

"Basketball," Mark said.

"C'mon!" Delilah pressed both of her soft, firm hands against his chest. Delilah worked out. She was crazy attractive. Her family was very rich.

"Don't get caught, girls." He began to pull away—

—but not before Delilah pecked his cheek. Daisy pretended to look at the nation's new flag that was flapping in the wind.

"Party at my house, Friday night," Delilah called after him.

I wish I were them, he thought, jogging to St. Max's front door, *with their wall of cash that pays for their three-story mansions and layers of security.* He never talked about it, of course, but everyone believed that Delilah's parents knew both President Holder and Vice President Thompson. Powerful Mr. Samson worked hard to stay in the good graces of whoever might someday be in charge. In the meantime, his daughters drove sports cars and their foreign investments were protected.

Mark pressed the buzzer at the front door, and one of two armed men, each 6'5" and 250 pounds of muscle, buzzed him in.

Still, he thought, Delilah and her family are survivors. Her dad, ugly as a mud fence, went from business to government, getting raises the whole time. Her mom, always gorgeous, married up. Delilah had her parents' eye for prizes. *And maybe she likes me,* Mark thought, but he was under no illusions: she didn't like him for his family or personality. *She's talking herself into liking me because she thinks I have the potential to go pro.* And these days, there were no greater heroes for the nation than its Olympic athletes.

"Hey, how's our conquering hero?" Officer Matt asked him.

"How's our three-point man?" asked Officer Dan.

"Good," Mark said.

"Glue of the team," Officer Matt said.

"That's right," Officer Dan echoed. "Team captain."

Do they know something? In the school's security zone, Mark gazed at a portrait of Edith Stein, another murdered saint. With a little shock, he realized that the camera close to the portrait was turned the wrong way; it no longer faced the parking lot.

Paranoia rippled through him. Every step of the way this morning, someone had taken out the cameras: on the train. In Eastgate. In St. Max's parking lot. *That's good,* he tried to tell himself, *because I can't afford to be mixed up in what happened.* An investigation could endanger his whole family. *At least Jason will keep his mouth shut.*

"Rough day, huh?" Officer Dan glanced at the clock. Mark had missed the first two hours of school.

"You know it," Mark said. Kids were late all the time. "Did I miss anything at St. Max's?"

"No, thank God." Pete looked at his partner and shook his head.

"We like boring days," said Officer Dan.

"Thank you, officers," Mark said, took his pass, and side-stepped them.

"You take good care of yourself," Officer Matt said.

So that's how it was going to be, then, Mark thought. Because if Delilah and Daisy had bloody photos from Eastgate, that meant half of the school had seen them. And there was no way these two cops hadn't.

But, apparently, the authorities' official line of murk was going to be: *nothing happened.*

Which meant: the story wasn't going to be on the news. Discussing it would be done in whispers. *It didn't happen.*

Just like G.J. Dasch's disappearance. In fact, just like G.J. Dasch's whole existence.

Erased.

~

Skipping the last five minutes of second hour, Mark swung by Coach Bliss's first office instead, the one near the chapel and library. Decorated with banners from three national championships in four years, and countless photos of his athletes who now played for the pros, this office was really a trophy room, designed to awe visitors.

But on the back wall, in the most prominent position, Coach only had one photo: with President Holder slinging his arm around his Coach's shoulder. Coach also had one where he stood with Vice President Thompson, but he only displayed that when Thompson supporters visited St. Max's.

Keep moving, the woman with the scar across her jugular said, *or I'll kill your brother.*

Mark shuddered. *I don't have time for basketball,* he thought, peering inside Bliss's glass door. *Mom, Maria, Jason, and I have to leave this country.* He'd been weighing options for weeks now, making inquiries in the most careful way: he only dared to ask his richest friends when they were high or drunk, and not likely to remember. Sometimes, he also borrowed someone else's computer, and tried to get to illegal websites, to get information, but even when he found something helpful, within a day, the website would vanish as though the feds had taken it down.

Mark knocked, peered inside the door's window, and in the shadows, a St. Max alum and now-national athlete floated on a poster. The alum soared above ordinary people, above everyone's fears; he was a god who might someday bring glory to Holder in the Olympics. *He probably lives in a mansion with armed security*, Mark thought. *And has a jet.*

If Mark had a jet, the first time the plane traveled to a border city, he'd just keep flying into foreign airspace, and defect. *Even though they say all of our neighbors are worse*, Mark thought.

Bliss wasn't in. *I have to catch him before the assembly*, Mark thought.

The bell rang, and students populated the halls. Younger and immature kids laughed and gossiped, but older kids spoke in whispers, heads down, showing each other photos from the massacre at Shenanigans.

"Mark," Heath Grimjack bumped shoulders with him. "You okay?"

"Great."

"Delilah Samson says you arrived late."

"Jason," Mark said. It bothered him a little, how easily he lied.

"You hittin' that?" Heath asked him.

Mark frowned. *Does he mean—* "No."

"What are you waiting for?" Heath asked. "She wants you bad."

"Does she?"

Heath cracked up laughing. "Delilah and every other girl. C'mon, man."

"O-kay," Mark said sarcastically. The best way to get Heath to shut up was to mock him.

"You never tell us anything," Heath said. "When you're probably getting it twice a—"

Mark rammed his elbow into Heath's lowest rib. Heath tried to be tough and not gasp, so Mark jabbed that pressure point again. Heath winced.

"Doesn't hurt." Heath tried to sound casual, but he was pale.

"Rumors hurt people." Mark nailed Heath again, and his friend turned green. "People like you."

"Fine. You could have just asked." Heath hooked his arm, entangling Mark. Heath's eyes indicated another cluster of teenagers showing each other forbidden photos from Eastgate.

Sixteen dead before the police got there, someone whispered.

And then the police let them kill sixteen more.

Good!

No. Not good. They're choosing sides. They're with the Yellows. How do you think the Yellows got all of those guns in the first place?

The Black Zone.

The Black Zone! That's the one place without *a paramilitary. They'll kill every militia member they can find. Hell, they shoot military!*

I'm telling you, the Yellows and the Blues get their guns out of the Black Zone.

You're so full of sh—

With effort, Mark wrenched himself back to paying attention to Heath, whom he had known since kindergarten.

Heath was on track to be valedictorian. He was saying, "—half these chicks think it's the end of the world. You think they wouldn't like a roll with Mark Wingfield before doomsday?"

Mark sighed. For a valedictorian, Heath had an amazingly narrow set of interests, and they all revolved around girls and booze, neither of which he ever seemed to get anywhere near. Mentally exhausted, Mark decided to destroy this conversation. He pulled Heath close as they reached their third hour class. "Between the two of us," he whispered, "there is someone I like."

"Who?" Heath asked eagerly.

Mark shook his head at Heath. "If I tell you, can you keep it to yourself?"

Heath was nodding vigorously. Meanwhile, Mark smiled pleasantly as three girls walked past him and Heath, and entered Mr. Mosley's classroom. They genuinely smiled back. In his peripheral vision, when he made eye contact with the first, he observed that the second looked him up and down. Mark waited for them to go inside, and then turned back to Heath.

Heath, however, was checking out the girls. "Every girl," he murmured. "Every girl wants you."

Mark's fingers stabbed Heath's rib, right in the bruise. Even as Heath winced, he didn't stop grinning. "If you found your dream girl," he said discreetly, "can you send the rest of them my way?"

Shaking his head, Mark ushered Heath into calculus.

Their instructor was forty-three, bald, aerobically fit, and always revved up. He skipped the prayer, got their attention, and said, "What I'm about to show you could be disturbing."

Here we go, Mark thought. *One of his tangents.* Mosley

was always showing them videos that told them what to think and how to live.

Mosley pressed a clicker. The lights dimmed, and a picture of a cold, blood-encrusted hand filled the screen. A senior girl gasped.

"I've been saying this all day to every class," Mosley barked, "because you deserve to know: these photos are a masterful fraud."

Several people murmured. Mark sat absolutely still.

Mosley slowly zoomed out. The hand belonged to a man's corpse, his blue shirt stained with two gigantic Rorschach inkblots of blood, like a splatter pattern against a wall at a crime scene.

As Mosley got closer to revealing the face, the girl across from Mark was trembling. Mercifully, Mosley stopped at the neck.

"It's a fraud," Mosley said. "I can prove it to you."

Mark recognized the corpse's build. This was the man who'd chased them onto the roof at Shenanigans before he, Jason, Matt, and Shannon leapt across the open air to Cabaret. He had the same sickle tattoo, and the same bulky torso. His thick arm hair was now matted with dark, dried blood.

"Photoshopped." With a laser pointer, lingered on each of six bullet holes in the man's shirt.

I wonder what his name is, Mark thought. He felt depressed. He thought of the golden pickaxe on Mom's kitchen floor that morning—the sign of someone who belonged to the Yellows—and he worried all over again, feverishly, about what his sister, Maria, might be entrapping herself into.

"Why would anyone fake this?" Heath's voice came out of the darkness.

"Good question." In the darkened classroom, Mosley's face basked in the reflected silvery light from the screen. "Because they want you afraid."

"Who? Holder?" a girl asked.

"*No.*" Mosley looked at the girl with stark disbelief, and she shrank back. "People against the authorities." He switched his tone, and gave them his I'm-confiding-in-you expression. "We all know our society has gone through hard times, although you've had it easy compared to the previous generation. But it's been hard ever since you were born."

"Yeah, but this is nothing compared to what happened during the Fracturing," said Heath.

"Exactly!" Mosley said forcefully, which had the effect of shutting Heath down, for which Mark was grateful. He didn't need Heath's version of what had happened long ago. "They want you to feel afraid. But crime has been falling every year since you were born."

Mosley pressed the clicker, and the screen flashed to a downward graph.

B.S., Mark thought.

"But why would people *do* this?" the girl asked again. Mosley waited, but she didn't speak.

"Do what?" Mosley barked.

The girl didn't want to talk.

Mosley stood. Everyone's eyes were on him as he stood perfectly still, his body language authoritative, his glare probing each person in the room.

"Everything's going to be all right," he said in his comforting baritone.

"The photos…"

"The photos are fake. I know the freshmen are sending them all around the school. It's horrible thing, what people are doing to our delicate fourteen-year-old children.

People are sending each other grotesque photos, with no regard for who they're frightening. For no reason! It's malicious. That's why I just showed you that the photos are fake."

You showed us nothing, Mark thought.

"I just demonstrated that crime is going down. That chart was published in *The Era.* It was verified by the state and national governments."

"But who would *lie* to us this way?" Ruth Weinstein. She was on the verge of tears—

—and as convincing as she seemed, Mark had the strangest intuition that she was crying about something else. *Doesn't she...*

Didn't she date G.J. Dasch last year? Before Rachel Rosendahl? he thought.

"Listen." Mosley said very calmly. He had a deep bass voice like a late-night radio psychologist who sought to soothe the masses. "Things are turning in the correct direction, and a few people who have always benefited from mayhem don't like that. This city—this whole country—is becoming enlightened. Crime is down, education is up, the economy gets better every year, and that makes selfish people very angry."

"Why didn't they just leave ten years ago?" Heath asked.

"Because they had it better here." Mosley dismissed the selfish, angry people with a wave. Then he changed his composure back to the strong father explaining things to his children. "Listen: you're the seniors of this school." All eyes were on him. "I need you to be leaders. I need you to show your classmates and the younger kids that these photos are a malicious con. I wouldn't be surprised if—"

Picturing the man shot in front of him, and how Jason

could have been killed, Mark couldn't take it anymore. "Mr. Mosley's right," he interrupted.

Everyone stared at him.

"You know what I'd do if I wanted to cover up a massacre in Eastgate. After all of the people died and the police mopped up the last of the paramilitaries, I'd release hundreds of photos myself."

Clearly confused, Mosley opened his mouth, and closed it.

"Mildly doctored photos," Mark said. "So easy to do with software. Take real photos of bodies, add one photoshopped bullet wound, and then people will say the whole thing is fake. And put out crime statistics that say murder is down when in fact it's up."

Mosley's hands shot to his hips. "Just what are you saying?" he barked.

"I'm saying you're right," Mark said in a calm, level tone. "Everyone can see that. We can tell these photos are fake. There was no gun battle."

"Right—" Mosley began.

"But if there were," Mark raised his voice, "I'd flood everyone's phone with photos with just one false detail apiece so that anyone who examined them could claim they aren't real."

Mosley clearly wasn't following, but a boy behind Mark stifled a laugh. Ruth Weinstein looked at Mark with a shocking amount of gratitude, as if to say, *Finally.*

"The key facts revealed by the photos appear to be authentic," Mark repeated. In the darkness, he could see kids suppressing smiles. They knew he was challenging the official line. "That's what they *want* you to believe."

Mosley stood ramrod still, like a soldier you saw on the news, a Grand Marshall leading a parade in the Capitol.

"Yes," he said. "And I'm counting on *you* to help calm this school down. Because whoever put these out there is very selfish."

"Absolutely, sir," said Heath. "Selfish people are bad."

"Thank you," Mosley said. "Because—"

Abruptly, an alarm blared. Ruth Weinstein gasped and knocked several pencils onto the floor. As red light flooded and pulsed, and the kids startled, Mosley gripped his clicker, and the screen flashed to a photo of three bloody corpses sprawled half-on, half-off the curb, their limbs bent unnaturally.

When Ruth Weinstein shrieked, Mark whispered to her, "It's all right."

Hastily, Mosley sent the bloody image away. His desktop appeared, and the class saw his neurologist wife, three young children, and golden retriever, all outside of his three-story house, inside of the gated community, Weissensee.

"It's okay," Mosley's deep bass voice boomed. "It's a routinely scheduled fire alarm."

"We'll probably step outside and get shot," Ruth murmured.

"Stick with me," Mark whispered.

"Follow along!" Mosley shouted. He swung open the door and led the class into the second floor hallway. Sunlight streamed in through the bulletproof glass wall even as the alarm blared and red lights flashed.

"Walk calmly. Walk *quickly*!" shouted the school's disciplinarian, a white-haired man who played rugby thirty years ago. The younger kids were afraid of him.

Everyone is on the verge of panic, Mark thought. The walls were getting overcrowded because the kids weren't moving toward the stairs.

"Outside," the disciplinarian shouted.

"Go, go, go, *go!*" barked Mosley.

Straight into a shooter, Mark thought. In the strobing light, painting people's faces, some kids were freaking out, while others trembled in place, frozen in a rictus of fear. But Mark noticed that many seniors were actually gently placing their arms around the younger kids, and talking to them gently.

"Teachers first!" yelled the disciplinarian.

Mark saw Mosley reach the steel door that led downstairs to the back quadrangle, which he knew was empty, because the second floor hallway's entire right-sided wall was made of glass, and they could see the quadrangle from the second floor. But Mark thought, *there is no way I am going outside.*

He felt ashamed of himself, but as his classmates reached the bottom of the stairwell, and Mosley bravely opened the door, held it, and yelled, "Now, now, now, *now!*" Mark saw something he dreaded for the third time that day: the red dot on the above, monitoring camera, suddenly went out.

They aren't recording what happens next, he thought. His mind scrambled: it was a blur of thoughts about Mom, Maria, and Jason. *Who will protect them?*

He made an impulsive decision. As his classmates reluctantly stepped outside, past Mosley's wind-milling arm—and nothing happened—Mark slipped down a darkened hallway. It led deeper into the school.

Not going outside.

He'd find a closet. The most important thing, he believed, was protecting his family, and that meant staying alive, not following the rules.

Terrified amidst the klaxons and light that painted him, Mark glanced up against the camera. It was still off.

If the camera turns back on —

He didn't finish the thought. Because he'd be caught evading fire alarm protocol. For anyone other than a star basketball player, that would get you two weeks of out-of-school suspension. Worse, the police would get involved because, these days, it was a crime, and it came with hundreds in fines. Even for him, there would be a hushed-up investigation.

They'll interrogate me. They will want to know why. They'll probe everything I've ever done.

He knew where he was going: a janitor's closet. He'd hide out until this was over. He'd think long and hard about where he could get a plastic gun, the type that the metal detectors couldn't pick up. More importantly, he'd seriously work to get his family out of this country —

What the hell?

Forcing himself to stop suddenly, he lurched, and nearly tripped. By the edge of the chapel, he yanked himself backward. He hid behind an oak wall.

Someone's in the fishbowl, he thought.

He got his breath under control from the sprinting. He wiped sweat off his forehead. He dared to look.

A blonde senior girl was at Mrs. Melnitz's computer. *Rose Scholl.*

Mark pulled back, lest she look up and see him.

What is she doing?

In the shadowy gloom outside the chapel, he peeked again. Her fingers were flying. And then she hesitated —

She's going to look up —

He pulled back. Hidden and plastered against the wood, his arms outstretched. Maybe she had that creepy feeling of being watched.

Because whatever she was doing, she obviously wasn't supposed to be doing it.

Suspicions flew through his mind, each wilder than the last.

He liked Rose; he'd known her since kindergarten, at St. Mary's. They both were friends with G.J. Dasch. Like his family, her family was poor; he had no idea how she afforded this school. *Maybe she's stealing money right now.*

He glanced at the camera's red dot bulb. *Still dead.*

Whatever she was doing, she was taking advantage of the firm alarm, and the cameras being off. *That* was gutsy—had she known this was going to happen? Because a fire drill only lasted seven to ten minutes. Did she have it timed? And how did she know the cameras would be off?

Unless she turned them off.

And as fast as her fingers moved, she clearly had gotten into Mrs. Melnitz's system, which had access to every system in the entire school.

Panting, Mark wanted to glance at her again and search her face for clues, but he needed to not stare, because he didn't want to alert her.

Rose was smart; he knew that. She moved in different circles than he did: he with the athletes, she with the theatre crowd, although they both took AP classes. She was also cautious: Mark had never seen her lose her cool. She could act just like any other girl, but mostly, she flew below the radar. She never said anything too interesting. And yet, her peers hung on her every word. They followed her lead—even though she never appeared to be leading at all. *She leaves no fingerprints,* he thought.

For a fraction of a second, he peeked one more time. Thirty yards away, her fingers were flying.

How did she break into Mrs. Melnitz's computer? he thought. *Wouldn't the school secretary have the most sophisticated encryptions of anyone at St. Max's?*

The puzzle pieces came to him: Rose's father was a cop. In fact, he was a former SEAL. He walked through dangerous neighborhoods; Mark had seen photos of him after an ugly fight. Rumor had it he singlehandedly took down three armed men at four a.m. just this year. His left arm had a burn mark and he had a scar along his neck from a bullet. He was fearless and smart.

Did he teach Rose how to hack into the school's private system?

And maybe Mark was wrong, but now that he thought about it, he wondered why Rose always appeared to be vigilant and agile. Like a top athlete, she had situational awareness. Her attention was never casual; she was always surveying her surroundings. In any room, she always seemed to locate herself between two exits.

What exactly did her father teach her?

Mark peeked. Abruptly, he saw Rose spring to her feet. He yanked himself backward. He couldn't tell, but it looked like Rose's hand reached to the side of the keyboard, and then shot to her pocket. *Is that a flash drive?*

Hoping she hadn't seen him, he slipped inside the chapel. His thoughts still not coalescing, he gazed at the crucifix.

A man bleeding out, his limbs pinned down, his life not his own…

The chapel door was opening. Frantically, Mark crouched behind a marble pedestal that elevated a statue of St. Stephen.

Wedged between the chapel's stenciled glass wall and a marble pedestal, Mark caught the entrant's reflection in the chapel's glass wall:

Rose Scholl.

Why did she come in the chapel?

Terrified she would see him, watching her in the reflection, he hunched down until he couldn't see her. *If I can't see her, she can't see me.*

At least, he hoped that was true.

And yet, he couldn't help but peek. She had her eyes closed. She was praying.

And then, abruptly, the klaxons ceased, and the red lights in the hallways died. The ordinary lights came back on. But on the camera overhead? The red dot stayed off.

Mark watched Rose make the sign up of the cross and stand up as though nothing had happened. She even genuflected before zipping to the exit.

When she opened the door, Mark heard the conversations of other kids. Now was the time to not get caught out of place. He hurried to join the crowd.

His goal was to make it back to calculus without anyone paying any attention to him. Taking the hallway from which he came, he quietly blended into the hundreds of students filtering in. No one asked him anything.

The cameras above were still dead. When they didn't reboot, Mark suspected that meant they were down for the count.

Rose, he wondered, *how did you do all of that? And why did you do it?*

When she disappeared up the stairs, her blonde hair swaying, he thought, *Rose can help my family.*

She's our way out.

CHAPTER FIVE
Gatherings

Rose dreaded all-school assemblies, and today was worse than usual. St. Max was delaying the start of fourth hour today, and sending kids to the gym. Stone-faced, she met up with Sophie, and they followed hundreds of kids down the hall, past the chapel, and when they neared the fishbowl, she made her expression as bland as possible.

Her heart was racing.

I want to run to the woods. But what good would it do?

But she kept walking, even though she would have to pass within inches of the old woman in the pantsuit and her two male assistants.

If anything, the conversations around her seemed noisier than usual today, as students seemed energized: perhaps by the fake fire alarm they had executed. They were laughing and jostling each other, even though the cameras were back on.

The principal was standing near the blonde. "We're looking into it," he said. He was forty years old, married, and had six children. He'd gone to St. Max's as a teenager, and spent his entire life in private schools.

"You don't have a backup system?" the blonde said.

"Did you ever think about tennis?" Sophie asked Rose, a bit too loud. She ramped up without waiting for an answer. She could tell Rose was listening in on the authorities' conversation, and she was supplying cover.

"We do," the principal said. "I don't have all of the details yet. We're already investigating what happened."

You had complete shutdown, Rose thought. *Because*

before I erased every recording across the school since six a.m., I also unleashed a virus that will keep the system off until you find and stop it.

"This is unacceptable." The blonde frowned.

"I'm having Chloe look into it." the principal dabbed bubbles of sweat on his forehead. "She's our IT—"

"I know who she is," the blonde snapped, "because I have a list of everyone who works or attends here, and what they do. We'll send in our people to help her."

Rose's heart skipped a beat. She'd erased everything—but what if she hadn't? *They'll make me disappear.*

"Do you know what's happening in the Capitol?" the blonde asked.

The principal's hands floated upward helplessly and he shook his head.

"They arrested six traitors near a construction site where the president was giving a speech." She scowled. "He was announcing a public works program, and creating millions of jobs, and the Blueshirts got in, somehow."

They'll investigate Dad, Gretton, and all of their friends, Rose thought. *Because of me. They'll catch me and investigate them.*

"Is everyone all right?" the principal asked.

"Yes, thank goodness," she said. "All six of them were shot before they could do anything."

"I'm sorry to hear that," he said reflexively.

She looked at him severely. Ten feet past them, now, Rose strained to hear.

"They would have killed the president."

"Did they get off a shot?"

"No. You can thank a secret service sniper for that."

Rose couldn't hear anymore. She whispered to

Sophie, "I want to go home."

Sophie nodded. They sat along half-court, three seats up, near the center of everything, where they would be overlooked. She hunched, her shoulders and chin collapsing into her body.

What would you do? Sophie's eyes asked.

Rose shielded her lips so only Sophie could see them. *Bust into the police net,* she said soundlessly. *Use facial recognition software to identify G.J.'s captors. And then try to learn where they took him.*

But Rose feared that even if she get into the police's system, they wouldn't know where G.J. was.

Sophie gave her a hug. "These sports assemblies are a waste of time."

Rose laughed ruefully. "That's what they wanted to do when they were children: grow up and waste other people's time."

"Well, they don't want us in a real history class," Sophie began, "where we might just learn—" She caught herself in time and shut up.

"St. Max Ava*laaaaanche!*" the principal exclaimed. He stood center court, a microphone making his voice boom. "Let's begin with a prayer."

Safely hidden among a thousand students, Rose glanced at the blonde observer, who stood along a wall. She stared impassively as the principal began.

"Dear Heavenly Father, we thank you for the gift of this community. We thank you for every person. We ask you to watch over each of us—"

The blonde was whispering to her assistant. Rose was looking right at the principal—but paying attention to her peripheral vision. She was struggling to read the old woman's lips, but the woman had shielded them. Frustrated,

Rose forced herself to pray.

"Do you think Mark Wingfield will play basketball?" Sophie asked.

"Yes," Rose said. "No. I don't know." Rose had heard the rumors. Mr. Star Athlete mentioned to one friend that he might need to get a job to help pay the rent. That "friend" had then told half of the team and a girl he was trying to impress, and the story flew around the school.

"Why do you care?" Rose asked. Mark was the last person on her mind; she was thinking about G.J.

"I don't know," Sophie said.

"You don't even like basketball."

"I go to the games."

"So you can flirt," Rose said. "You don't watch the court."

"I watch the halftime show," said Sophie. "I think he'll go out."

"He has to," Rose said. She shielded her lips from others. *It's how he pays his and Jason's tuition.*

Sophie's eyebrows shot up. *Don't say that.*

Rose shrugged. She was friends with Mark until junior high, when they drifted apart. They ran in different crowds, and she didn't like his crowd: a bunch of strutting boys who thought they were destined to go pro. She especially didn't respect the girls who hung on them.

Mark was different; he always appeared very heavy-hearted to her; she knew he worked hard for his family. Even so, they seldom spoke, anymore.

Rose closed her eyes and deeply concentrated. When she finished, she opened her eyes and said to Sophie, *Help me think of a way to go home early.*

Just walk out of an assembly? Sophie asked, incredulous as the drumline drowned out most conversations, and a dozen dancers center floor kicked up their legs.

I want to find out where he is, she said.

Sophie's eyes widened. She knew Rose meant G.J.

The dozen dancers formed a heart, which morphed into a butterfly. The peppy music mocked Rose's crashing mood.

Sophie didn't ask, *Did you see what happened to him?* She didn't need to ask.

Rose nodded.

Sophie and Rose both looked at the smiling dancers with sorrow. *Female trouble,* said Sophie.

I used that this morning.

No one will ask! Sophie said.

After everything that's happened today? Rose said. *If they suspect anything, they'll interrogate every person I came into contact with.*

Sophie hesitated. The dancers appeared to beam at both of them. Rose couldn't help but think about how several of them threw themselves at Mark Wingfield. And how girls like Delilah Samson hit the gym every day to make themselves attractive to him, even though she told everyone how much she hated exercise. All because, in six months, Mark Wingfield might be nationally known. Rose studied the dancers, and glanced at beautiful, rich Delilah, and thought, *He doesn't stand a chance.*

Your mom is sick, Sophie said. *You have to help her*

Rose shook her head. Her mom was very fit; with four kids, she didn't have time to be sick. The administration knew this.

Your dad called you out, Sophie said.

Why? Rose asked.

I don't know. Text him. Have him make up a reason.

Rose shook her head. *He thinks the safest place in the*

city for me is to be here.

Sophie sighed, the dancers finished, and the emcee cried, "Give it up for the daaaance *teeeeeeam!*"

When the applause faded, Coach Bliss took the microphone. "Thanks, Rufus. That was terrific ladies," he said. Bliss was a forty year old with red hair and a still-athletic build with long muscles that flowed and rippled beneath his suit and tie. "We're going to do something I've never done before. I want my athletes to join me—right here, right now. Nash! Lamar! Malone! Toby! Come down here."

Four boys, each at least 6'4", sprang from the front row. *Fast, flexible, and ripped,* Rose thought. Since birth, they ate better food than almost everyone else.

"Barq. Chuck. Pip. And—Mark Wingfield!"

An eruption of emotion as half of the teens shot to their feet and cheered like they'd won the championship. The whole performance looked staged to Rose because the band played what they called "The Standing Ovation Song." At this cue, instinctively, everyone around them jumped to their feet and cheered. Rose craned to see Mark's face. Instinctively, she looked where he liked to hide out: behind a crowd of unpopular kids nicknamed the tax collection agency. As people searched for him, Rose memorized the look on his face:

Dread.

As people pushed him to stand, he looked like a man who was suddenly handcuffed and forced to walk where he did not want to go. For an instant, Rose forgot all about Delilah Samson and the other girls who threw themselves at Mark Wingfield. Yes, their peers adored him, thousands would see this video later, and marvel hungrily at the lifestyle he was promised. Authorities would force teachers to give him A's; the government would open doors for him.

And yet, a complex story played out over his face. But before Rose could figure it out, he masked what he was feeling.

What are you thinking, Mark Wingfield? Rose asked herself.

She closed her eyes, and replayed back what she had just seen. *What did I see?*

Resentment.

Was that possible? *Aren't they giving him everything?*

She wondered, *What is underneath the resentment?*

She opened her eyes.

Fear.

Rose tried to understand what happening to Mark. On the surface, it looked like they were handing him a golden future; he had a shot at being a national hero. But Rose realized:

He feels used. He knows all of this talk about how much they love him—well, they don't love him. They'll use him, pump him full of drugs so he can play even when he's hurt, and he'll live under a microscope. He will live in a golden cage. And when he's no longer useful to them?

Well, she thought, *what do they do to everyone else who is no longer useful to them?*

Lost in thought, Rose startled. A man was *touching her sleeve.*

The principal, Dr. Clark, was leaning next to her. Sophie had gone so milky pale that she looked like she'd be sick.

"Rose, would you please come with me?" he asked.

Run!

"What—what's this about?"

"Don't worry. Everyone in your family is okay. Just come with me."

Follow him, Rose told herself. *And when you're in the hallway, sprint for the door—*

Against her will, Rose found herself standing. She didn't look at Sophie because she feared one or both of them would cry. She took note of the school's five cops, who each stood by different exits, their .44s in their holsters. Dr. Clark discreetly led her past a thousand kids. A ripple of fear shot through six seniors in the crowd—Rose saw their fear because she knew—*knew!*—they worried she'd rat them out for their role in the fake fire alarm.

She fought off feeling dazed as she and Dr. Clark entered the hallway. By the exits, the old, blonde woman's two assistants stood whispering to each other in the center of everything as though they owned the school. They weren't discreet: they were arguing about paramilitary deaths in the Capitol that morning, how the media accidentally broadcast some footage, and which of the illegal YouTubers broadcast the events. Rose stopped listening; she couldn't concentrate. She eyed the nurse's corridor, and the exit to the parking lot beyond—

—where she'd witnessed G.J. being dragged away—

If I run, I could make it to my car—

Maybe. But that wouldn't work. They'd just arrest her on the highway.

"How's your dad?" Dr. Clark asked.

"Good." They passed the nurse's corridor. Rose noticed that the eye in the sky's red light was still dark. Apparently, the system was still down.

"Still walking the beat?" Dr. Clark sounded easy, casual.

He's an actor, too, Rose thought. Forlornly, she passed the nurse's corridor. Even though running was a bad idea, it was the only idea she had.

"I'm not sure what he does exactly all day." Rose hated to lie. So far, she hadn't.

"Well, I know he used to have street time," Dr. Clark said. His voice stayed relaxed, as though they were strolling and he had nothing in particular on his mind.

"I think it's a combination of things," Rose said. *A meaningless answer.* But she felt something horrible shift inside of her: she felt that there was a huge chance that wherever Dr. Clark was taking her, she wasn't coming back. *All I can do now,* she thought, *is try to protect Mom, Dad, Elisa, Hans, Warner, and Inge.*

She vowed to tell Dr. Clark nothing. She'd tell the old, blonde woman nothing. Wherever they took her, whatever they did to her, even if they tried to force her to comply, well, her father had taught her how to say nothing.

"How's your mom?" Dr. Clark unlocked his office.

"Great," Rose said.

"And your brothers and sisters?"

"Fine," she said. "Dr. Clark, what is this about?"

"I just like to hang with all of my students a bit. We haven't really spoken much since your junior year."

Rose furrowed her brow and struggled to remember if she'd ever had a heart-to-heart with Dr. Clark.

"You're about to graduate." He led her into his office, which was half of the size of her kitchen at home. Compared to a public school, the St. Max offices were tiny, and the décor was dated. When her parents went to St. Max's, it was a wealthy prep school. Now, it was held together with rubber bands and duct tape.

"Have a seat," he said in his friendly, energetic, innocent voice. She remained standing. When he closed the door, she wondered if it locked behind him.

Maneuvering around her, he sat down. His desk was

between them. Her heart racing, Rose soaked in the whole room. She could seize a Mont Blanc pen off of his desk and pierce his side with it if she had to. Or seize a decorative railroad spike off the wall and—

Abruptly, his expression lost all of its energy, and he looked sad and defeated. Suddenly, now that he was out of the hallway, with its dead cameras and the occasional person who wasn't at the assembly, he wasn't an actor anymore. The bags under his eyes now jumped out at Rose.

Dr. Clark picked up a photo of his family. For a moment, Rose thought he wanted to show him his tiny children, and tell her how much they meant to him. He seemed vulnerable to her. But instead of speaking, he pointed to a kill switch in the wall. He flipped it, and then pointed upward:

The red light on the camera overhead, which was on a separate system, went dead.   Rose's eyebrows shot up.

"We can speak freely," he said.

Can we? she thought.

"They're off," he said. "I wouldn't lie to you."

Her worry spiked. Mentally, she disciplined herself. With effort, she controlled her breathing. She needed to portray a worried girl, a straight-A student who had never been in this situation, so she put an anxious look on her face.

"Trust me, Rose," Dr. Clark said.

"Dr. Clark?" Rose's voice trembled. "Is my family okay?"

"They're fine!" He looked startled. "As far as I know. Why? Did you hear otherwise?"

"I—I don't feel comfortable here," she blurted, changing the subject. Her gaze darted everywhere. In his family photo, he and his wife relaxed in an idyllic meadow, surrounded by their six young children, each three years apart. His wife, Hazel Clark and four of their children had sandy hair; only Dr. Clark and a ten-year-old boy had black hair. "I want to leave."

"Nothing bad is going to happen. We just need to talk." He lay both palms flat on his desk.

"You haven't said—said why I'm here." She let her voice tremble.

He showed her both of his palms. But Rose didn't really believe all of the recorders were off. The camera's dead light meant nothing.

"Rose, you're special." She must have looked horror-struck because he rapidly added, "What I mean is, you're influential."

"No, I'm not."

"You are—"

"I have no leadership positions," she said. "I participate in choir and not much else." She didn't mention *theatre* or *improv*.

"Please let me finish," he said. "People imitate you. They act like you, talk like you, and look to you. You hint, they follow."

Rose contorted her face to say, *That's the most bizarre idea I've ever—*

"Rose, you know that St. Max is under crushing pressure."

She nodded. The school's debt only increased, and if it weren't for a few big donors, it would close. And one of those donors had just been arrested.

"The press publishes what they think is an expose every other week. They insinuate that we're hoarding the best teachers and most qualified students. They believe that despite all of the charity we do, we're an affront to the people's community because we're distinct."

Rose didn't dare nod, even though her parents said all of the exact same things. *I don't want a video of myself agreeing with these unpopular but common ideas—*

"When I started teaching as a naïve, fresh-out-of-college, idealistic history teacher—" From a premier Catholic college, now closed—"I really felt we were going to improve the world. In college, we read dozens of books like *Walden*, and had all-night discussions of how we would persuade the rich to share with the poor. We were going to clean up the culture. We wanted to insure dignity for every person, no matter what race, sex, identification, or creed. We were starting society all over again."

Dr. Clark's gaze had drifted to his family photo, and he lapsed into silence. Ten slow, agonizing seconds passed. When Dr. Clark gazed back at Rose, he looked inexpressibly sad.

Noble goals, she almost said. But she wondered: *is he trying to get me to feel sorry for him?*

Because his college dreams weren't any different from what President Holder or Vice President Thompson were saying, even though they came from opposite parties, had nothing in common, and were on a unity ticket whose only pledge was to keep the nation together. *Everyone says the same things,* Rose thought. *Dr. Clark, the whole St. Max community, and all of our officials. They all pretend to want the same things, even though they never say what they want to do to us until the last minute.*

"Rose, our school and the larger community is on the edge."

She put an appropriately worried look on her face.

"The recorders are off," he repeated.

"Why did you turn them off?" she asked.

"You don't believe me," he muttered.

She said nothing.

His eyes lingered on his wall of meaningless awards. In the past, his medals and certificates symbolized something, but now they were just iron discs and sheets of paper. "Rose, someone you and I both admire and love is in dire trouble."

She pictured: G.J. wrenching himself free from the agents in suits. But the man sprinted after him, gripped his shoulder, and yanked him backward. G.J. stumbled to the ground, and the woman stalked toward him, and pointed her pistol between his eyes.

"Who?"

"Do I really have to say?"

You said we can talk freely, she said, her voice very soft, her face tilted down because she did not believe the camera.

He grimaced. She could read his face: he wanted her to read his mind. He wanted her to say everything out loud. And then he wouldn't need to risk anything; he wouldn't even nod. He'd just give her a look, and then she would do what he wanted, and, if there were any consequences, he would be able to deny that this conversation ever happened.

She wasn't going to play along. "I really don't know what you're talking about."

"I'm talking about our whole community, and what it needs. You do care about St. Max and the thousand students who go here, don't you, Rose?"

"Of course."

"You know what a lifeline this community is for thousands of alums, don't you? If we close, your friends won't just lose a safe school and a good education. Some people will lose their only protection from…"

The larger society, she finished for him. "How close are we to closing?" she asked.

He held his finger and thumb a millimeter apart. "I want you to think about it: we're not just talking about what some people say is the only real school in the city."

She nodded. If Harry Dent were any indication, the national schools didn't believe in accuracy of any kind.

"As flawed as we are, what would you say if I told you we were the only school dedicated to teaching upper level math or science? Where in English, we read real books, and not state-approved rewrites? Where in history class—"

We teach what actually happened, she thought, thinking of Mrs. Stein.

"The world grew dark since I was a child, Rose." He glanced at his family photo. For an instant, he looked lost in thought. His gaze appeared to linger on each of his children's photos, and he appeared to grow increasingly worried. "This school is a tiny candle in the midst of a very long night. But a candle we are. And eventually, all nights come to an end."

She said nothing.

"But in the meantime, Rose, I need you to persuade Mrs. Stein to cancel that play."

"*Helen Keller*?" Rose asked.

"No, not the official school play." Dr. Clark frowned at her, and she realized she'd feigned a little too much ignorance. "You know which play I mean: the off-campus play."

"I have no control over Mrs. Stein," Rose said.

"You can influence her."

"She won't listen to me."

"Rose, do you want them to take her?"

"Take her *where*?" She was thinking of G.J.

He suddenly lost color, and his look became accusing, as if to say, *Why would you ask me that?* "Just tell her to call it off, Rose."

"Dr. Clark, I'm just a high school senior," Rose began. "She's an award-winning director, playwright, actress, and teacher. Assuming she even is involved in a...*forbidden* play...why would she listen to me?"

He visibly wrestled to control himself. Against her will, Rose shrank back, her hands instinctively hovering, discreet but ready for anything. *If he attacks me, I will punch his jugular, bend his wrist backward, force him to the ground, knock him out, and slip out the door—*

He'd gotten control of himself. "I think you've played dumb enough. Do you care about Mrs. Stein?"

"Of course."

"And your peers?"

"I love the students here."

"And their parents?" he asked.

"I love the St. Max community," she said, "*and what it stands for.*"

He frowned. "And what does it stand for?"

"It stands for freedom of conscience," she said, "and all of the other things that support that."

He was visibly wrestling with himself. Because he knew what she was implying: a few people dared whisper about the old set of rights that their school depended on, that Vice President Thompson reverently touted, like freedom to gather as a group, freedom to think for yourself, and freedom to defend yourself.

Rose watched Dr. Clark force himself to be patient. "We have to have solidarity," he said. "We have to think about the whole community."

Rose said nothing.

"If Mrs. Stein doesn't call off that play, she's going to force me into a choice I don't want to make."

Rose raised her eyebrows.

"If forced to choose between her and the community," Dr. Clark said. "I will fire her. By tomorrow. And it will be for her own safety."

"You can't do that," Rose said.

"I'll have to."

"She'll sue," she said. "For…for…" The words wouldn't come.

"Wrongful termination?" he asked. "No, she won't. She doesn't have the money to hire a lawyer. And if she forces me to do that, then she'll finally understand how I'm trying to help her."

"*Help* her?"

He sighed. "It's simple, if you think about it. She can cancel the play, keep her job in a bad economy, and we can fend off the inspectors for a little longer."

"Until they think of something else. They don't like her Holocaust class."

He ignored that point, and continued: "Or she can be selfish—and you can be selfish—and she can 'make a statement.' A statement that—no matter how much I admire it—just puts a target on our backs."

"I thought we were already a target."

He stood up, apparently not able to contain himself. "Rose, I get that you're well-read, and that your father's a cop, and you know more about how the system used to work than most people. But I am asking you right now to stop arguing with me and think about Mrs. Stein and the fact that she is handing the people who want to shut us down everything they need."

"So, Mrs. Stein doesn't get freedom of expression. But Vice President Thompson says we have freedom of speech."

He grimaced at her. They both knew she was being

sarcastic.

"It's a historically accurate play."

He took a step to his left as if he wanted to maneuver around his desk and confront her, and then pulled back.

"You were telling me about your idealism in college," she said. "Are you saying that's over? Now you give up your standards, and do what you're told?"

He was struggling to contain himself, she knew. She felt like she had better not provoke him any further.

"I want to speak with my parents," Rose said.

He shook his head. "After you speak with Mrs. Stein."

"You can't forbid that."

"Rose, you have a four-year-old sister, don't you?"

Something about his tone chilled her. *Are you threatening—*

"And Hans goes here, of course. And your older sister is in a fast-track school, studying to be a nurse."

Rose's older sister, Elisa, had wanted to be a reporter, but that was a stupid career choice these days. Better to have skills that were useful anywhere.

"Dr. Clark," Rose said slowly, "I wish you wouldn't talk about my family."

He sat again, picked up his own family portrait, and let his eyes linger on it. She had the feeling he was dragging out the moment, because the silence felt unbearable.

"How do you feel about your family?"

She startled. *Are you threatening—*

"Because you're acting like you don't care," Dr. Clark said. "You do you really want the authorities to have a record of you calling home in the middle of the day—on the day the state said they were going to put in their own cameras?"

And on the day that we had an unauthorized fire alarm? she thought. "They're doing that?"

"Yes," he said. "Don't tell anyone that."

Then why are you telling me?

"They've always downloaded all of the recordings from our cameras," he said. "But now they want more."

She felt sick. *So they can get us—*

"Everything is at risk, Rose: your family, my family, everyone. Every student, their parents, the whole community. We have to do some things we don't like."

The old, blonde woman came to mind, and what she had said to Mrs. Stein: *We'll see whether funds should continue to be wasted on these classes that don't move the needle.*

"Elisa, Hans, Warner, Inge, your mom, your dad," Dr. Clark said. "I don't like saying any of this out loud. But they're in your hands. Because—"

Because the authorities will threaten anyone they need to if that gets them what they want—

She hung her head. "I'll speak with Mrs. Stein."

He exhaled, his shoulders sinking. She thought he was going to say *thank you,* but instead, he said, "This needs to happen immediately."

She nodded. She felt sick.

"Can I go, now?" she asked.

"I know it's distasteful." He circled his desk and held open his door.

She stood. They made eye contact. She looked at his blue irises—

—and she had the strangest feeling that he knew a lot more than he was letting on. And that he wanted a lot more than he was saying.

"Is that all?" she asked, probing him.

His face hinted at something. *But what?* she thought.

He nodded. But as he moved and opened the door for her, she felt he was lying.

"Thank you," she said, because that's how students said goodbye to adults at St. Max's. Class ended, and students said, "Thank you." It was respectful. It embodied the mystic cords that united them together.

She stepped into the hall. Her thoughts felt jangled, chaotic. *What just happened?*

Because this can't just be about Mrs. Stein. I can't believe a school principal is enlisting an eighteen year old to do anything important. And she had already told Mrs. Stein not to do the play. *What does he really want?*

She felt agitated. *Does he know I caused the fire alarm? And that I took the cameras offline? Is he just trying to read me?* She couldn't figure out Dr. Clark.

You're influential, he had said. Mentally, she retraced her steps from the entire day. *What does he know?*

Of course, the old, blonde woman had threatened him. She and her assistants threatened the whole school. And he insinuated that she was risking her whole family.

What do you really want! She shuddered. Were they watching her more closely than everyone else? Had they penetrated her encrypted app? Did they know about her plastic gun?

She fought with herself. She wanted to bolt out the door, run to the parking lot, make a call to her dad and mom…warn them…

When, from nowhere, two strong hands seized her.

Both of her feet left the carpet, and she lost her balance, but the man—whoever he was; she couldn't see his face—had her in an iron grip from behind. She almost screamed, but strong fingers covered her mouth. She twisted, but it all happened in a second. With one arm around her waist, he lifted her off the ground, and they both shot backward through a doorway, and into a room she had never been in, a janitorial closet.

Her assailant's foot flew out and he kicked the door closed. She fought like a wildcat, but in an instant, she was on the floor, face down, and his knee touched between her shoulder blades. *I could scream,* she thought, but this was another one of the school's soundproof rooms, installed long ago, during the Fracturing. No one would hear.

This is my fault, she knew. She hadn't paid attention to what was around her. She'd let Dr. Clark make her feel scattered, and she hadn't paid enough attention to what she was doing, and now bad things were going to happen.

She didn't even know who her attacker was.

CHAPTER SIX
Center

Half of the people in the gym were chanting his name. Feeling sick, Mark stood up among the unpopular kids where he had been hiding.

"Mark. Mark. Mark."

He edged his way toward the center aisle, aware of everyone's gaze, the boys with naked admiration, and many girls with total attraction.

"Mark. Mark. *Mark.*"

As though their fate depended on him. Not that anyone had told him that *directly*—but Coach Bliss had wrapped his arm around Mark's shoulder and hinted at how many dollars the donors gave the school because they loved basketball.

"Mark. *Mark.* MARK!"

When he stepped onto the gym floor, the chanting intensified.

He approached the center, people sprang to their feet, his former teammates seized his limbs, and yanked him toward them—

STOMP STOMP *CLAP!* Hundreds of kids put their hands and feet into it. One of Mark's teammates playfully punched his sciatic nerve. He winced—

STOMP STOMP *CLAP!* STOMP STOMP *CLAP!*

"You couldn't do it without us," said Chuck Wade. Others laughed.

"Glad you did the right thing," said Toby.

"Any more of this 'reluctance' crap, and we'll destroy of you," said Maurice Pip.

"Shhh, idiot," Lamar told Pip.

His teammates pulled and nipped at his shirt like birds, and their fingers pecked at his skin as they each tried to yank him in their direction.

"Mark. *Mark.* MARK!" STOMP STOMP *CLAP!*

In the deafening noise, Lamar said, "We're going to state!"

"State's nothing," said Nash. "I'm going to the NBA."

"Glad you made the right decision." Lamar slung his arm around Mark's neck in a sleeper hold. "Now I won't have to soak your house in gas at 3 a.m. and burn you to death for wrecking our lives."

"Mark. *Mark.* MARK!"

Against his will, two guys hoisted Mark upon their shoulders. When the cheers grew more frenzied, Mark blushed, and jumped down from his teammate's shoulders. As his feet landed, his knees bending, he noticed Dr. Clark discreetly shepherding Rose Scholl out of the gym.

And now she vanishes, he thought.

Cold sweat streaked down his sides. He didn't think he could feel more cornered—but if they were coming after her, did that mean they had video of him, too, observing her? *What are the penalties for not ratting her out?*

"Mark. *Mark.* MARK!"

First Dasch, now Rose. But he was sure she'd covered her tracks. *How does she pull it off? What is it about Rose Scholl?* Everyone else thought the same way—like they couldn't bear what was happening, so they all just went along with it, and scavenged what they could out of life for themselves. *But Rose...*

"Mark. *Mark.* MARK!"

Her friends were separate. People listened to her. It appeared that they did as she suggested—but he couldn't recall a single time she'd ever voiced an opinion. On social media, she had an account that she seldom updated, only posting cat videos. And yet, she somehow created her own climate. When she walked into a room, the weather changed—

Why was she in the fishbowl when everyone else was outside?

"All right," Coach Bliss said. The forty-year-old, muscular man in a tailored suit approached his circle of athletes. He was the sun and they aligned themselves around him. He pushed a palm downward, and a thousand people hushed. When it was as quiet as a wedding chapel upon the entrance of a bride, Bliss exclaimed, "Ladies and gentlemen, I give you the St. Maximillian Kolbe Avalanche varsity boys basketball team!"

An explosive cheer erupted again from hundreds of teens, as drill team girls did synchronized flips in the air. Bliss met Mark's gaze. He winked as if to say, *I've got you now.* Leaning in, Coach confided, "I'm glad the rumors weren't true."

It was all Mark could do to keep the fake smile on his face.

Bliss pushed a hand toward the floor, and hundreds of people sat down.

"Thank you. We can't make any promises, other than we will work harder than we ever have before. We will give every last drop of sweat and blood to bring you glory. Thank you."

Ordinarily, the team captain might speak, but apparently, Bliss didn't trust Nash, so he handed the microphone to the emcee, and he led the team to their front row seats—

—and as the last round of cheers faded, Mark felt

Bliss's hand atop his shoulder. It felt not even remotely like his father's.

"And now," the emcee boomed, "the varsity *grrrrls!*"

As a cheer rose up, Bliss abruptly steered Mark toward the exit. The door swung shut behind them. The noise abruptly got cut in half.

They were alone. Bliss locked eyes with him.

Mark did his best to reveal nothing.

They stood between two locker rooms. Bliss's hand returned to Mark's shoulder. "Thank you, Mark," Bliss said casually, but his face was darkening. Mark didn't know what to say, so he let Bliss guide him toward the coach's private rooms. "You gave us quite a scare, son."

"I didn't ask for this," Mark began, but Bliss put a finger to Mark's lips. He gestured for Mark to open the office door. Mark complied. Bound, Mark went where he did not want to go.

New furniture. Awards hanging on the wall. Bliss's team photos from his own college years. Bliss's team had won nationals four years in a row, with Bliss being the second-best man on the team, but an injury had kept him out of the pros.

"Have a seat."

Mark glanced around anxiously. "Shouldn't we be at the assem—"

Bliss waved that off. "What do you think?" He touched his walls.

Mark felt shocked. Steel stripes ran from the ceiling to the floor. They blocked any parabolic microphones. And from a wall safe, Bliss retrieved the most expensive, illegal signal jammer that Mark had ever seen.

"We're in a bubble," Bliss said. "We can speak freely."

"I tried to find you this morning," Mark said, "to tell you I can't play."

"I know. That's why I avoided you," Bliss said. "To help you not make the biggest mistake of your life."

Mark felt a surge of anger and was about to speak, but Bliss retrieved an envelope from his pocket and pushed it into Mark's hands.

Golden handcuffs…

"Open it."

Hundred dollar bills. A bundle of them. Mark looked up, shocked.

"Mark, you're already doing a lot of good for this school."

Mark kept himself from counting the money.

"That's six months' living expenses for your whole family," Bliss said.

More like a year, Mark thought. "Where did you get this?"

Bliss looked at Mark like he was naïve.

But rumor has it the school is on the verge of collapse, Mark thought. "Mom will never let me accept this," Mark said.

"It isn't a gift," Bliss said. "You've earned it."

Mark shook his head.

"She'll accept it," Bliss said.

"You don't know my mom."

"With all due respect, son," Bliss said, patting Mark's knee, "yes, I do. I know, and she knows, that your neighborhood is 'protected' by a flimsy barbwire and electrified fence. I know your neighborhood can barely pay for a few aging guards. I know that your mom, you, and your sister have four jobs between you and that you're two months behind on the rent. And I know you're here on an athletic scholarship."

"Academic scholarship," Mark said.

Bliss smiled. "Yes, you're smart. So, you're smart enough to know that when Clark tells you that your scholarship is 'academic,' what he means is: 'athletic.'"

Mark's thoughts smashed together like cars in a pileup. *Because smart kids are a dime a dozen,* he thought. The nation didn't want any more STEM, and it stigmatized selfish parents who wasted money on private schools when they could put that money toward the people's community. *But it loves athletes who will bring their new country glory in the Olympics—*

"I can't just tell my mom that I came home with—" he hesitated "Twenty *thousand* in cash…"

"You added wrong, Einstein." Bliss smiled gently. "It's thirty."

The thought came unbidden: *I could pay a coyote to get us out of the country with this.*

But that was theft. And while there were stories of people going away with coyotes, no one ever heard the ending to any of the stories.

"Your mom sees this coming," Bliss said. "But if it makes you feel better, you can bring out a few bills at time for the first few months."

"I can't keep this much cash in our house. We live—"

"We've already delivered a floor safe to your house," Bliss said. "It weighs thirteen hundred pounds. Maintenance people from the school will install it in the basement floor tonight and seal it in the concrete, all an hour before the curfew. I'll be there myself."

Because you've done this before.

"I will personally drill a hole in the concrete, drop it in place, lock it in the ground with fresh cement, take away the debris, cover it up with a rug and put your sister Maria's bed on top of that. She sleeps in the basement, right? You get broken into, no one even knows it there, let alone can open it or take it."

No. No, no, no, no— Mark glanced out the window toward the woods, where he'd been just ninety minutes ago. Where he'd seen G.J. Dasch fighting to not be taken away. *This only ends badly,* he thought. *Even if I do make it to the NBA*—

"Son, I can tell you're reluctant," Bliss said, "so let me spell it out for you. With the right coaches, you've got the talent to be one of the all-time greats. You've already set records. You'll break more records. Your family can live in a neighborhood with steel walls and ex-SEALS as guards."

—they'll own me. And they discard every athlete when they're through.

"You'll win the Olympics. And then it's money, and mansions—"

If our country even participates! Abruptly, Mark had a fantasy of being on foreign soil and defecting. He'd never come back.

Except Mom, Maria, and Jason would be stuck here.

"Glory and fame for your country," Bliss was saying, "and safety for your family. Especially for your sister."

What do you know about Maria?

"And—do I have to tell you this? You'll save this school."

Bliss glanced at the thick wad of bills in Mark's hands. Now Mark wondered how much other cash was already flowing St. Max's way.

Because of me.

"And it's more than just the money," Bliss said. "Do you think they'll want to shut down a school that creates

Olympic winners?"

But I don't care about saving St. Max, he thought. *I have to get Mom, Maria, and Jason out. And I want to see Dad again.*

If he's alive.

Bliss was waiting for Mark to speak. When he didn't, the coach sighed. "If you don't do the right thing," he said, "you and Jason can kiss all of those *academic* scholarships goodbye. Your mom will lose the house. Your sister—"

Mark's dark look worked as intended: Bliss shut up about Maria. Because Mark couldn't bear to think that Maria might be dating a—

"I've given you a lot to consider." Bliss leaned back. "It's only fair that I give you fifteen minutes to think about it."

Unbelievably, Mark's coach stood up, strode to the door, opened it, and stepped through. After it latched shut, Mark heard a key enter the lock, and then a mechanical click. The hair on his arms stood up; he realized he was locked inside.

How many conversations has Bliss had like this? Mark started counting other St. Max athletes: Ray Felder, Sam Williams, Ben Greenberg—all semi-pro. Joe Clipper: straight to the NBA.

Clipper was dead, of course; nearing the end of his career, he'd said few vague things that some people interpreted as disloyal. Then there was the tragic train accident, the flags flown at half-mast, and the state funeral as the country mourned a national hero.

This desperate school, Mark thought, *with an undisclosed number of kids on hardship 'scholarships' since the Crash. Rumor said it was well over 70%...*

How does it stay open? Mark wondered. *Is there that much under-the-table money coming in?*

Click. Startled, his heart ramming his ribcage, Mark whirled to the office's other door, which led to Bliss's second little room. Astonished, Mark watched the door glide open—

—and then Delilah Samson sashayed through.

Mark was too stunned to speak.

She smiled demurely. Since seeing her in the parking lot, she'd curled her hair, touched up her face, and rolled her skirt. She was so elegant that she appeared to float.

"What are you doing here?"

She laughed as though she found him delightful, glanced at Bliss's chair, rejected it, and tiptoed her way to the couch and sat next to Mark. "Bliss told me to wait until he left," she said.

He shrank back to the couch's armrest. "This is a Catholic school," he said.

She laughed. She was very attractive. She and her trainer worked out every day.

"Delilah—"

And gazing up at him frankly, she closed the gap. Inches separated him from this girl with long, flowing, dark hair, an inviting smile, and a tight body.

They get their hooks into you—

"I have—" he started to lie.

She stopped his mouth with a kiss. He found his body responding against his will. Her hands touched his shoulder blades. His hands floated to her silky hair. Everything about her was perfect: her looks, her touch, and her slender, toned curves. She'd always been sweet to him. She was a little stuck on herself, but maybe that was just the ignorance of growing up in a protected neighborhood with her insider parents. *Delilah Samson was taught to always land on top—*

He sprang to his feet.

"I have a girlfriend," he said.

She smiled playfully. "No, you don't."

"I do."

"Who is it?"

"I don't want to say."

She patted the seat next to her. He noticed that, sometime while they were kissing, her shirt became untucked. He held his breath. *I didn't do that.*

"We just started dating." For some reason, Rose Scholl popped into his head, but of course he and Rose weren't seeing each other.

"You're a terrible liar," she said. When she crooked her finger, he instinctively took a step toward the young woman considered to be the most attractive person at St. Max's. When she rose, all he would see was her immaculate skin.

"We have a whole ten minutes," she said.

And they were kissing again. Her hands played along his back—

—and a minute later, he broke away, again. *This is so bad,* he thought. Bliss, the school the cash, Delilah—what else were they going to throw at him until he did what they wanted?

They'll expel Jason if I don't. But if I do, we'll never be free of them—

Except the bare skin of her arms made his fingertips tingle.

Would it really be all that hard to fall in love with Delilah Samson? Maybe we can make this real, he thought. *She certainly wants me.* His mind was racing, and his body was ignoring what he wanted it to do. He wanted to just talk to Delilah, to tell her his worries, to say that he was terrified for Maria because she probably was giving herself away to someone in a paramilitary. He wanted to tell Delilah what had happened that morning. *If I could just trust you…*

Her fingers explored his hair.

"Bliss's coming back," Mark said.

"Not until I tell him to," Delilah said.

"You said ten minutes."

"Shhh," she said, and kissed him.

I have to stop, he thought, but he wanted to do things he shouldn't, with this girl who appeared to be offering everything because she expected him to go pro —

—where they would own him—

"Do you ever just want to talk to someone?" he asked. He was stroking her hair.

"Maybe while I perfume you and wash your feet with my hair?" she said teasingly.

He must have looked at her like she was crazy because she laughed. "I love to talk," she said in a husky voice. "We can talk. For *hours*." She smiled seductively. "After."

Right then and there, he wanted to lift her off her feet and lay her down on the couch.

But even though he didn't, too much time passed. Eventually, he said, "Bliss's coming back in—" He sprang back when he saw the clock. *One minute.*

Smiling like she owned him, she straightened her clothes and said, "Mark you know we've always liked each other."

Embarrassed, he nodded.

"My mom says, 'Sometimes a man just needs a little push, and then he'll make you happy," she said.

And with that, she playfully pressed his chest, and then vanished into Bliss's other little room. Only now did Mark realize that the second room also had a second door, which led to the hallway that separated the looker rooms, and the weight room. Only coaches and referees used that door; Bliss always kept it locked.

Bliss arranged all of this, Mark thought stupidly, repetitively. He gazed in the full-length mirror. His clothes and hair looked like he'd stepped into a wind storm. Hastily, he put himself together—

—and finished just as Bliss re-entered. As ever, Bliss looked impeccable; his Brooks Brothers suit flattered his athletic build, and it contrasted professionally with his perfectly cropped auburn hair.

"Did you think about everything you can do," Bliss asked, "for the school?"

"I'll play," Mark said.

"Good!" Bliss pumped his fist. "You'll be happy you did. Get to class."

"Yes, sir." Mark opened and stepped halfway through the door.

"Mark," Bliss said, like a father reminding his son.

"Sir?"

"You forgot something." Bliss pressed the envelope of cash into Mark's hands. He gestured for Mark to jam it inside his pants; it was too thick for any pocket. Mark did so, and left.

In the hall, he heard the band strike up the school fight song, which meant the assembly had about eight more minutes. Mark began running.

Where am I going?

The money envelope chaffed. He glanced overhead. The cameras were still off. *Rose left them reeling,* he thought.

Mark felt like *he* was reeling. Wild thoughts collided into each other. *Where am I going?* Should he really go back to class? Shouldn't he instead run to the woods, get his gun, get Jason, get his family, get the hell out—

Abruptly, his phone buzzed. Mark didn't even reach for it. He knew it was Mom calling to fake-say, *Are you sure?* when what she really meant was, *Thank God.*

He didn't want to speak to her. Angrily, he shut his phone off.

Rose Scholl.

She had her back to him. She was shuffling along, past the offices, moving slowly, unlike she ever moved. At first, Mark had no idea what she was doing because he had never seen her look so purposeless before. It dawned on him that she was oblivious to her surroundings. She was lost in thought, fully exposed. *That's completely unlike her—*

Impulsively, silently, and desperately, he ran toward her. *If she can kill the cameras,* he thought, *what else can she do?* He touched her shoulders, apparently too hard, because she startled; she was completely surprised.

Rose lost her balance. In a second, with one arm, he gripped around her waist, hoisted her upright, and took control of her. With his free hand, he flung open a door to storage closet. *She knows things—things she's not telling. Her dad's a cop. He'll know people. He can get us out.*

He yanked her inside and kicked the door shut.

Now she fought like a wildcat. Her elbow rammed his midsection as hard as it could—

—he gasped—

—they tumbled to the ground.

Desperately, he twisted so he wouldn't smash on top of her. His breastbone stinging like hell, he stepped back and tried to be gentle—

—just as she whirled, and her foot shot out and rammed his quad with incredible force. He gasped again. "I just want to talk—" he began.

But he lost the ability to speak because suddenly she was up and striking him an unknown number of times: all he remembered was the hollow of his chest, which knocked the wind out of him. His head rang, his Adam's Apple hurt like hell, and his wrist was on fire, and he didn't even remember what she had done to his head. Dazed, he didn't know if she broke anything, or if he could even breath—

Her dad's an ex-SEAL—

And she was on her feet, her back pressed against the wall, and she had a plastic gun's barrel aimed at his eye.

As his chest heaved for air, the look on her face made him decide against getting up.

She waited.

He watched his own arms shade down from an angry, airless red to a less inflamed scarlet. "I just…" He started. He had to catch his breath. "I just want to talk."

"I will kill you."

"I'm staying on the floor," he said.

"Why did you grab me?"

"All I meant to do was touch your shoulders. And then you tried to run away, but I need to talk with you. I'm sorry!"

She looked like she didn't believe him. He tried to keep from babbling. "Because you wouldn't talk to me, otherwise." He wished his heart weren't ramming his chest like a caged animal. "You avoid people like me."

She was an excellent actress, he thought, but for a second, she failed to keep her guard up. *I'm right and she knows it,* he thought. *The last thing she wants is attention, and the whole community is watching me.*

"Who are 'people like you'?" she asked. He started to shift his leg, but she re-aimed her gun at his heart, and her face—already cold—now looked fatalistic, like he was forcing her to pull the trigger.

He decided to let his leg hurt. "People who get stuck in the public eye."

Her eyebrows narrowed. She'd decided that he was telling the truth.

"G.J. Dasch," he said.

Her face twisted up in a rictus of pain, but she hid it. Once again, her face was cold. "Speak," she said.

"I saw him get taken," Mark said. "I arrived at school late." *Through the woods, where I hid my own gun.* "Rose, I know we don't talk, but it's not safe here. I want you to help get my family out."

Her eyes widened. "Out of—"

She was making him say it. He nodded. *Out of the country,* he whispered.

"What makes you think I can help you with that?"

"Because you just flattened me when I had the jump on you. Because you have a plastic gun. Because your dad is an ex-SEAL. What else do you have?"

Her gaze searched him. When her eyes explored his, he suddenly felt absolutely exposed—as if she knew everything he had ever done. Ashamed, he thought of how far he'd gone with Delilah Samson. Something told Mark not to offer Rose any money because she'd be offended.

"I have a friend who is missing," she blurted.

He could tell, now, that she was fighting tears. *If she cries, rush her. Take her gun.* But he grimaced at himself. She'd shoot him—he was sure of that. *Why am I so stupid-desperate?*

"Look," he said, "the assembly is going to be over soon, and they're going to take attendance, and they are going to wonder where we are. But G.J. is your friend and my friend."

"I am going to count backwards from ten. You are

going to tell me everything you know and want," Rose said, "and when I reach zero, we are going to walk out of here, and I will decide if we ever speak again. If anyone asks me about you, I'll deny that I know anything. Ten."

"We have to get him back."

He saw hope in her eyes, but she shook her head. "No one ever comes back. Nine."

"Your dad. He can tap police records."

"The police have nothing to do with anyone who disappears, and you know it. Eight."

He cringed. *I'm a fool.* He was demanding favors from her while offering her nothing. But he blurted, "Look, I have to get my family out of this country."

"Seven." Just talking about getting out was treasonous.

"They want me to be their performing slave," he rattled, panicked, because he hadn't softened a bit. "They say, 'professional athlete.'" He stopped talking. He didn't know how to explain.

"'Performing slave.' Make Holder look good and you get a jet and…whatever…" She wasn't going to say *mistresses,* but he could tell from her revolted expression that that's what she was thinking. "That's your problem. Sorry, not buying it. Six."

"It's the truth!"

"Five."

"They just tried to bribe me!" He reached for the cash, to show her—

—her finger pressured the trigger—

—he stopped. "I have an envelope of cash."

"I don't want it. Four."

He felt like asking, *Why not?* But she was an honest cop's daughter. Maybe she knew something about how some people marked bills…or maybe they had some invisible chemical on them. Maybe they would later be able to trace and prove who had all of these illegal notes. Maybe they could blackmail him, now.

When I took his cash, I jumped right into Bliss's bottomless pit.

"For God sake's, Rose! You know the paramilitary violence that happened this morning at Shenanigans? The photos they're trying to tell us are fake? Jason and I were caught up in that! We were going to the train station and we nearly got shot!"

He rattled off the whole story. The woman who jammed a gun in his back…how he and Jason got away…the escape through the alley…the rooftop…the leap…the deaths. "I can't risk my family's life on the NBA. I have major problems right now!"

Her face softened. She wanted to help. But, subdued, all she said was, "Three."

Icy perspiration coated his skin. He only had one option left. "I saw you in the office on Mrs. Melnitz's computer. I saw you in the chapel afterward. You and I were the only two people inside St. Max's. You shut all of the cameras down!"

She looked horrified. She looked vulnerable. He wanted to protect her—

—except he was afraid she'd shoot him.

"Never mention that again. Two."

He hung his head. He was spent. This was worse than this morning. At least this morning, he'd always had someplace he could run. He had no doubt she'd shoot him with her silent gun and leave the corpse for someone else to find. That's what he'd do to her if that's what it took to protect his family.

"I will…" He faltered. "I will do what you say. You tell me what to do, and I will risk my life to get G.J. back. You can even sacrifice me. Just get my family out. I know you can."

"I told you," she said, "I can't."

She looked at him—she was relentless—but he also knew she was an excellent actress, and smart. Whatever she was feeling—pity? anger at how he'd seen her? fear of where all of this would lead?—she was hiding it.

"Please," he said.

"Don't talk to anyone," she said. "Expect nothing. Wait for me to contact you. One."

She gestured with the barrel of her plastic gun for him to stand. He stumbled; his leg was killing him. One more gun-flip and he opened the door. He hesitated—

—and her fingertips touched his back, and he instinctively stepped into the hall.

She wanted me to go first because of the cameras. "Don't worry," he said, "they're still off."

"Hurry," she said, and he picked it up.

He sensed no one behind him. Five, ten seconds passed.

From the gym, the fight song climaxed, and noisy students streamed into the hall, in no hurry to get to class. Mark waded into the crowd—

—and reluctantly became an actor himself. A teammate hung on his shoulder cute junior girls whispered to each other as they saw him coming, and underclassmen gazed up at him, awestruck. Bliss had done it again.

Don't talk to anyone, Rose had said. His solar plexus and jugular still ached from where she had spiked him with her sharp elbow. He wondered just how much martial arts training her father had given her, because he was sure she'd targeted his pressure points.

Wait for me to contact you, she had said.

He looked down at his wrists. She'd sent incendiary pain blazing through his body through them, so much that he'd nearly passed out. His wrists were still a sickly shade of pale. Unbidden, he envisioned them with shackles.

Maybe I should just do what they want, he thought. Because all he'd done with Rose Scholl was put her on high alert. *What is she going to tell her SEAL father and his cop buddies to do?*

He was shaking. He needed to get himself under control.

I need to get our family out of this country.

But how? With Bliss's money? Was that even possible? He wondered if he could find a coyote? And how could he even persuade mom, Maria, and Jason to go along? The only stories the approved media told about the coyotes all ended in death.

Don't talk to anyone. What Rose said came back to him.

He waited in the hall for the assembly to end. He felt hopeless.

Expect nothing, she had said.

But then had also dangled a dust mote of hope at him, because she had also said, *Wait for me to contact you.*

The paramilitaries. Coach Bliss. Delilah Samson. Rose Scholl. His life, he decided, was in far too many other people's hands.

Something needs to change—fast.

CHAPTER SEVEN
The Hidden Map

Not speaking to each other, Sophie and Rose strode to Rose's car. She wished she had her old windows back.

Dad had found tinted windows in a junkyard; once, they were on a drug dealer's car. But, distractedly, Rose remembered that the governor changed the law himself, bypassing the legislature and the courts, due to the emergency and his temporary powers. Dark windows became illegal overnight, which forced her dad to reinstall the old ones. Now, inside of her own car, Rose felt totally exposed.

At least she kept the bulletproof doors.

"What did Clark want?" Sophie asked fearfully.

"Sorry." Rose held up a finger, turned on the radio, and put it in drive.

"Fellow citizens," said President Holder. It was three-thirty; he spoke every afternoon. Mom asked that Rose listen to him.

"I am here with Vice President Thompson. The unity government faced a serious challenge today," he began. "In what appears to be a coordinated nationwide attack, Blue paramilitaries assaulted unarmed civilians in six cities today, including the Capitol. Using illegal firearms and stronger ordinance, they attempted to murder civilians, damage the people's property, and slow the workings of your government."

Thompson spoke; like Holder, he had an urbane baritone. "The death toll of innocents could have been appalling. Ordinary workers striving to build our community found themselves under fire."

Holder: "But due to the efficiency of our police forces, newly re-trained and enhanced by the army, not a single life was lost: *not a single life.* These terrorists and Island sympathizers found themselves neutralized—"

Rose shut it off. Same old lies. Sophie, too, was shaking her head. This was not what the photos going viral around the school had revealed. At least sixteen died in Eastgate; what did that mean for the rest of the nation? And Holder only criticized the Blues—he would never mention the Yellows because they supported him.

"Your mom is obsessed," Sophie said. "Making you listen every—"

At that moment, Rose's phone rang. The screen lit up with Mom's photo. As Rose avoided the highway and took the slow way home—her parents didn't want her on any well-traveled roads—she and Sophie started laughing.

Rose clicked accept. "Rose," Mom said. "You're not anywhere near G-29 or G-33, are you?"

"I'm on 39th and heading east," Rose said.

"Don't go near G-29 or 33," Mom said. In the background, two news people were arguing on TV about when the Blues would be finished off, and if generous President Holder made a mistake in making Thompson his VP in the new unity party. This was tricky for them to argue, because the majority hated Thompson's party, which barely made the legal threshold that allowed it to exist. Further, no one sane criticized Holder. Rose could picture her mom anxiously clutching the phone, peeking out the window, while also keeping an eye on ten-year-old Warner and four-year-old Inge. Unbidden, what Wingfield had said popped into her head:

I have to get my family out of this country.

"Mom," Rose asked, "why are we still here?"

Silence. Rose could picture her mom processing that question, and deciding it was too dangerous to answer.

"How far are you from the intersection of G-29 and G-33?" Mom asked instead.

"Ten minutes east."

"Rose—"

"Don't worry! I'm getting farther away every second."

Sophie sighed: *Parents.*

"Come straight home."

"I have to drop off Sophie."

"Sophie, sweetheart," Mom said, "do you want to stay at our place tonight?"

"Um," Sophie said, "Let me think about it."

Rose found it tempting. They had a lot to discuss.

"Your father said there are calls coming in from neighborhoods that *never* call in," Mom said. "I don't want to scare you, but there was a murder in Brentwood and an armed robbery in MacAllister that involved a shooting. And in Eastgate—"

Rose knew all about Eastgate. Unbidden, again, she thought of Wingfield:

You know the paramilitary violence that happened this morning at Shenanigans? Jason and I were caught up in that!

But after Weissensee, where the ruling class lived, Eastgate was the safest part of the city. It was one of Holder's "Crown Jewels": the premier shopping district represented everything that was best about their new unity government: perfect gun control, sleek housing, and a thrilling nightlife. "Eastgate," Holder had said when he visited their city, "represents the best of our new society."

"—thirty deaths," Mom was saying.

"Thirty?" Rose exclaimed.

You can even sacrifice me. Just get my family out, Mark's voice said.

"With over forty injured. They can't estimate. They don't know. Half of them ran off. Your father spent the morning chasing them down."

"Is he all right?" Rose blurted. She didn't know why she asked that. She crept past a police car parked by a library. The cop inside aimed his radar gun at her.

"He's fine," Mom said. "They weren't going to send anyone in until after the firefight." Rose nodded. The police department contained firefights; it didn't intervene because they were outgunned. They had armored vehicles and flak jackets, but they'd also found landmines and rocket launchers in the paramilitaries' lairs. The paramilitaries' deadliness was not public knowledge.

"Sophie?" Mom said. "How about it?"

"Okay," Sophie said.

"Good," Mom said. "Call your mom or she'll be sick with worry."

"Mom," Rose asked, "why are we still here?"

"What do you mean?"

"In this country?"

A pause. "I don't understand."

But Rose knew she did. "It's violent," Rose blurted.

"Our whole family is here," Mom said.

"Well, why aren't we figuring out a way to get everyone out?"

"Rose," Mom sounded even more anxious, "I don't even know where to start. Your grandparents on both sides, your aunts and uncles, your cousins, the St. Max community—"

"We should get as many people out as possible," Rose

said.

"I don't think we should be discussing this," Mom said, her voice rising in pitch.

"Like an underground railroad."

"Sweetie—"

"Dad said this app is secure."

"I know, but they have parabolic listening devices. Your car could be bugged."

"Mom, you have to trust Dad. If he says our signal jammer is good, then you have to believe him."

"I do believe your father, but our house could also be bugged." Mom's voice was getting ragged.

"Mom…"

"How would we even get out?" Mom asked, sounding even more frustrated.

"I don't know." Rose pushed a hand through her hair.

"Where would we go?"

"I don't know," Rose said. They were surrounded by hostile nations, fragments of the country they once were, a country that their grandparents remembered as a beacon of hope, but their parents recalled as disintegrating into violence. "We could pay for a—"

"Stop," Mom said.

—*coyote*, Rose thought.

"We can discuss this at home," Mom said.

"We can go to the Island," Rose said.

"Seriously?" Mom asked.

"Rose!" said Sophie. "That's the worst nation on earth."

"Rose, I don't know what has gotten into you," Mom said. "Just hurry home. I love you."

"I love you," Rose said. Mom clicked off.

Sophie sighed, exhausted from listening. "Your

family can't afford a coyote for even one person."

"I know."

"And I don't know why you said the Island. You were the one who showed me that documentary!"

"Yeah," Rose said. Everyone knew the Island was a closed society, with no information going in and little coming out. Everyone at St. Max's, her friends in public school, the church, Holder, Thompson, the media, most of the YouTube channels—they had all documented the nightmare nation that was the Island.

"I'm amazed that the people who made that film got out alive."

"I suppose."

"Remember that twelve-year-old boy that they put on trial? What did the authorities call themselves? 'The Committee for Public Safety'?"

"Yes."

"And how they framed him for murder? And then sentenced him to death by starvation? They're sick!"

"That's what the show said."

"And now you don't believe it? But the video is banned. Holder doesn't want us to see it because it's so gruesome. Guillotines, buzz saws..." Sophie shuddered.

"And yet we saw it," Rose said.

Sophie paused. "Just what are you saying?"

"I don't know." Rose fluttered one hand. "Just that the same people who say, 'Don't trust the Island' aren't giving us reliable information on anything else."

Sophie sighed. Rose knew her friend was exhausted from the day. "Your family can't afford a coyote for even one person."

"I know." Both sets of grandparents had already mortgaged their houses to send their grandkids to St. Max's, which was also giving them a break on tuition because of favors Dad had done in purging a few people's police records. "But we have to do something."

They rolled past a strip mall. The armed security watched them from behind their iron bunkers. The parking lots were barren today.

"Such as?" Sophie asked.

"But if we stay here," Rose said, "society is only going to get worse. They will close St. Max's—"

"They won't close it." Sophie bit a fingernail.

"Dr. Clark said we're under scrutiny."

"We'll pass. Clark won't let it close."

Rose thought of the hassled, desperate principal, who clearly wanted to enlist her into…something. *But what?* she thought. She glanced at her closest friend—

—and decided she couldn't tell her about what happened in Dr. Clark's office, or what happened with Mark. *I have to protect her.* Because: what if they got suspicious of Sophie? What if they interrogated her? What if they threatened her family? Rose decided: for now, it would be better if Sophie simply didn't know.

I can't expose her.

Abruptly, Rose's mood crashed. She felt horribly alone.

I have to protect you.

"Clark thinks I can somehow talk Mrs. Stein out of putting on the play."

"It's off-campus!" Sophie exclaimed. "At a church. Nobody's going to go to it."

Rose nodded. The topic was too incendiary.

"No one will even go out for it," Sophie said. "A play about people betraying their families? Forget it."

"I won't," Rose said. She watched Sophie's face wash

clean with relief. Because ideas were forming in her mind. She was creating plans—

"How did Mark Wingfield react at the assembly?" Rose asked.

"Wingfield." Sophie shook her head in disparagement. "About what you'd expect. A bunch of girls fawning all over Mr. NBA. Half of them think if they become his baby mama, they'll be set for life."

"I mean, how did *he* react?"

"'How did *he* react'?" Sophie paused to think. She turned to Rose. "He looked shocked. Like he didn't want to be there."

Rose recalled her conversation with Mark. *I have to get my family out of this country.*

"He was weird." Sophie looked puzzled. "They're handing everything to him, and he can't hide how distraught he is. Like he'd rather mop floors."

Performing slave. Rose recalled an athlete who had died in a car crash just two years ago. Everyone loved him: he had gorgeous dreadlocks, a charming smile, and even though he was only 22, he was happily married, famously faithful to his wife and home every night by six, and they had beautiful twins.

But Rose remembered: he'd said a few controversial things where he defended someone else's right to free speech. "I don't have to like what someone says to know I like free speech," he'd said. His coach had to put out a statement saying, "Russell has accomplished so much for our country in such a short time that people forget that he's just a kid. He's learning. Cut him some slack. He won't do it again."

But people strung together video clips of him frowning or smiling mischievously and juxtaposed the images with those from Holder's speeches. Russell hadn't actually *said* anything. He wasn't even reacting to Holder. But the *appearance* of rebellion—

Rose remembered the lowered flags. The public was in grief, until a spike in paramilitary violence stole everyone's attention and made them forget all about Russell.

"I bet they stuff Wingfield's pockets with money," Sophie was saying.

Rose nodded. "In kindergarten, he was my best friend," Rose said.

Sophie laughed. "That's right. You were teeter-totter buddies."

"We could balance the board where we were both floating in air." Rose smiled. "When we played hide'n'seek, we could always find the best spots. We could play with a dozen other kids and always make it back to home base without ever getting caught."

"Then his parents got divorced," Sophie remembered. "And his dad had to move away. Where did he go?"

I have to get my family out, Mark said.

"Rumor has it he went to the Island," Rose said.

Sophie's face lost color. "I don't believe that."

Rose shook her head. She didn't know what to believe. That was fourteen years ago, during the Fracturing. After that, her parents told her the economy collapsed, the paramilitaries appeared, and the government endlessly changed hands. Just last year, there were four parliamentary elections, until, out of desperation, Holder and Thompson— opposites—formed a Unity ticket to save the nation. Holder's party had more seats, so he became president. But their fringes—the Yellows and the Blues—didn't accept this compromise, so they returned to the streets.

Abruptly, Rose turned sharply. "What are you

doing?" Sophie asked.

"Going to the police station," Rose said.

"*What?*"

"Sophie," Rose said, suddenly very serious, "I have several big favors to ask you."

Sophie swallowed. "What are they?"

"Things are already going to be chaotic when we get there. Go in first and make a scene."

"'Make a *scene*'?"

"Start screaming. When you see someone who's in handcuffs, cut up, and covered in blood, that's when you start freaking out."

"Someone *'covered in blood'*?" Sophie looked aghast.

"There's always someone like that at the police station."

"There is?" Sophie shuddered.

Rose nodded. "I will enter seconds after I hear you."

"Why?"

"You're going to have to trust me."

"What? No!"

"Sophie, you're not going to want to know," said Rose.

Sophie's eyes went wide.

"This is about our friend," Rose said. Instantly, she regretted saying even that. With her eyes, she communicated: *If anything goes wrong, you will not want to know what I was up to. They will take me, too. I will disappear. When they question you, you don't want to know anything.*

Rose wasn't sure how much Sophie understood, but in the meantime, radiated anxiety. Rose could smell it; it was like a pheromone.

"Okay," Sophie said slowly. "Society's going to hell, anyway. It's only a matter of time before they come for all of us. She touched Rose's arm. "Why am I at the police station?"

"You came with me. I came to see my father."

"Why didn't you come in with me?"

"I was about to," Rose said, "but I was thinking about calling my mom again."

"Why didn't I wait for you?"

"You wanted to pick up a job application."

"I *did*?"

"The police are the only local people hiring," Rose said. As Rose rolled into the police station's parking lot—also nearly empty, like usual—their mood dropped. They fell silent. From the backseat, Rose retrieved a special makeup kit.

"My father says, ironically, that the police stations are actually the least surveilled places in the city," Rose said. "They have some say in what camera gets placed where. And they're good at 'accidentally' breaking equipment and taking forever to fix it."

"They don't want a record of what they do?"

"Why would they?" Rose asked. "Dad says there are a lot of dirty cops. But they also get told to take on the paramilitaries even when they're outgunned. If they don't do everything perfectly, the politicians scapegoat them. Everything the police do is a no-win situation."

"What are you doing?" Sophie asked.

"You don't want to know."

Rose finished applying blush to her cheeks. In the rearview mirror, they glittered just a little now. She dabbed Sophie's cheeks with the same.

"Even with their broken cameras, take precautions," Rose said.

Sophie nodded: keep your head down, like usual.

If I can, I'll erase any record we were even here, Rose thought, but did not say.

"What's in the makeup?" Sophie asked.

"Don't ask," Rose replied. Sophie nodded—bits of metal, but not enough to set off the metal detectors. Between giving their hair a different shade with a special chemical, and the filaments in the makeup, Rose's obvious goal was to mess up the facial recognition software.

Rose watched Sophie inhale—and forget to exhale. Her closest friend was trembling. Rose wondered if Sophie could handle this. As she watched her friend reach for the car door, she blurted, "Stop."

Sophie looked at her.

"Don't," said Rose. "I changed my mind. I can't ask you to do this."

"Rose." Tears formed in Sophie's eyes. "G.J. disappeared today. I know that, at some point, you're going to be next. And then I'm going to lose my mind. I'm going to live in fear, if you want to call it living. And then in a few weeks or months, I'm going to be next. Everyone we care about is going to vanish, and we won't be able to talk about it, until it's finally us. We'll just live these fake lives where we just fake-smile, read between the lines about what we're supposed to do, and give them our souls. I can't. I can't live like this and always wait for them to show up."

"You haven't even told your parents," Rose said. "You deserve a chance to say goodbye."

"We said goodbye a long time ago," Sophie said, "because they aren't brave like you." Sophie opened the door.

"What are you going to do?"

"Shriek and go crazy," Sophie said. "And count on you to get us out."

Rose held back tears. She wanted her actress friend to compose herself. *If I cry, we'll both lose it,* she thought. She strode for the police station. "I'll count to thirty and follow," she said.

When Sophie reached the police station's public entrance, Rose retrieved something that looked like a tiny hairpin from the makeup case, but was in fact a sophisticated lockpick, and followed.

~

Sophie passed through the civilian entrance's metal detector. A female security officer frisked her.

"Where do I apply for a job?" Sophie asked.

As the guard looked at her resentfully, Sophie's gaze darted around the spacious room, which was twice as big as the school's fishbowl. She only saw seven people, mostly secretaries.   Mounted on several walls, an electronic board showed a map of the city. Many neighborhoods bled with red light; black skulls and crossbones showed today's death toll; a chart tabulated murders, firefights, assaults, and arson. Rose had shown Sophie pictures of the crime board; today, the numbers were the highest Sophie had ever seen.

"Far left." The security woman stared resentfully. "They won't hire girls your age."

"Thanks," Sophie said. She didn't point out that she was eighteen and that the law said she was eligible. She walked toward the counter.

Two cops wrestled a dazed man through a backdoor. His face was streaked with blood, and his forehead still bled. One cop's truncheon was encrusted with red—

—and Sophie shot to her tiptoes, terrorized in place, and screamed.

The bleeding man appeared to startle out of his stupor. Everyone froze, and stared slack-jawed at the high school girl—

—who screamed again, in a bloodcurdling cry, her shudders wracking her body uncontrollably, as she wailed and wailed again, apparently terrified.

~

Outside, Rose felt relieved: her parking lot was empty; the officers were out, trying to contain the paramilitaries. She retrieved one of her father's metal keys and unlocked the door.

As she opened it, from down the hallway, Rose heard a woman crying bloody murder. Even with her new metallic highlights and glitter makeup, she kept her head down. She didn't want any camera to capture her.

The woman down the hall screamed again. She sounded terrorized.

Rose sped up. She hoped Sophie could buy her about ten minutes.

~

To Sophie, even the bleeding man looked alarmed. He turned to look at her—

—and when she looked at the blood dried on his face like a Rorschach inkblot, she wailed again in panic, absolutely losing her mind.

Two officers in black rushed toward her, but she was stumbling backward, trying to get away from him. *He could be a rapist I saw on the news,* she thought. *A killer.* She tripped against a chair and landed on the floor.

The officers tentatively touched her shoulders. She jumped back as though bit by a rattlesnake. "He's bleeding! His head is *cut open*. Why doesn't anyone *help* him?"

"Shhh, shhh, shhh, shhh young lady," said an older officer, who was incredibly muscular for a bald, white-haired man. His powerful arms offered a hug—

—but she couldn't stop looking at the bleeding man any more than a driver could take her eyes off of a burning wreck along the side of the highway. "Help him," Sophie finally managed to say, her voice barely under control. "Help him. Why doesn't somebody *help* him? *Help him.*"

~

Sprinting down the isolated hallway to the chief's office, Rose wasn't sure how she would find clues about G.J. But—as she heard Sophie's performance—she hoped she'd recognize what she needed when she saw it.

She passed six doors. When she was five and Dad brought her here, the leaders of various departments occupied those offices, but that was long ago. Since then, the state abolished most departments, converted the rooms to interrogation cells, and the leaders were put back on the streets. Official reason: knitting a more unified community meant more cops in the neighborhood.

But the first real reason, according to Dad, was that murders kept going up. Ever since the Fracturing, young men and women joined the paramilitaries, swelled their ranks, and the police department needed every hand on deck.

But that wasn't the only reason. *Who pays the paramilitary's salaries?* Dad asked. *I thought everyone was broke.*

The powers above the police department didn't like

local cops digging into financial crimes. Instead, they put more cops in cars. Dad's friends found themselves handing out speeding tickets and otherwise keeping the employed compliant. The employed kept society running. The authorities wanted them working, paying taxes, paying fines, and otherwise pinned down so they didn't have energy for anything else. *Just keep them productive…*

Rose pushed those thoughts aside. She retrieved a cloth from her pocket and turned the chief's doorknob.

Locked.

The government gets its money from somewhere, Dad said.

She bent at the knees, retrieved a lockpick made of the most durable plastic, and she tripped the lock. She slipped inside.

She'd been to the chief's corner office many times with her dad. He had the only window in the station. The window, big as a sofa, was made of bulletproof glass, and it gave him a view of what was once a garden behind the station. They walked with state officials between chrysanthemums and crocuses, and had private conversations. The frequent watering was supposed to reassure the officials that no electronic recording devices were present; as cops, they could have honest talks.

The chief's computer was tempting—and she'd need to erase any pictures of herself and Sophie—but her gaze explored the room, instead. In his sixties, the chief wrote things down, displayed photo of crime scenes, and drew diagrams on white boards. She looked at the polished oak furniture, and the photos on the wall of the chief beaming with President Holder. The chief always had photos of himself with the president—but past presidents were no longer in favor, and those photos were shredded, she knew.

She strode toward his desk, her eyes widened in horror. *G.J.—*

The chief had two color photos of her friend. She had his professional headshot. And second, she saw G.J. in a neighborhood she didn't recognize. His hair was light brown, not black. His eyes weren't their natural blue, which always dominated his photos, but a dull color. *He's wearing contacts to change his eyes,* she thought. He had acne in the photo, unlike real life. His unfamiliar clothes were shabby, nondescript.

Ordinarily movie-star handsome, G.J. now looked utterly forgettable.

What are you up to? she murmured.

The photo captured him looking over his shoulder as though he feared getting caught.

She read an index card nearby:

G.D.

* I.Q. 142.

* Home library of illegal books in a former bomb shelter, hidden behind a basement door, which is hidden behind a shelf of tools.

* Hacker. (Underlined twice.)

* Known associates: P.M., E.S., K.F., and T.B.

* Person after person says, "Almost never says anything controversial or even interesting."

She was sure "G.D." was G.J. Dasch. And she also felt like she knew what that last bullet point meant: G.J. was too cautious for his own good.

She also felt P.M. might be Peter Müller. *But who are E.S., K.F., and T.B.? Evey Stevenson, Klara Fogarty, and Thomas Berger?*

Except for pictures from a shooting maybe a week

ago, the chief's desk was otherwise empty. The computer's screen saver displayed a picture of an isolated lake, where Rose knew the chief, his wife, and four sons went fishing.

That's where he sinks the bodies, her father once joked, but that led to Rose's paranoid mom asking Dad ninety minutes of questions while Rose and her sister, Elisa, secretly listened in.

I don't think he's on the take, Dad had said.

Are you sure? Mom replied.

He's the last honest chief in the city, Dad said, *and he's paid a price for it. The feds talk about 'integrity,' but their version of integrity is—*

Rose took photos of the picture and notes, and saved them in the encrypted part of her phone. She also sent them to her computer at home. If anything happened to her, she hoped her parents would be able to break into her machine, and learn what she had learned.

And then she took a big risk.

On the chief's keyboard, she typed in what she hoped was still his password.

Because the old guys, like her father, knew the chief's password. And Rose had casually observed the chief type it in. All the while, she'd been pretending to make casual conversation with her father, but she'd memorized it just the same.

Success.

Fingers flying, she loosened a hidden command, built into the system, to wipe out all of today's videos. That was easy. She'd seen the chief do it. Her dad knew the codes. Anyone who knew the chief from before the Fracturing knew the codes. They had an unspoken arrangement to save each other. The old guy—the SEALS—didn't like the new regime. After a few drinks, a few of them even said out loud why they became cops in the first place, how everything had changed, and what they'd like to do about it…

Relieved, Rose shot through the doorway to the Puzzle Room. She'd been there many times, too, with Dad's strong hand on her shoulder, and the kindly chief drawing his finger from photo to caption to map on the entire south wall, which they used to diagram difficult cases: a wall of pictures, descriptions, locations, arrest records, and questions.

Except: the back door was locked.

It was never locked.

Rose inserted her pick in the mechanism—but, dismayed, she realized that in this old-fashioned office with oak furniture dating back forty years, giving it the feel of a judge's chambers—the Puzzle Room's lock was state of the art.

Do I break the door?

Hands trembling, listening to Sophie's wails, she realized she didn't have much time.

If I don't hurry, I'll never see G.J. again.

She tried for ten seconds before she accepted that she couldn't pick this lock. So, as Sophie's voice faded, she retrieved her gun and fired.

Gingerly, she slid the door open and stepped inside.

Staring at the wall, she zeroed in on G.J.'s photo. But she froze in place:

As her gaze widened, she saw hundreds of photos; the wall was full. The chief had also rolled in two more whiteboards, each the size of a picture window. The diagram, a complex web, swallowed the whole room.

~

"He's all right," the burly older cop said to Sophie, whom he had turned away from the bloody convict.

"Are you sure?" Her gaze skittishly danced around the opposite wall and a group of black and white photos. Someone had forgotten to take down a picture of a discredited former president beaming in front of the nation's former flag, before Holder changed the flag.

"Man, shut up, you dumb twit," the convict said. "Unless your spoiled ass wants to pay my bail."

"Shut your pie hole, you dumb criminal," his guard said.

Sophie jumped and shivered.

"Get him out of here," someone said.

I hope I gave you enough time, Sophie thought.

~

Rose shook off how startled she was, and started taking photos of the wall.

G.J. was one photo; a line connected him to a man in the center. Ten people G.J.'s age radiated from the photo of a blond man, perhaps thirty years old. Rose recognized six of them. Three had gone to St. Max's; the other, a public school. She hadn't seen them in months. Of course, no one asked about what had happened to them.

Hastily, she took a dozen shots. She captured the whole wall and all of the whiteboards.

Blue, yellow, or black lines connected dozens of photos to each other in a complex web. The chief had written dates beneath many, and had printed "MISSING AS OF" or "DECEASED" above others.

She gasped.

A separate section listed a dozen seniors from St. Max's. Three were presumed missing. She remembered the last day she had seen Klara Fogarty—because the next day, her boyfriend, Thomas, was hollow-eyed—he'd clearly been crying and he was whispering a few reckless questions like, *Who last saw her?* Rose remembered trying to pull him aside and get him to act like nothing happened. She remembered because that was the last day she had seen him.

A week later, Dr. Clark had forwarded an email—written almost but not quite in Thomas's voice—stating that while the family had moved a thousand miles away, he'd always loved St. Max's, and was an Avalanche first and last, etc. Of course, whoever wrote the email neglected to add Thomas's new email or phone number.

Three of these twelve are missing, Rose thought. The other nine still attended St. Max's. The chief had placed question marks after each of their names.

Her eyes drifted to the top of the whiteboard. The name listed?

Mark Wingfield.

~

"See?" the burly cop gently steered Sophie's shoulders to look at the convict. An officer guided the handcuffed man toward a little room. "They're taking him to the nurse's station where she'll stitch him up."

"Okay," Sophie sniffled.

"Why did you come here, anyway?" an older cop asked gently, a father-figure.

"To apply for a job," Sophie said.

A laugh escaped two secretaries. Even the father-figure cop couldn't stop smiling.

"Are you sure this is the right place for you?" he asked gently.

They were all struggling not to laugh. "Well, it seemed like a good idea before I walked in." She gave a nervous smile.

The room lost it.

~

Slipping her phone into her pocket, the twenty photos she'd taken already sent to an encrypted server, ironically located in this station's basement, Rose left the Puzzle Room and closed the door behind her.

Sophie had stopped shrieking a full minute ago. *Why didn't I leave earlier?* She shot down the hall. She was nearly at the officer's private entrance—

"Stupid girl," an older woman said.

"That's how they raise them in Brentwood," a man's voice said. "Naïve and spineless."

Their shadows appeared on the wall. Frantically, Rose realized: *They are rounding the corner.*

Rose shot out the officer's door. Lightning fast, in the afternoon light, she swung the door closed as fast as she could, stopping it an inch before it slammed closed. Then, she glided it shut.

Please God, don't let them see what I just did—

She dared not return to her car—not here. Running down a side street and ducking into an alley, she texted Sophie. They could meet on 13th and Hess, under a canopy of trees, where the omnipresent cameras would not be able to record that Sophie would be picking Rose up. Of course, someone could always trace her route from the station to the trees—but she was gambling the police would have their hands full, as is.

She withdrew and pressed her gun to her chest as she ran. She did not want to be caught by surprise by anyone dangerous. Most likely, he wouldn't be the only person taking advantage of the alley's lack of cameras.

As she emerged on a street of liquor stores, payday loans, and pot shops, she picked up speed. She would run a mile and Sophie would pick her up.

And all that time, she thought about the five people above the line: G.J. Dasch, Peter Müller, Evey Stevenson, Klara Fogarty, and Thomas Berger. And she thought about the man at the very top: Mark Wingfield.

Despite the warm day, she felt chilled, and a shudder rippled through her. Mark had nabbed her just a few hours ago. He seemed sincere when he asked for her help. Rose trusted her judgment: he was genuinely rattled.

And she wondered: Why does the chief have him at the top of the board?

CHAPTER EIGHT
Loxley

Ninety minutes earlier

When school dismissed, Mark was the first one out the door. In the forest, he peeled back the moss, picked up his .44, and jogged a mile to the train station. He would ride to Jason's school, take his little brother home, and—

He didn't want to dwell too much on the next part.

At the train station, the security guard winked at him. As Mark walked toward the metal detector, the guard shut it off. These bribes were expensive, but more than ever, Mark needed his gun.

He wrinkled his nose as he sat on one of the torn plastic seats. He realized: *This is the same train Jason and I were hijacked on.* The cops must have investigated, of course, because, on the floor, Mark found a bit of yellow and black police tape that said: DO NOT CROSS. And the car smelled like bleach. *They must have tried to washed out the blood*, he thought. But they missed some fluids, because on the walls, Mark saw a few encrusted, red blotches.

He hoped Jason would be on time.

~

Five minutes later, Mark's metro rattled and screeched its way into Platz station, which was a block from Jason's school. When the car halted and the doors parted, Mark exited the car and stepped on the platform. Instinctively, he pressed himself against the brick walls and observed the scene:

Fewer people than usual.

Those present were rushing.

Everyone seemed paranoid: they rushed to get on or off the train; they bolted up the stairs; no one was reading. Instead, they eyed each other.

They are staying home, Mark realized. Like the people at school, the commuters knew about the paramilitary deaths that morning in the least likely part of the city. More importantly, they knew *the officials were denying anything had happened.*

He glanced at the clock. Where was Jason? Looking around, he saw two people whom he knew were old friends; they huddled together, whispering, and then hurried up the broken escalator. Mark decided that, most likely, the only people out in the city were those felt like they couldn't help it.

Jason trotted down the escalator into the metro's cavern. He was easy to spot in his beige school slacks and navy polo. Mark waved him over.

"No school tomorrow?" Jason asked him as a metro rumbled toward them.

"There's school," Mark said.

"Aw, c'mon." Jason looked him in the eye. *What if there's another battle?*

"You know, I've been thinking that an alternate route is quicker," Mark said.

Jason sighed.

"Learn anything?" Mark asked.

"I learned you went out for basketball." Jason gazed up to Mark eagerly.

"This is our stop," Mark said. When Mark got off the metro, he realized he had yellow-and-black police tape stuck to his shoe.

As he peeled it off, he noticed: no more than thirteen people scurried about the metro's cavern. Several clutched ratty coats; they stuck to the shadows and ran from the light.

"C'mon," Jason said. They walked up the stairs so they could switch platforms. In the dim lights—the subways had been brighter and cleaner when Mark was a kid, riding with Dad—he looked at Jason's face. He *really looked* at his brother.

This dumb fourteen-year-old is learning all of the wrong lessons, Mark thought. He and Mom tried to get him to concentrate on school and their shrinking community, but Jason was losing his innocence. And not the innocence Mark wished he would lose. Mark wished maybe Jason would be a little lazy about his work—but do it, anyway. That he'd roll his eyes when his religion teachers warned about the dangers of lust—but that he'd still respect the girls. But Mark believed Jason would end up like dozens of others: radicalized.

Soon to be underemployed, Jason would live at home, like Maria, who had been a straight-A student. All three kids played by Mom's rulebook: go to class, get a job, and work for promotions. Society said it needed your labor and money for the common good. But as people joined paramilitaries, following rabble-rousing speakers, the Wingfields increasingly felt defenseless. And getting caught with a gun? They'd make you disappear.

Meanwhile, the people whom Holder deemed undesirable either got out, or they lived underground. Mark knew of at least three houses where the wrong kind of people—people deemed unsympathetic to the new society— lived in basements or attics. They hadn't stepped into sunlight since Holder's party won the last election. He imagined they wanted to escape, but the rumors were: the military shot every coyote that they caught.

"What?" Jason asked.

Mark shook himself out of it. Apparently, he'd let his gaze linger a little too long on his younger brother's face. He'd always loved the oblivious kid.

"Just thinking about what a punk you are," Mark said. In that moment, he made up his mind.

"Take our subway," Mark said. "Go straight home. Don't let Maria or Mom leave. I'll be home tonight."

"Where are you going?" Jason blurted, alarmed.

Mark glanced both ways in the desolate cavern. "I'll tell you later," he said. "Get out of here."

"Mark?" Jason's face twisted with unexpressed emotion.

"I'll be back by six." He gave Jason a shove.

He watched his brother shamble toward the escalator. The kid was dragging his feet—until, apparently, he realized that if he didn't hoof it, he'd be stuck on the platform for another twelve minutes, which was plenty of time to get caught up in something ugly.

He waved goodbye. With his face contorted with confusion, Jason didn't wave back. Mark exhaled, feeling defeated. He knew what Jason was thinking, because he was thinking the same thing:

What if I never see you again?

~

Mark had never taken the black line. It led toward the most decayed part of the city, stopping short just one mile from a No-Go Zone. Immediately, as Mark boarded the train, it felt like he had entered a different world.

The train was *crowded.* Surreptitiously checking each

person out, because everyone was a potential threat, Mark knew they were all working class. Most of them probably lived in century-old houses, others squatted in the shadows, and others lived in the weirdest apartment towers he had ever seen. The towers were built like canisters, and every apartment was shaped like a wedge. Mark had been inside of one, and gone to the top. The tower's center was actually was empty, and he'd looked down thirty-stories to the ground. The drop gave him vertigo. Random conversations echoed upward; people hung clothes to dry over their railings; single parents tried to keep their kids away from drug dealers.

Abruptly, the metro brightened, and Mark shielded his eyes: the subway train emerged from the tunnel, climbed an elevated track, and soon was riding close to an eighteen-foot cement wall topped with barbed wire. As it pulled into the station, Mark warily glanced around:

While they were in the dark tunnel, someone had placed a black plastic bag over the camera.

In his two-year-old jeans and thrift store t-shirt, Mark felt conspicuously overdressed. Unlike a lot of people here who worked for a living, he had clean fingernails and teeth straightened by childhood braces. Feeling like a sheltered prep schooler, the star of the St. Max basketball team, who might be NBA-bound for the glory of President Holder, Mark waited for thirty people in sooty overalls to step onto the platform.

The afternoon sun was already blood-red. He reached inside his pocket and touched his .44. Inside of his pants, the envelope of cash chaffed. With dismay, he realized he didn't even know who he was looking for. All he knew was: he had to start in the lawless part of the city.

All around him, pairs of working people glanced at

him. When he caught them staring, they pretended they hadn't noticed him.

On a post overhead, a camera hovered but did not stare: the lens was shattered as if someone had nailed it with a fastball.

Mark hurried down the street, stepping over crushed plastic whiskey bottles and drug butts. He aimed for the nearest bar. One block later, past a state-run liquor store, a smashed camera lay on the pavement.

Mark picked up the pace. When he entered high school, the police came to this neighborhood. The mayor said that he'd inherited the No-Go Zones, but Mark knew they were ballooning. That was both good and bad: the residents smashed the cameras, chased away the cops, and the last time a paramilitary risked attacking one, only a few got out alive.

Mark steeled himself. *Just me and my .44,* he thought.

On a street corner with a bar, a church, and hardware store, he stepped inside a cavernous pub called Green Fish. Making eye contact with and nodding at a bouncer, a man nearing forty with basketball-player muscles running to fat, Mark acknowledged the 6'11" man, and stepped past him—

—but the man stood up and held Mark back by fingering Mark's shoulders.

That's his left hand, Mark realized. He watched the bouncer's right hand discreetly slide into his leather jacket's coat pocket.

"Nice coat," Mark said. Leather was outrageously expensive; Mark hadn't seen a new coat like this one since his childhood.

"Where do you think you're going, son?" The former player smirked at him.

"I have something for you." Mark raised both of his

hands to his chest. "If you help me."

"You're too young to be here," the bouncer said. But his eyes followed Mark's right hand as it drifted toward his shirt pocket. The bouncer's eyes brightened as Mark produced a hundred-dollar bill.

"I want to talk to Loxley," Mark said.

"He's busy." The bouncer glanced around to make sure no one saw him crumple the bill into his pocket. "Shouldn't you go home? Don't you know true evil is raining down all over the city?"

The bouncer jerked a thumb to the TV bolted above the bar. It was tuned to an illegal internet channel. The anchors and reporters never showed their faces, and the videos were raw, but they showed footage from peoples' phones that captured army brutality, paramilitary violence, politicians sneaking into their friends' wives' houses late at night—all kinds of news that the authorities ignored or denied. Mark couldn't hear the screen, but the ticker-tape listed off multiple cities now under paramilitary seize. "Look at what's happening."

Mark handed the aged-out basketball player another hundred. "Five minutes with Loxley," he said.

"Four." The bouncer accepted the bill and shoved it inside his pocket with his middle finger. His other hand remained inside his leather pocket—the snub-nose of his hidden .38 clearly pointed at Mark. "Upstairs. Tell him Sparkles sent you."

Mark strode past a dozen people, every one of whom had an illegal gun poorly hidden inside his coat or beneath her waistband. As they sized him up, he revealed just the handle of his own .44, and he put a hard look on his face. They pretended to ignore him and let him pass. But it bothered him: they were clearly wondering why Sparkles was going to let him see the boss.

When his father had brought him here a decade ago, this was a very different place—harmless—but at the time, the bathroom had a window you could slip out of, and the kitchen had a door that led to an alley. And upstairs had a fire escape.

The top stair was broken; the walls had gouges. Standing on the second-to-last stair, Mark knocked. People were laughing inside.

Mark knocked louder.

"What?" a man's voice cried. A girl's laughter faded down.

"Sparkles sent me."

"How much you pay him?" Loxley asked.

"He let me in cheap," Mark said. He peered into the eyehole, but it was made of one-way glass.

Mark heard two electronic locks click. Loxley, apparently, swung the door toward him. It looked heavy; with a glance, Mark saw the backside was actually made of inch-thick steel. *Are you expecting a rocket?* Mark wondered.

"'Four minutes'?" Loxley started laughing. He was lean but muscular; maybe thirty; brown-haired and brown eyed. *Nondescript,* Mark thought. *The rumors are true. He can blend in anywhere.*

The girl, mid-twenties, however, had a .22 with a silencer pointed at him.

Loxley's gaze flitted to Mark's .44, and he chuckled. "Come in," he said. "Point that at the floor," he said to the girl, who warily did so. Loxley swung the door shut behind Mark.

The room appeared modest: a bed, a desk, and several paintings of hyenas playing poker. Mark seemed to remember a safe being behind one. Six loaded .38s rested on a coffee table.

"No, really," Loxley said, "how much did you pay him?"

Mark hesitated.

"Spit it out," Loxley said. The girl stared at him, her hair dangling far past her shoulders; her bangs somewhat obscuring her eyes. She still had her finger on the trigger. She looked athletic; Mark doubted he could draw his gun before she shot him. "You already burned through thirty of your two hundred and forty seconds."

"Two hundred," Mark said.

"Ha ha ha!" Loxley laughed. He glanced back at the girl, who, easygoing, laughed with him, but her behavior seemed feigned to Mark. Mark had no doubt she wanted him to *think* she was letting down her guard.

"Refund," Loxley said, handing Mark the same amount, in hundreds. "Sparkly is a chiseler. He ain't gonna like it when I take ninety percent of what you gave him."

Is Loxley high? Mark thought. He'd never seen anyone behave like this.

Loxley's clear eyes probed him. "What can I do for you?"

Mark hesitated.

"One hundred and seventy seconds," Loxley said.

"I need a coyote," Mark said, "to get my family out of the country."

"How many people?"

"Four. My mom, my twenty-one-year-old sister, my fourteen-year-old brother, and me."

"What if you only have enough money for three?"

"Then I'll stay here."

Loxley nodded thoughtfully. "Everybody normal?"

Mark must have looked confused, so Loxley added,

"No handicaps or crazies?"

"Everyone's fit and healthy," Mark said anxiously. "Can you do it?"

"Kid, I just met you." Loxley looked at him sarcastically. "We don't do illegal. This is a neighborhood bar. We're lucky we're still open—taxes, and all." He winked, and the girl cracked up.

"My dad used to come here," Mark said. "Joseph Wingfield."

Loxley's eye lit up. "Auburn, square-jawed, brown eyes, freckles? Eagle tattoo? In construction?"

No wonder he's in charge, Mark thought. *That was fourteen years ago; Loxley had to have been about sixteen, and yet he remembers.* Mark nodded.

"Where do you want to go?"

"Across the closest border."

"Into *that* outhouse?" Loxley winked. Mark could tell Loxley was being sarcastic. "You know what they say about *them.*"

Mark shrugged. He could tell Loxley didn't believe the official news reports, either.

"What makes you think I know any coyotes?" Loxley asked.

"Dad said you worked for Hudson," Mark said. Hudson used to own this bar. He died nine years ago—an apparent suicide.

"Good man, Hudson," Loxley said reflexively. "You know a lot, kid."

Loxley's tone was relaxed, but his eyes said something different. Mark looked away; he knew they were sizing each other up. Further, Mark knew Loxley understood what Mark was implying: Hudson had his fingers in all kinds of pies, none of them legal. Unable to control himself,

Mark accidentally eyed the fire escape.

"Tell you what," Loxley said. "I don't know any coyotes. But if I were you, I'd take my family to Pier Thirteen in the Warehouse District. I'd have eight thousand per person. I wouldn't bring more than a backpack, and I'd be prepared for them to confiscate it, and strip-search each of you. It's gonna get awkward, but that's one reason he's the best. Don't mention my name."

"What's his name?" Mark asked.

"Aspwater," Loxley went on. "Crewcut, about fifty, has an earring."

Mark nodded.

"But maybe you shouldn't go at all," Loxley said casually. The girl raised one eyebrow at Mark as if to say, *Think about it.*

"Why is that?" Mark asked.

Loxley slung his arm around Mark's shoulder. Despite how loose and casual the older man was, his gesture gave him away: Loxley was deceptively quick and strong. *Which martial art does he know?* Mark wondered. Because it felt like he could put Mark on the floor and snap his neck in a second.

"I liked your dad, Mark," Loxley said. "I like you. He used to bring you and your sister here. I don't know if you remember that."

Even though he was four years old at the time, Mark remembered Loxley: a laughing sixteen-year-old with his arm around a full-grown woman.

"So I'll tell you this. Something cataclysmic is coming."

Mark stared. If Loxley meant stepped up paramilitary violence, that was already happening.

"Where?"

"Everywhere."

"Like a revolution?" Mark asked.

Loxley flicked his wrist. Mark took that to mean Loxley was batting away the idea of any paramilitary having the brains or firepower to take over anything. How Mark knew that was what Loxley meant, he couldn't say, but the willowy woman had also stopped swaying, and was nodding almost imperceptibly.

"Something else," Loxley said.

"Like what?" Mark asked.

"Something like what happened fourteen years ago. The whole country fell apart. You're too young to remember that, but maybe your momma told you. I know the schools won't tell you."

"My mom doesn't like to talk about fourteen years ago," Mark said, but he didn't add: *Because that's when Dad left.*

"Well, long story short, this used to be a good country. A big country. Lots of states. Our country was just a few of them. And Albert Holder was just a nobody. A dropout, unemployed, homeless for a time, no friends, no family, a crack user, but never an addict."

The girl was nodding.

"But he caught on. He started rabble-rousing. He started a paramilitary. They're all scum. You know that. They all want to terrify people into blind obedience. He joins the Yellows, and he tells the country they're being attacked by outsiders, he denounces anyone against his 'people's community' as a traitor, and he rides the wave to under forty percent of the vote. But we'd switched to a parliamentary system, so that put him over the top. People like him tore the whole system down."

"Does that mean you like the Blues?" Mark asked. He

knew he should get out the door, but he was fascinated by what Loxley was saying. A few of his teachers, like Mrs. Stein, came close to saying this, as did that relentless bookworm, Hanson Davis, but most people danced gingerly around the topic. But Loxley was just being blunt.

"The Blues!" Loxley laughed. The girl even smiled, but Mark could tell that both paramilitaries disgusted her. No one in the Black Zone liked the paramilitaries. "They're the same as the Yellows. They all want our money. We're all just supposed to follow orders. 'For the people's community.' 'For the common good.' If they believed in the 'common good,' why do they all want to close down the internet and the churches? Why don't they let anyone have a different opinion? Why do they want your guns?"

"You go to church?" Mark asked.

"That's personal," Loxley said. "Listen, it was a good system before the Fracturing. Some people voted and the leaders let you run your own life. You could travel internationally and take your money with you. But too many liars won elections. And then they spent the next fourteen years here fighting amongst themselves. They'd curse the paramilitaries, but everyone knows Holder's in with the Yellows, and his VP is in with the Blues. It's all for show. They get their voters riled up one way or the other, but they don't mean anything they say. They just want you to swallow their lies. They tell us there's a crisis, the people are under attack, and they get us to do whatever they want. It's the same with all of them."

Mark started to ask a question—because everything Loxley said fit with what he had pieced together on his own: that the president, the VP, the Blues, and the Yellows might have all preached a good game, but what they really wanted was total control—but the girl was shaking her head at him.

For some reason, that warded him off.

Loxley glanced at his grandfather clock. "Time's up, kid." Loxley was pulling him toward an iron door by the window. Underneath the wood paneling, Mark noticed a gap in the wood. Underneath the paneling lay more metal. The whole room was apparently steel- or lead-lined.

"But—"

Smiling, Loxley swung open the door. A cold gust hit Mark in the face and made him shiver.

"That's three hundred," Loxley said.

Mark glanced down the fire escape.

On the surface, it looked rusty—but standing on it, now, Mark saw that the rust was an incredibly deceptive paint job. Like the room, the girl, and Loxley himself, the fire escape was something other than what it first appeared to be.

Mark envisioned Loxley shoving him over the railing. He might scream on the way down, but he'd break his spine on the concrete, and he'd be found in a junkyard car, like Hudson was nine years ago. But someone had also shot Hudson in the heart, and the gun was in Hudson's dead hand. The police hadn't cared about Hudson's death, Mark remembered, and he knew they wouldn't care too much about his, either.

Mark paid the man.

"This is a dangerous nation," Loxley said. "I'd go to Saxet. Everything they say about Saxet is 100% backwards, just like everything they say about anywhere. But you might be better off just not leaving your house until it all shakes out."

"What's going to happen?" Mark asked.

"Holder's gonna make his move," Loxley said. He was swinging the iron door shut. "So, take a different way home."

And Mark was left standing on the fire escape. The fake rust—the clever paint job—looked like dried blood.

At that moment, Mark's phone buzzed. He glanced at the screen. The call asked him for permission to download "Dolls with Layers," an illegal app that he'd heard about: supposedly, not even the government could hack it. If this was real, and not a trap, then someone who had access to very sophisticated communications wanted to talk to him.

He ran down the fire escape. On the ground, in an alley that cut in four directions, he saw no one. Apparently, people steered clear of Loxley's alley.

Mark pressed *accept*, and an icon of ceramic dolls, one inside of the next, pixel by pixel, coalesced on his screen.

And then he answered the call.

CHAPTER NINE
The Black Zone

"Lady," Mark said.

He was shocked to see Rose Scholl. She was a passenger in a car; from the canopy of trees in the background, he believed she was somewhere between St. Max's and her house, but he couldn't really tell.

She looked grimly satisfied that he had answered, and that he was discreet enough to not use her name. "How did you push an app to my phone?" he asked.

"Don't worry," she said. "It's unbreakable. We can speak freely."

Exiting the four-way alley, Mark pressed himself against the red bricks. Nearby, someone had painted a golden shovel and pickaxe, and someone else had drawn a black X through it. Mark took in the cityscape:

Two women in miniskirts stood on a street corner; they forced Mark to walk fast in the opposite direction. "I doubt that," he said. Twilight approached, and the creepy-crawlies were coming out. He stepped over a dead police dog. *I need to get to a bus, or call a taxi—if one will come.* The problem would be finding an honest driver, and not someone who would try to rub him. He kept one hand on his hidden .44.

"State of the art encryption," she said, "from my dad."

"So the police can get in," Mark said.

"What? No," Rose said. "I'll prove it. My name is Rose Scholl." She swallowed. She looked nervous, stating her name over the app. "We're wasting time. You wanted me to help you. Well, I want to help you, now."

"Why?" He was trying to listen—this was important—but a block away, a plain brown Impala idled at a red light. On its passenger door, someone had hand-painted the logo of the metro's only taxi company. No other companies were allowed, but individuals got around that with a variety of symbols. When the police asked questions, the drivers played off their designs as art.

Two bruisers, covered with gangland tattoos, eyed him from a boarded-up shop. One clutched a rebar with a chunk of cement still stuck to its end. Mark thought he'd dressed down and kept his head down, but compared to the locals, his worn, torn jeans were new. Mark was too rich, too well-groomed, too naïve: he stuck out like a choirboy in a slum.

His breath caught in his chest. *Gotta take a chance—* He ran to catch the taxi.

~

Rose looked at Sophie for reassurance, but Sophie was concentrating on turning right on a pothole-infested street. The car rattled as she crept along past their third patrol car in three minutes.

"What is going *on?*" Sophie looked brittle with nerves.

Rose had a sinking feeling. Obviously, the police had called up every officer, every reserve, and every part-timer. Something bad was happening.

"Because I need your help," Rose said to her screen. Mark held his phone close to his face, but he was trotting, then running. He was someplace with gutted shells of buildings. On the streets: men with prison muscles. So far, she hadn't seen a single cop.

What are you doing in a No-Go Zone? she nearly blurted.

"Help with what?"

"Mark," she said, "I located our mutual friend."

"G.J.?" he exclaimed. Immediately, he dropped his voice. "You found him?"

Abruptly, Rose's screen flashed a dark red with a yellow border. "Required Viewing," came across the screen, along with the new symbols of Holder's government: an eagle surrounded by golden pickaxes. As the new national anthem sounded, Sophie jumped.

"You found him?" Mark repeated, over the blare of the news.

"Just a sec," Rose said. She was trying to close down the news app.

"My fellow citizens," came the voice of President Holder, "I wish I could say good evening, but it is not. Something horrific has happened. Something that attempts to strike at the heart of who we are. Insane, malicious reactionaries—with aid from foreign governments—have set fire to and burned down the national parliament."

Images of the majestic building, with its Greco-Roman architecture dominated the screen. And for an instant, despite everything they needed to do and the criminal actions they had taken all day, Rose and Sophie were mesmerized:

The parliament's curved dome had a hole blown in it as though it had been hit with a missile. An explosion suddenly happened—a loud bang, like a tanker-truck of gasoline suddenly ignited—and the dome collapsed as they were watching. Firefighters scrambled on the ground, but they were too few, and their equipment looked useless.

Ambulances shrieked nearby.

"I'm sorry," Rose said to Mark, "I can't make it stop playing."

~

As Mark tried to listen to Rose, he beat four toughs, each of whom held rebar with chunks of cement on the end, to the Impala.

"Just a minute," he said to Rose. He muted his phone. He approached the driver's side—

—the middle-aged man rolled the window up an inch.

"I need a ride."

The man shook his head, and he wouldn't turn off his car radio. The president was speaking: "—you are seeing footage from an hour ago. The best estimates are that the fire started from within. Once the blaze started, firemen could not put it out. The arsonists appear to have used Thermite mixed with volatile chemicals. This is a weapon of war, illegal according to every international convention—"

Hastily, Mark risked being stupid, and tried to discreetly show the man a hundred dollars.
The four with rebar were sizing him and the driver up—

—the leader saw Mark's note, and started walking across the street—

—Mark showed the driver a second note, the driver nodded, pressed a button, Mark heard the backdoor unlock, and he scrambled to get inside. The driver put it in gear.

"Whoa, whoa, whoa, whoa," said the leader. He hit the cement top into his calloused palm. "Where do you think you're going?"

"No trouble," the driver said.

"—our first responders tried to put out the fire—"

The driver tried to turn down the radio, but he was shaking, and accidently tapped a station-change button. The president continued speaking.

"This is our block," said the leader.

"You can have it." Mark pointed his .44 at the man's face.

"B.S.," a second man said. "That kid won't shoot—"

Mark took careful aim and fired. The leader's rebar flew out of his hand and clattered to the street. Everyone jumped back.

"I have five bullets." Mark kept the gun trained on the leader. "And I don't miss. Get out—"

"—are investigating—" Holder said. The driver finally turned off the radio.

"—of the way," Mark finished.

The toughs backed up in four different directions. "Drive," Mark said to the nervous taxi owner, who hadn't moved even though two toughs were no longer blocking his car.

"Don't shoot," the driver said.

~

"Mark, get out of there," Rose whispered. Sophie's fingers anxiously covered her lips.

The split screen only showed the roof of the Impala; apparently, Mark had set his phone on the seat.

"—we already have arrested a suspect," President Holder went on.

"Drive," Mark shouted, his voice coming through Rose's speaker. They heard tires squeal. A rumbling engine drowned out the president.

"Can you turn Holder off?" Sophie asked. She turned into a neighborhood of rowhouses, near a trailer park. Those people lived without a security fence. A band of men, in their thirties, patrolled the neighborhood on bicycles. Unlike in the Black Zone, most did not carry illegal firearms. They were doing the best a law-abiding citizen could do.

"I wish," Rose said. "Mark?" she asked.

~

"Thank you," Mark said.

The driver hastily tossed Mark his two hundred dollars back. "They're yours," Mark murmured, subdued.

"No, sir," said the driver, who looked to be in his fifties. Mark read his nametag: Korben Houston.

"You earned them." Mark gently placed the bills on the front passenger seat.

"Where to?" The driver mopped his brow.

"—we will give the citizens of this country a full report after we have completed an impartial investigation," President Holder was saying. "But as we learn all of the facts, no doubt our enemies and others will propagate many lies. You will hear conspiracy theories. These lies exist only to undermine your faith in our elected government, which serves you. Our enemies will seek to turn us against each other, and destroy our unity—"

"Will you shut off the radio?" Mark picked up his phone. "Rose, I'm back."

"You can talk?" Rose asked. Nervously, she avoided making eye contact with yet another patrol car's driver; the police car passed them in the opposing lane.

"—our top priority is to arrest the traitors—" Holder went on.

Rose watched Sophie's shoulders rise; her friend was a bundle of nerves.

"Accordingly, we have activated those National Guard who are part of local police forces—"

"I'll say," muttered Sophie, who had just passed her fourth police officer in ten minutes.

"I can talk," Mark said.

"Mark, we found you-know-who, and we need your help to pick him up."

"Where is he?"

At that moment, a siren blared. Sophie jumped. In the rearview mirror, Rose saw the black-and-white that had just passed them strobe the neighborhood with its lights.

"Rose." Sophie was white with panic. The cop car was executing a three-point turn and coming after them.

"I thought you said this line was encrypted," Mark said.

"It is," Rose said. A block back, the police car accelerated toward them. Sophie looked like she was in shock. "Pass us," she muttered. "Please, God, let them go after someone else. Pass us…"

"I have no idea what you're up to," Mark said. "I don't know how you got into my phone. I don't know you." Rose froze, dismayed. Mark was reciting clichés in case they were being recorded. Because *every* non-encrypted call got recorded.

"Mark, this app is safe," Rose repeated. "It's from outside the country. G.J. is being held in a place called Lubyanka Prison. It's a transfer station. I just learned this an hour ago. Everyone we know who has ever disappeared— they all go to Lubyanka, first. It's in Oak Meyer, which is brilliant, because few people go there." Officially, Oak Meyer suffered a toxic waste spill fourteen years ago;

unknown parts were still lethal. But unofficially, Rose's dad said, the official story was a fake story propagated by the government because they were doing things in Oak Meyer that they didn't want people to see.

"I have no idea what you're talking about," Mark said.

"Peter Müller. Evey Stevenson. Klara Fogarty. And Thomas Berger. Everyone who's ever disappeared that people can't talk about. I saw a map of the missing on the police commissioner's wall!" Rose spoke fast. "Mark, you have to help us get G.J. back!"

"I think you're high and hallucinating," Mark recited. "You need medical help, Lady. We never talk to each other in school. I don't know why you'd call me or why you have this number—"

"Mark, apparently G.J. is smart enough to help you get what you want—"

The cop car now rode their bumper, blared it's siren in a different key, and soaked them with an intense blue light. Sophie gazed at Rose helplessly.

"Pull over," Rose said.

"I have to go," Mark said.

"Mark, wait. I can talk my way out of—"

Click.

"Damn it," she said.

Sophie lurched to a stop, her foot jostling and then slamming on the brake. The car bounced and ricocheted as it scraped the curb. Rose helped a trembling Sophie shift into park.

The officer turned off his lights, exited his car, and was approaching Sophie's window.

"Rose." Sophie was shock white. She shivered as a drop of sweat coasted down her temple, and dropped on her collarbone like rain.

Rose crossed herself.

~

Mark clicked off. "Eastgate," he told the driver, but the man pulled behind a former apartment complex, now just a fire-scarred building with smashed windows and trash barrels in the parking lot, where homeless people lit their fires.

"Sorry, kid," the driver said. "Get out."

"I gave you two hundred," Mark said.

The man tossed it back. "And I returned it—twice. Kid, I never picked you up. I never saw you. I never heard any 'encrypted' conversations."

"That call? That was nothing. That was just my friend playing a joke," Mark said, improvising. "Mr. Houston—"

"Get out!" the driver shouted.

Mark pressed his snub-nose to the man's neck.

"You are not going to shoot," the driver said.

Mark hesitated.

"You're a good kid, or your friend wouldn't have called you."

"She isn't my friend," Mark said.

"And I have a wife and three kids. A good young man like you is not going to shoot a working man like me and leave that man's wife a widow with three orphans."

"Why won't you help me?" Mark asked.

"Listen to the damn radio," Korben said. "Holder declared martial law. The roads will be crawling with cops even here. He'll probably send out the damned army. Anyone on the road is a fool. This car is going in one direction only, and that's east." Deeper into the No-Go Zone, and the opposite of where Mark lived. "I have to get home and defend my family."

"What the hell am I supposed to do?"

"Hole up here for a few days," Korben pointed at the charred complex. "Call your family and then lose your phone. Don't get shot."

"Drive," Mark said.

But Korben turned off the engine, hopped out of the car, and opened Mark's door for him. Frustrated, Mark lowered his gun. Korben had read him well: Mark wasn't going to shoot an innocent father, and that meant he also couldn't steal the car.

An air-raid siren went off. They both startled.

~

"That's Officer Peter Graham," Rose said to Sophie. With dread, they watched the late-thirties cop lumber to Rose's car.

"You know him?" Sophie was biting a nail.

"He joined the force the same year as Dad. Dad says he's mostly a good cop, but he complains all the time. He's got a short temper."

"Great," Sophie said.

"It's because he thinks he's the last honest man on the force," Rose said. "And his son went missing."

Sophie bit her lip. Because she was moving to roll down the window, Rose spoke fast: "He and his wife didn't handle that well and got divorced. Just answer all of his questions honestly, but don't tell him anything. If you just hesitate naturally from time to time, I'll speak, and he won't realize he asked you a question, and not me."

Sophie closed her eyes, inhaled, and nodded like the

actress she was. When she opened them, she portrayed a fragile but innocent teenager pulled over for reasons unknown to her, and not an eighteen-year-old woman who, with her best friend, broke the law every day.

Lt. Graham rapped his knuckles against the car door. Sophie scrambled to compose herself. "What seems to be the problem, offi—"

"What the hell are you dumb kids doing on the road?" Next to his ponderous gut, Graham's hand rested on his holstered, tiny caliber pistol.

"Going home, Officer," Rose said softly.

"Well, you're late, aren't you?" His arm swept toward the neighborhood. In the distance, they heard an air-raid siren.

"We're on our way," Sophie asked.

"School was out hours ago. Why is your radio off?" His eyes were bloodshot. From the passenger seat, Rose smelled beer and fish on his breath.

"We—" Sophie looked to Rose.

"We haven't had it on in a while, Officer Graham," Rose said, making sure her eyes lingered on his badge. "We needed to concentrate on the road."

Graham cussed. Sophie blanched. "You stupid kids. Some foreigners burned down the parliament. In the last thirty minutes, they put in martial law. Didn't your parents call you?"

"My dad is busy," Rose said. "He's on the force, too."

"Well, then you should know better." Graham frowned. "Unless Mommy always told you that you're *special*."

"I guess we had our phones shut off," Sophie said.

To Rose, Graham now looked like he smelled blood in the water. "You're not supposed to be out. We've got—" He waved an arm—"Problems."

Paramilitaries taking advantage, Rose thought. The curfew siren was a warning that the police or media would never say out loud, but it meant the army could shoot on sight, and the media would bury the story.

"Wait here," Graham said.

"My dad is Officer Scholl," Rose said. "Please call him."

Graham's angry eyes lit up like a shark seeing chum, and Rose realized she had made a mistake by mentioning her dad. Fearfully, she watched him; it wasn't hard to tell what he was thinking: *Straight-arrow Scholl's daughter was violating a stay-at-home order while the city burns. Maybe the daughter isn't a goody-goody like papa. Maybe Scholl himself isn't on the up-and-up.*

"Don't go anywhere," he barked.

Rose and Sophie watched Graham lumber back to his patrol car.

"What is he going to do?" Sophie asked nervously. She looked on the verge of tears again. "If he takes us in—" She frantically reached for her phone.

Rose placed a restraining hand over Sophie's screen. "Do everything I say," she said.

~

As Mark watched Korben speed away, a sudden explosion rattled the ground, drowned out the curfew sirens, Mark lurched to stay standing, and several blocks away, a two-story-high ball of flame erupted.

What the—

Secondary explosions came next. They sounded like cars or furnaces igniting, and blowing themselves apart.

Mark shot inside the nearby abandoned house. When a floorboard snapped beneath him, he leapt sideways and hopscotched to solid wood.

In the gloom, he looked around. Broken furniture, shattered windows… Everything looked old…

…except for footprints in the dust. He also saw food wrappers from a grocery store.

And, suddenly, he was making eye contact with a girl. She was maybe seven years old. She huddled near several crates by the brick fireplace.

He pointed his .44 at the ceiling his right hand, and placed his index finger to his lips. She nodded.

"I'm leaving," he whispered. By the fireplace, he saw two more kids, and a woman in her mid-twenties; probably their mother.

Mark stepped backward.

~

After two minutes of watching Officer Peter Graham sit in his patrol car and stare at his screen, obviously reading their files, Rose saw the 39-year-old open his door and push himself outside. He plodded toward them.

"What kind of a cop is pulling over teenagers while the rest of the city burns?" Sophie murmured.

Graham touched Sophie's door, then stepped back, his hand touching his tiny .22. "Get out of the car."

"What?" Sophie asked.

"Sophie, it's okay." Under Graham's gaze, Rose opened her door. She had both hands in the air as she stepped out. Looking reluctant, Sophie imitated Rose.

"Give me the keys," Graham growled.

"Officer, we haven't—"

"Give them to me!" he snarled.

As he jammed them in his hip pouch, he added, "You rich kids think that just because you go to private school and your daddy, Miss Scholl, is a show horse cop with a bunch of *commendations*," synonymous with *crap*, "that you can break the law. How do you afford private school, anyway? Is it because your daddy's an accountant, Ms. White?" he asked Sophie, glaring. "Is he on the take?"

"No." Sophie was trembling.

"Hands on the vehicle," Graham said. When Sophie hesitated—she clearly didn't want to get frisked—Graham's face grew dark.

"Officer Graham, I know where Tommy is," Rose said.

Graham froze.

"Your son. Tommy," Rose said.

Graham gaped at her. His hands were twitching. They touched his tiny .22, drifted away, and tapped it again, *rat-a-tat-tat*.

"He disappeared fifteen months ago," she said. "I saw his picture. In a diagram of the missing. It's a web of over a hundred people."

"You're lying." Graham looked shell-shocked.

"A card beneath listed all of the details. Thomas Graham, age seventeen. Son of Peter and Lauren Graham, divorced couple. Mother has little contact with son. Son known to make provocative statements. Perhaps associates with—" Rose recited two names. "'Can't control his mouth. Potential powder keg.'" She cringed. "Sorry about that quote, Officer Graham."

"Where did you read that?"

Rose hesitated. "If I tell you, will you let us go?"

"Princess, I am fresh out of patience. Tell me!"

Rose shook her head. Graham spun Sophie around and shoved her against the Impala. "Rose!" Sophie pleaded.

"Okay!" Rose cringed. She had to have the courage to see this through, or Graham was going to take them in. Dad had told her about fifty-time losers like Graham: if he could bag a cop's daughter for doing something wrong, and if the ensuing investigation of Officer Scholl led anywhere, who knows how many rewards would come his way?

"You know how the chief has a private room in the station? For sensitive cases?" she asked. "I saw it on his wall."

"No one's allowed in that room."

Slowly, so that Graham could see her hands, Rose retrieved her lockpick, and displayed it.

Graham looked sick. Rose watched him think. She couldn't tell if he were going to be sick, angry, or what. "The chief let your dad in that room?"

"I know where they took him. I know where they took Tommy," Rose repeated.

"Gah." Graham stepped back, and shoved a hand through his hair. "Do you know how much I've been digging?" he muttered, perhaps to himself. "Do you know how I've risked my life, talking to lowlifes and hoping they wouldn't rat me out? And all this time, getting nowhere? Hell." He twisted, looking at the sky.

Do I dare? Rose thought.

But Graham drew his tiny .22. "You're taking me to him."

"No," Rose said. "I will tell you where he is. In exchange, you need to let us go."

~

"I won't hurt you," Mark said to the woman and her three kids, all under the age of seven. "Leave us," the mom commanded.

Mark shook his head. In the twilight, he sat on the dirty floor near the kids. The mom shrank back, but Mark set the gun on the floor. Mom pulled her two boys into her, but they all startled as a siren abruptly flared, out of sync with the slow, wailing curfew signal.

"I'm just a high school kid," Mark said.

"You look like a man."

"I'm eighteen."

"Why do you have a gun?" the woman asked.

"Everyone around here has a gun."

"But you're not from around here," she said.

"It was my father's," Mark said.

"What do you want?"

"To get home," he said. Abruptly, the four-year-old boy crawled toward him. Mark rested his palm atop the gun to keep the kid safe.

"Alex!" Mom said. "Get over here!"

Little Alex looked at Mark.

"I'll keep him safe," Mark said. "Where's your husband?"

The woman grew shaky. She looked like she might cry. "Vanished," she said.

"I'm sorry," Mark said. "My dad vanished fourteen years go." The boy snuggled next to him.

"That's different," the woman murmured.

"True," Mark said. He glanced around in the fading light. "Were you trying to get home?"

She shook her head. "My company closed and we couldn't pay the rent. We were on our way to my sister's when—" Her hand rose, stalled, and plunged to the floor.

Extra paramilitary violence, Mark thought, *and rising unemployment.* The news said joblessness had dropped to thirty percent, but in Mark's neighborhood, half of the people didn't have work. He wondered how long this woman and her family had been squatting here.

"When do you think it will be safe to go out?" she asked.

"I don't know. Someone burned down the parliament," Mark said.

Her eyes widened—they both knew that was the worst event since the Fracturing. Mark watched the mom instinctively glance around: usually, when the Blues and Yellows went at it, the Black Zone was actually the safest place to be. Because most people here were armed, the paramilitaries faced random snipers from dozens of rooftops. Once, an entire squad of Yellows stalked someone into an abandoned furniture store—and a bomb exploded, dropping two stories on them. That was the last time Mark had heard of a paramilitary stepping into the Black Zone.

"I'm Mark. What's your name?" Mark asked.

"Elyse," she said.

The boy snuggled in Mark's arms. Despite himself, resting in this century-old house, a remnant of his father's country, built long before the nation split into the breakaways, Mark imagined what the house must have looked like: two stories and a basement, like an old farmhouse he'd seen in books, with a fireplace, three bedrooms shared by a big family, kids always coming and going, people playing, working, building, planting, tinkering, lots of noise, friendly arguments, teasing, hugs, and a mom and a dad. On the mantle: a family photo surrounded by religious icons.

Elyse wasn't much older than he was—maybe 25. His

own mom had her three kids by that age. "What did he do?" Mark asked.

"Firefighter." Her kids snuggled with her. The police siren had faded, but the curfew siren still waxed and waned. She traced a finger in the dirt. "We married when we were eighteen. But it wasn't what you think." She motioned toward the tallest girl. "Mallory came along a year later."

Firefighter. Stable job, Mark thought. *Supposed to be, anyway.*

She reminded him of Maria, who had been engaged to a cop when she was nineteen. Maria, like Elyse, had planned ahead. In school, she'd made A's, developed practical skills, and dated a man who was going places. *Until the night of the shooting, and we lost Maria's fiancée—*

"Are they in school?" Mark asked. Because if she moved—if she made it to her sister's—what would happen, then? Safe schools were unaffordable. Mark felt for her. With her dark hair, her resemblance to his mom was uncanny. *Could they move in with us? Just temporarily?*

The little boy, Alex, was asleep, now. Mark's heart ached for the four of them. He hungered for his own family.

His phone vibrated. He retrieved it. Elyse looked apprehensive. Mark glanced at the screen.

Unbelievable, he thought.

~

Abruptly, Graham swung his tiny .22 from Sophie's chest and stalked toward Rose. But as he moved his arm, he was slow. As he moved it to aim his pistol at her heart, she bolted toward him.

Jugular—

Underneath the canopy of trees that blocked any

cameras, four of Rose's fingers shot straight below his Adam's Apple. Shocked, he sucked for air. As his arms flailed upward, her palm smashed down on his nose.

Sophie shrieked, but an instant later, Graham's pistol clattered against the street and all 250 pounds of him landed hard on the boulevard.

His eyes wide with horror, he looked for his gun, but Sophie had kicked it away.

"Stop." Rose now held her own plastic gun.

"That's assaulting an officer." Graham panted on the ground. He was clutching his throat and rubbing his nose.

Sophie handed Graham's tiny .22 to Rose, which Rose slipped into her pocket.

"I want to help you find Tommy," Rose said. *Because we're going there, anyway.*

"Rose." Sophie's voice shook as she moved to stand behind her friend. "What did you just get us into?"

"Give me my gun," Graham said.

"Do you want to find your son or not?"

Graham struggled to shove himself to standing, but he winced when he put his left hand on the ground. Rose could tell he'd hurt it when he'd used it to break his fall.

"You'll get yours," Graham grunted, "your highness."

"Stay down," she said.

"You're not going to shoot a police officer." He twisted himself to all fours. But before he could push his bulk upward, Rose fired.

Graham lurched and twisted. He was back on his rump. A cloud of dust rose an inch from where his hand had been.

"Spoiled fat cat," he panted.

"I want you to think about what my father taught me

for the last fifteen years," Rose said. "Martial arts. Sharpshooting. And I want you to think about how motivated I am."

"To do what?" Graham demanded. "Kill an honest cop?"

"I *found your son,*" Rose said. As Graham stared at her venomously, she saw something else in his eyes.

Fear.

"I get it," she said quietly. "You're afraid. You think you can't have him back."

His eyes grew wide, and a little emotion cracked through his tough exterior.

"But maybe you can," she said.

"What do you want?" Graham looked uncomprehending. "What does your father want?"

"Get in the police car!" Rose fired her gun.

Graham's hand flew to his head. She had blasted off strands of his shaggy, brown hair.

"You're crazy!" But he scrambled.

"Rose," Sophie sounded forlorn, "what are you doing?"

"Hand Sophie your keys," Rose said. Graham did so.

"Open the back door for him," Rose said to Sophie.

Sophie did so, and Graham got in, where he sat behind the bulletproof glass that separated him from the front.

"I'll drive," said Rose, and climbed in. She pressed several buttons; she turned off the car's cameras, erased the last ten minutes of footage, and darkened all of the windows. It wouldn't do for anyone to see two young women in the front seat, and a uniformed officer captive in the back.

"Your father will lose his job," Graham said. "And

you'll get life for this. A very short life."

"Are you going to report me," Rose asked, "if we get your son back?"

"Nobody comes back," Graham muttered.

Rose started the police car and put it in drive.

The windows, Rose knew, functioned like a one-way mirror: tinted on the outside, but they could see the street clearly from the inside. As she drove, Rose retrieved her phone and made a call.

"I hope that's your dad," Sophie murmured.

"Sidekick chick, her dad can't save you," Graham said. "But if you let me go, I can forget all about this."

A burst of static, and then the cop radio said: "Blue paramilitaries have taken over Tomfooleries restaurant in Eastgate," a dispatcher said. Rose turned it down. To the east, they saw the sky light up, and they heard a distant explosion. A column of black smoke rose in the sky.

"I don't know if you figured this out," Rose said, "but we all have bigger problems than that."

~

Staring at the photograph on the screen, Mark hesitated, then clicked *accept*. "Rose," he said.

"Are you all right?" she asked.

"Great," he said. In the darkening house, Elyse and her children's eyes grew wide.

"You're not home," she said. "Unless your electricity is off."

"Are you *driving*?" he asked. "There's a curfew."

The picture on his screen swept in a panorama. Rose was showing him that she was inside a police cruiser. Sophie White was her passenger. Mark gasped.

"My guess is, because of the curfew, you're stuck somewhere," she said. From his phone, Mark heard more sirens; apparently, the curfew was citywide. "Let me pick you up."

He had a thousand questions: was the cruiser her father's car? Did she steal it? What was Rose doing out? Why was Sophie with her?

And did he just now hear a *man's* voice in the car? She hadn't shown him the backseat. Behind the bulletproof shield, did she have a captive?

"What do you want?"

"Same thing as before," she said. "I want you to help me rescue our friend. Where are you?"

"Why?"

"Because we can't live like this!" she said. "We can't just abandon people we've always known." But then she hesitated, and he felt like she was holding something back. He didn't know what—but it was obvious that, whatever it was, she didn't want to say.

"Rose?" he asked. "What's really going on?"

"I'll tell you in person."

His thoughts flew rapidly. He was holed up in a crumbling house in the Black Zone. If a fire swept through the neighborhood, if a gang came, or if a paramilitary battle spilled into these houses, then he, Elyse, and the kids were all dead.

"Tell me now," he said.

"We need each other, Mark," Rose said plaintively.

That's your problem, he thought. He'd only help her after he knew his own family, and Elyse's family, were safe.

"I'll help you," he said, "but you have to give me the police car whether or not we get G.J. out."

Graham laughed out loud. "*Aaaaand* they're all high,"

he muttered to himself.

"What do you want the car for?" Rose asked.

To get to the coyote faster, he thought. His family would breeze right through the curfew like it was air.

"Fine," Rose said.

"Rose!" Sophie exclaimed.

"They'll swat you down like flies," Graham said. "And then they'll execute you."

Who is that? Mark wondered. Rose wouldn't show him who they'd captured, but the voice sounded middle-aged. *He sounds like he orders people around—is it a cop?* Oddly, Mark found himself hoping it was: *If she can outsmart a cop and take his car, what else can she do?* For the first time, he felt like he might be able to get his family out of this country.

"I'm at 87th and Columbus," he said.

"Be there in ten to fifteen," she said. Abruptly, he heard her sirens flair. His screen pulsed out red and blue flashes—

—and then Rose hung up.

~

` With a little bit of reprogramming, Rose disabled the cop car's interior camera, and the tracking device that let the station know where it was. She then turned on the GPS. A map of the metro emerged, lit up seventeen-inch screen between her and Sophie. She gasped.

Graham muttered the foulest curse word Rose had ever heard. "It's gotten worse."

The map bled with red dots—reports of assaults, smashed shop windows, and burning churches and synagogues. Larger yellow triangles collided with blue trapezoids—street clashes between the Blue and Yellow paramilitaries. Black flags nearby showed police positions; often, they remained a safe four-to-six blocks away.

Rose accelerated and turned right on Hess Street. They were six miles from Mark. She could weave through a path of empty roads.

"Turn left on Rudolph," Graham said. Rose frowned. A police substation was on that road.

"So we can get caught," Sophie blurted.

"No, genius." Graham sighed. "Because there's more to this city than that map." He pointed contemptuously. "Those roads will be empty. Those cops all be out protecting our leaders. How else would they get their kickbacks?"

"Then why don't we see any police presence in Weissensee?" Sophie pointed to a gated community that once belonged to the wealthy, but now were occupied by the ruling class.

"Because like us, they'll have their trackers off, Brainiac," Graham said. "Do you think the fat cats will want a record of their homes being overprotected while the city gets torched?"

Rose nodded. What he said made sense.

"You can't possibly believe him," Sophie asked Rose. "Do you?"

"Since you're going to get us all killed, anyway," Graham said, "could you at least take this road now? *Please?* As a special favor to the honest cop that you jacked in the throat?"

Rose veered onto Rudolph. "I don't believe this," Sophie muttered. Rose accelerated. "We're probably speeding right into a trap."

"We're not, wizard," said Graham.

Rose glanced at the screen. Someone had reported a fire near St. Max's. As far as she could tell, the authorities were letting it burn.

Rose turned on her blue-and-red lights, and floored it.

~

Mark glanced at the time. Five minutes until Rose arrived. The little boy, Alex, slept in his arms.

It must have been hard, he felt like saying to this beautiful, 25-year-old woman who had three children, who had lost her husband. *How did you get by?*

"How did he die?" Mark asked.

"Saving us," she said. "He ran into our building, which was burning."

"From arson?"

Elyse nodded. For as long as Mark could remember, almost all fires were arson.

"Everything's going to get worse," Elyse said softly so as to not wake her children. She raised her head, indicating the whole city. "Steven said the fire department couldn't keep up. And it wasn't always the Blues or Yellows, or the gangs. He told me that a lot of the evidence showed something else."

Mark felt cold. He felt like he knew where this was going, but he decided to play dumb. "But the news said the Blues start fires."

"Steven said they're the ones the government wants you to hate because they're associated with the Nationalists." Thompson's party. "But he found evidence that some were started by the army."

"Why?"

"They want the chaos," she said. "They want people afraid."

Mark nodded. Living where he did, behind a fence,

he saw glimpses of the violence plaguing the city. The media and the authorities liked to slant it, but Elyse wasn't saying anything he hadn't heard before.

From a few blocks away, they heard gunshots. They startled, but then eased back to where they were sitting. *12-gauge shotguns,* Mark realized. Old-timey weapons, probably kept by shopkeepers and homeowners.

They waited: no further firings. Mark noticed the building that was torched five blocks away now no longer had flames rising into the city. It had either been put out, or it had died in a controlled burn. *The Black Zone takes care of its own,* he thought.

His eyes were drawn to Elyse. Her resemblance to Maria was freaky. Same black curls, blue eyes, immaculate skin, flat waist—

Abruptly, they heard a car roll along the street. As Mark strained to see out the broken window, his phone buzzed.

"Be right out," he said.

"Hurry." Rose clicked off.

Without waking the boy, Mark picked him up and laid him against his older sister. The kids stirred; Elyse's eyes searched him as though she were trying to figure him out.

"Heath Grimjack is my friend at school," he said. "He doesn't know anything about where I went tonight, or what my plans are, but if you ever get in a jam, contact him." Mark handed her five hundred dollars. Elyse's eyes popped. "Good luck," he said.

He felt her gaze lingering on him as he left.

~

"Clark Kent on a pogo stick," Graham muttered as they watched Mark step out of a man-sized hole on the house's side.

Rose wished Graham would be quiet. His nonstop complaints were getting on her nerves. Ignoring the cop, Rose watched Mark. He was clutching a .44, and he looked up and down the blocks of ramshackle houses before running to Rose's police car.

Rose opened the bulletproof window one inch. "Don't let him out," she told Mark, and unlocked the left rear door. "We need him."

Graham shook his head. "Where'd you meet this preppy?" he asked. "You go to the prom with one guy and come back with him, instead?"

"Get in," Rose said.

"You never told me you kidnapped a cop," Mark said.

"Yes! She kidnapped a cop! Thanks for noticing!" Sophie exclaimed. "Do you want to get in, or do like standing in the street?"

Rose could feel—she could see—silhouetted faces wrapped in shadows, staring down at them from second-story windows. She looked into Mark's eyes. He grimaced, then climbed in, closed the door, pressed himself against it, and leveled his .44 at Graham.

"My dad works with him," Rose said, and shifted into drive.

"Is he honest?" Mark asked.

"You bet your prep school ass," Graham said. "All honest cops ride in the back."

"What's he doing here?"

"We're helping him save his son."

Mark looked skeptical. He clearly thought Graham

looked fatalistic about his chance of survival.

"Where are we going?" Mark asked. "What's the plan?"

"We are going to take advantage of the curfew," Rose said, and explained what she wanted to do.

When she finished, the car was absolutely silent. Even Sophie, her best friend, didn't defend her. As Rose left the Black Zone, because it was safe to be a cop again, she turned on her flashing lights and took it up to sixty miles per hour.

"Preppy boy," Graham said to Mark, "it's been nice knowing you."

CHAPTER TEN
The Transfer Prison

The transfer prison looked like every other factory in the Garment District of the city. It even said Triangle Company on the front marquee, and it had two display windows that showcased models in simple flower-print dresses, new for the working class. Four stories tall, it had loading docks in the back.

Rose parked in the lot's furthest corner, underneath a tree. In the distance, they heard something eerie:

Silence.

"Guys," Sophie said, "I don't like this."

"Have you seen any cameras?" Mark asked.

"Not one," Sophie murmured.

"That's not good," Graham said.

Reluctantly, everyone followed toward the front door.

"Repeat the plan," Rose prompted.

But he looked at the others first. Finally, Mark said, "I'm a prisoner."

"Kind of," Rose said. She removed the bullets from Graham's tiny .22 and gave the cop his weapon back.

"Your trust means a lot," Graham said.

Rose ignored him, and handed Sophie and Mark a pair of handcuffs each. She had already removed the locks; they would look clamped shut, but Sophie and Mark, who were now putting them on, could spring them open at any time.

If need be.

"We are literally walking into a secret prison," Graham said, "if you can believe what you saw on the

Chief's walls."

"I believe what I saw," Rose said.

"The place will be crawling with dirty military officers, guys who get rewarded for making people disappear."

"I know." Rose assigned them roles. Mark and Sophie would be in handcuffs; they were new undesirables arrested by Holder's secret police. Rose and Graham stood behind them; Rose would portray an informer, compromised a long time ago. Graham was a cop who appeared to work for the city, but really worked for Holder.

"And we'll just stroll right through them," Graham said. "Maybe Sophie here can ask one of them out on a date."

"No. We won't 'just stroll through.'" Rose frowned at Graham. "They'll question us. Let me do the talking."

Graham threw up his hands. But he calmed himself, and pointed his empty pistol at Mark's back. Rose didn't trust Graham with a loaded weapon. For reassurance, she touched the plastic gun in her pocket.

As was written on the chief's whiteboards, they approached the front door. Of course, with the curfew and the riots, no one was in the shop. A single bulb made the mannequins look gray. In their simple dresses, they looked like statues in a museum from long ago.

Rose slid a scarred welcome sign aside. Underneath the sign lay a keypad. Sophie and Mark each raised their eyebrows. Graham rolled his eyes. So far, the whiteboard was right.

She punched: 022733.

Nothing.

Everyone stared at her apprehensively. The hair on the back of her neck stood on end.

The chief had tacked up several codes on his wall. Rose tried another: 013033.

The door stared back at them.

"You must be number one in your class," Graham said. "You realize if you type the wrong code too many times that a SWAT team is going to swarm around us and—"

"Shhh," Mark elbowed Graham, who shut up. Just because they couldn't see any cameras didn't mean they weren't being filmed.

"Rose?" Sophie asked her.

Her confidence dropping, Rose struggled to remember what she saw. The chief's pattern of photos and descriptions, was so intricate, with arrows connecting hundreds of people in a web like the world's most complicated decision tree. *What was that third code?*

She entered: 030533.

A latch released and the door opened a crack. They stepped inside.

In the red light, they saw mannequins that wore peasant dresses suitable for farmers and factory workers. Past a sales counter was a door. Hesitantly, Rose urged the others through it.

On the other side was a long, dimly lit corridor that, far off, glowed with white light. "Free at last," Graham muttered.

Rose watched Sophie and Mark tense with fear. They were all afraid. If they stepped into this corridor, they could easily be sealed inside. All the secret police would have to do is seal both ends.

"Ready to die?" Graham asked.

Rose turned to him. *Tommy,* her lips said soundlessly. He was still angry and afraid—but he nodded.

As they approached the bright room, and Rose saw pulses of light, they heard President Holder's voice: "—our swift retaliation is already underway. Even so, the public must respect the curfew: it's the law. For your own protection, go home. Seal off your windows and doors in case of gas attack. If any unknown person knocks on your door and begs to be let inside, deny them."

"Ahem," Graham said to the mustached man behind the counter. About thirty, he looked bony. In the corner, two much stronger men played a video game and shared a bottle of clear alcohol.

"We've regained the upper hand," the president continued. "We've captured the arsonist, who acted alone. But others tried to use this moment to attack our hospitals, our firehouses, and supply chains. In short, the arteries that—"

"You picked a bad night," the bony man said to Graham.

"Tell me about it," Graham grunted.

"We're here to see the Captain, and one more." Rose recited another code from the chief's board, one that revealed her as an informer. Sophie and Mark played their parts by looking terrified—but a little hopeful, as if they'd been told if they cooperated, all of this would go away, and they could go back to their normal lives.

In the background, Rose noticed the man had a wall of screens. Half showed the news from six media outlets, but the news was all the same: the nation's brave troops were beating back the paramilitaries—although one showed the smoldering shell of the parliament. It hadn't just been consumed with fire. The walls had blown outward as though, inside, someone had planted several bombs. Inspectors crawled through the wreckage where dozens of small fires still burned. *They won't find anything*, Rose thought.

The man's other screens showed half-shaved, ordinary people wearing street clothes, sitting or trying to sleep in tiny rooms that blazed with white light. Some were crammed four to a room. No room had a mattress; just wireframes to lie down on. Bare walls, no toilet, no sink, no sign of food. The screens shuffled through a series of cells. An old woman. A tough-looking man. And then—just for a second—G.J. Dasch.

But Rose remembered it all: G.J. lay on the floor because there was no furniture. He shielded his eyes against the searchlight-bright illumination. And then his image was gone, replaced by a boy no older than twelve in a different cell.

"The Captain, and one more?" the bony man raised both eyebrows—a surrender gesture. "Let me see…"

They all stared at the screens, watching as the images of prisoners flickered by: three women and one man in a cell—clearly afraid of each other. Obvious criminals. A guy on amphetamines who was ranting; he jerked his shoulders as he yelled at the ceiling. But Rose watched the bony man, and memorized the sequence he typed.

In one cell, Rose briefly glanced a white-haired man in a green military uniform with multiple epaulettes. Rose suppressed a shudder: the man was staring straight at them. But Rose knew he was staring at his reflection; one-way glass separated them. *That's General Hukov*, Rose suddenly realized.

Hukov had been famous for forty years, long before the Fracturing. He'd served the old nation. After the separations, he stayed loyal to his region. And at first, he'd received even more promotions.

But now, he was a bony, old man. He looked ten years older than his actual age. Rose wondered what they accused him of. He used to show up in the news every so often, always doing something they praised. And now, she couldn't remember the last time she'd seen him. This national hero had just simply faded away.

The others in the cell were mesmerized by live footage of the military kicking down doors in a Hanover apartment, and then the military spraying the room with gunfire. "Room four-twenty," said the bony man on the screen.

Rose nudged Graham. "Thanks," he said.

"You're too young to be an informer," the bony man said to Rose.

"You have no idea what she's capable of," Graham said.

Rose noticed the armed men in the back had finished their game, and weren't starting a new one.

"You know very well there are informers younger than me," Rose said, and recited an identification number she had rememorized from the chief's Puzzle Room. "And you know I can't talk about it."

"Room Thirteen." The room branched in three direction. The bony man handed Rose two keycards, pointed toward a middle corridor, and buzzed an unlock button.

The tough guys started a new game and appeared to ignore Rose's group. She led the way.

Graham gave her a discreet but meaningful look. Sophie kept up the silent suffering act of quivering, and looking like she was struggling to contain her tears. Mark looked bleary and defeated.

Did you time them? she communicated silently to Graham.

He nodded. He, too, she knew, had memorized the rotation pattern of the internal surveillance system. The screens shuffled through the cells and the hallways.

We have thirty seconds, and then we'd better be back in that hallway, she whispered, and opened a door to room 104, and shot inside. The others rushed in after her.

They were in a server room, the hub of the prison's computer system.

"I don't know, Rose," Sophie said.

"Tommy." Graham grimaced. He looked ready to kill. "I saw him. They have him in a cell with those animals."

Rose scrambled from computer to computer. "What are you doing?" Mark asked.

"I'm replacing the camera feed from certain hallways," she replied, "with a continuous loop showing the corridors being empty." They needed freedom to move without being monitored.

"Will that fool them?" Sophie asked.

"Not for long," Graham growled. "Dumb as they are, playing their games and being glued to the propaganda channel instead of doing their jobs, they'll eventually wonder where we are."

"Rose! Hurry!" Sophie was jittery, springing on her toes.

"Done." Rose did a quick search. "Your son is in Room 202," she told Graham. Graham pushed Mark down the hallway. Given his manner, Rose felt relieved that Mark had a loaded .44 in his pocket.

"G.J. is in Room Thirteen," Rose said.

"C'mon!" Sophie said.

"Wait," Rose said to Graham and Mark, who were already halfway back in the stairwell. She raised both eyebrows, and gave them a significant look. "The hall cameras are now showing a loop."

"And that other thing?" Graham asked.

"It's triggered," Rose said. "We have ten minutes."

"You did it, then," Graham muttered, a little shocked.

"Let's go." Mark yanked Graham along.

Rose hastily erased all evidence of their presence, and triggered the event. *Under nine minutes,* she thought.

"Let's go." She pulled Sophie's hand toward the threshold.

~

Mark bounded up the stairs three at a time. Graham struggled to keep up. When they reached the top, the heavy man looked ready for a heart attack.

Mark slowed the pace. Room 202 was just steps away. When they reached it, Mark swiped the keycard Rose had given him in the basement. The lock clicked open—

—and someone flung the door back, and four young men rushed Mark and Graham.

~

Rose and Sophie sprinted upward, and had to zigzag through a maze of corridors. They reached Room 13. Rose unlocked it.

G.J. lay curled in a ball on the antiseptic white tile. Only now did she notice that they'd taken his belt and shoes.

"Rose! Sophie!" He struggled to get to his feet. "What are you doing here?"

"C'mon." Rose seized his arm. "We have to leave."

"What?" He looked at the camera in the corner.

"It's dead," she said. She pulled his arm—

—but he was fighting her. He was skinny and short, no more than 130 pounds, unlike Mark, but he had a wild man's strength.

"Rose, stop!" he said. "You're ruining everything!"

~

As a stocky boy rushed him, Mark threw a basketball elbow below the man's breastbone. He hit the soft hollow and the man doubled over.

The punks we saw on video, Mark thought.

"Tommy," Graham said. He had done something very fast, some kind of martial art, and a second man was on the floor.

As the third man charged Mark, Mark's left foot shot around his assailant, hooked his ankle, and Mark floor-swept him. The third man crashed down on his friend, who grunted in pain.

"Peter?" Tommy asked.

"Don't call me 'Peter,'" Graham said.

Only now did Mark draw his .44. Sweating, he took stock of the situation: he hadn't expected any of the prisoners to attack. *How stupid are they?*

"We're here to get you out," Mark said.

"Let's skedaddle, son," Peter Graham said.

"What the hell are you doing, senile old man?" Tommy shouted.

"Getting you out, you ungrateful fool," Peter snarled. He seized his son's arm.

~

"We don't have much time," Rose said.

"You shut off all the cameras," G.J. said. "You infiltrated their servers."

Rose nodded. "But it's only so long before—"

"—they figure it out or the system reboots," G.J. said. "Rose, I appreciate—"

"No. Not reboots," Rose interrupted. "I triggered a full-on power failure."

G.J. went white. "Every cell will unlock." He began to stammer. "Do you—do you realized who you're turning loose?"

"A lot of ordinary people. Let's go!"

"And professional killers," G.J. said. "The best thing we can do slam the cell door closed and hope they can't break the lock."

"We don't have time to argue!" Sophie seized G.J.'s arm.

"I'm not going!" G.J. tore himself free. "Forget you ever saw me. Rose, Sophie, get out of here!"

~

"I made a deal with them," Tommy said, and pointed to the unconscious three men on the floor, all of whom were twitching.

"With *them*?" Graham put his weight into it and jerked Tommy into the hall. "You moron. Your teachers were right."

"What the hell," a voice cried from the end of the hallway.

"What the—" Graham began. A man in uniform was hurrying toward them.

"Good job," Tommy muttered. "*Father.*"

"Shoot him," Graham hissed to Mark.

Everyone will hear a gunshot, Mark thought. In a split second, he made a decision he hoped they wouldn't regret: while aiming his .44, he sprinted toward the man. As his target reached for something on his belt—Mark was not sure what—Mark shot to top speed.

~

"Leave me alone!" G.J. cried.

Rose regretted this even as she did it, but her hand shot forward, and she twisted his wrist backward, her thumb on a pressure point, and drove him to his knees. G.J. gasped, and looked up in shock at what his lifelong friend had done to him.

"Rose!" Sophie lost her color.

He tried to talk, but instead sucked for air. She didn't know what was worse: how nauseated he now looked, or the shock of betrayal in his eyes.

"I am saving your life." She lifted him to his feet and yanked him into the hall. Always underweight, he didn't have the energy to resist.

"My life is not important," he finally gasped, but her fingers on his neck threatened to clamp down on a pressure point and send insane levels of pain through his nervous system, and he knew it. She'd render him unconscious if she had to, and she and Sophie would lug the 120-pound boy out together if necessary.

"Yes, it is." Sophie pushed them toward the stairwell. "Go!"

"You have no idea how bad you've screwed everything up," he said. "I'm on the inside, now, Rose!" G.J. said. "Put me back and let me do what I can!"

'On the inside'? she thought. *Is that even possible?*

"You're a prisoner who was curled up on the floor."

"I had to let them think I was beaten. They're co-opting me," he said softly. "Rose, they are sending us out of the country. They have a network of prison labor camps that aren't even in our territory. They're in foreign nations—territory that Holder has conquered."

"Holder's *at war* with another country?"

"Places that can't resist," he said. "Tiny states. This is what I was researching for weeks. Why do you think everyone's so poor? The army gets most of the nation's resources."

"And now they think you work for them?"

"They will. You have to leave me here! Listen, I'm too valuable. I can manipulate any computer system. They figured that out. That's why they took me."

Rose shook her head. "You're betting you'll be able to fool them, and they won't just kill you."

"Rose, I can do this." He was pleading.

"No," she said decisively. "We are going three floors down to meet with the others, and we are getting on the street."

"I can do this!" he said. He tried to tear away, but her fingers dug into his wrist's pressure point, and in an instant, he looked weak and pale.

As they dragged him along, he said, "I can slow down their acquisition of slave labor. I can get the prisoners more food. Most get under 500 calories a day. Rose, *please!*"

"Let's go!" Sophie yelled. She seized G.J.'s arm and yanked so hard that he lurched into the hallway. "You're so smart, you can do all of that from the outside."

"Hey!" he said. But Rose and Sophie were forcing him down the hall.

"She's right," Rose said, gesturing with her plastic

gun.

But as they reached the stairwell, she worried that, somehow, she was making the wrong decision.

~

When Mark collided with the guard, the man's phone bounced against the floor like a hockey puck. He pistol-whipped the man hard. The man's knees wobbled and he crumbled to the white tiles, unconscious, twitching.

"Weak," Tommy muttered.

"Shut it." Graham was already pushing his on toward the stairwell. "Or he'll do you next."

"Just shoot him."

As they shot down the stairs, Mark fretted. *Ninety seconds until—*

When they reached the bottom of the stairs, Rose, Sophie, and G.J. saw Mark, Graham, and a tattooed, skinny man emerging at the opposite stairwell. "Twenty seconds," she shouted.

As Graham cursed, they all picked up speed, racing back the way they entered. Mark caught up with her.

"We'll have to shoot our way out," he said.

"No, we won't. I saw a map in the server room. We'll take the alternative path: the escape route."

"Escape route?"

"In case—"

And, at that moment, what Rose had programmed happened:

The power failed.

Every light died. Simultaneously, they heard hundreds of clicks from the door locks. They were in near-total darkness.

"Hands on each other's shoulders," Rose ordered. "Follow me."

And then, abruptly, they heard a whooshing sound, like a furnace switching on, and the halls were irradiated with red light.

Graham cursed.

The backup generator and system, Rose knew. She kept leading them toward what looked like a closet door. But it was not a closet door.

And then the red light died. *It worked,* Rose thought. She had also taken out the backup generator.

In near darkness, she opened the door. It led to a closet—but in the back, by the light of her phone, she found a keypad. It looked dead, but it was supposed to be on a third and separate system—one that she had not disabled.

From the hallway, they all heard noise. Doors were opening; voices were rising.

"Hurry," Mark said. Rose could smell Graham's son close by; the skinny man emitted a pungent odor.

All over the pitch-black prison, they heard it: distant shouts, doors opening, and a trample of footsteps.

"They're loose," Sophie gasped.

Rose entered a code. When she heard a latch pop, she pushed the brick wall open. She shielded her eyes.

A series of red bulbs, which interrupted the pitch-black closet and hall, lit an otherwise dark stairwell. "Down these stairs," Rose said, and hurried down.

The others followed; she glanced back and saw Mark swing the door shut behind them. The cacophony from above now was muffled.

"Cinderella, I hope you know what you're doing," Graham panted. "I saw some confirmed killers upstairs. Some lovelies that I put away myself."

"And some librarians and firefighters," G.J. said, "who got on Holder's bad side."

"Screw the librarians!" Tommy exclaimed.

The stairway crooked left, led down thirteen more stairs, and ended in a steel door. Abruptly, the muffled noise from above grew a lot louder and clearer.

"Here! Down here!" a bass voice echoed from above.

Pop pop pop. They heard gunfire, and someone cried out.

"Rose!" Sophie yelled.

"Shhh!" Mark said.

Rose flung open the door. Immediately, the smell of rotting meat hit her like a puff of hot air from an oven.

A loud shriek from above. Many shouts; lots of trampling. Rose could not tell what was going on, but she pulled Sophie forward, and into a sewer.

"Gah," Sophie said. The smell was hideous, and the damp air made it cold; Rose shivered.

When they all stepped down into the curved floor, into two inches of foul water, Mark pulled the door closed behind them. His hands felt along the edges. "I can't lock it," he said. But he reached into the muck, found two rotting tree limbs and a brick, apparently swept into the sewer, and he placed them in front of the door.

Shielding his nose and mouth, Tommy started cussing, and it seemed like he'd never stop. "What the hell," he finished. "It *stinks.*"

"It smells good compared to you." Graham shoved Tommy's shoulder. To Rose: "How much farther?"

"We're a soccer field away," Rose said. From her pocket, she handed Graham his bullets back. "Hurry."

They waded along in the muck as fast as possible, the odor nearly doubling Rose over. Soon, thirty yards back, they heard people ramming themselves against the door, and muffled shouts.

"They'll shoot us," Tommy muttered.

"You first," Graham said. "I've already been shot."

"Shhh," Rose said. The bricks and limbs had blocked the door with scraped against the concrete, and they heard splashes as, one by one, they fell into the sewer water. Even from a hundred yards away, Rose wrinkled her noise; the odor reminded her of dead, rotting reptiles. "Press yourself against the wall."

"Give me a gun," Tommy hissed.

"You? You'd shoot yourself," his father whispered. "Give it to me."

In the near darkness, all they heard were voices, cusses and the tree limbs Mark had placed scraping the cement before landing in the dead water.

"What the hell?" a voice echoed. Rose and the others pressed against the damp walls. Something creepy touched her shoulder.

"Uh. Gah! It *reeks*," a voice echoed from down the pipe. *Reeks...reeks...reeks....*

"It's a sewer. They do that," his companion replied. *That...that...that...*

"Damn it," Tommy muttered—

—and his voice echoed off of the curved sewer walls.

"Imbecile," his father whispered, and held his son back, in a shadow, pressed against the slimy wall.

The three men whirled. Their silhouettes pointed straight at them. All three raised pistols and pressed themselves against a wall.

"Identify yourselves!" one shouted.

Abruptly, Rose heard three shots; in the curved sewer, the bullets boomed like cannon fire. *Graham just fired,* she realized. Two of the silhouettes cried out and fell to their knees; the third raised his arm.

"Gun!" Mark cried, and pressed Rose against the wall with one arm. With his other, he was holding back G.J., who held back Sophie.

The third silhouette started firing. Rose flinched but she aimed carefully. Graham had left her no choice. It all happened quickly: she wondered how much the third man could see; the sewer only had a dim red bulb every twenty yards, and they were against the curved wall. The enemy bullets echoed like miniature bombs; chunks of cement burst from above; Graham was emptying his clip; she feared Sophie or G.J. would get hit by a ricocheting bullet—

I don't want to kill—

She aimed for the man's chest, and fired. Her gun recoiled in her hand.

Nothing happened. The silhouette twitched but remained standing, remained firing. *What the heck?* She was sure she hit him.

She wondered: is he wearing a bulletproof vest? Graham pressed himself against the wall. "Shoot," he hissed. "Shoot!"

Rose thought about where a vulnerable spot would be: a leg. A hard shot to make a hundred yards in near darkness. She fired—

—the man shrieked, and there was a clattering sound, and then a splash, as though he'd lost his gun, and it collided against the cement walls before falling into the sewage.

"Run!" Graham said. He pulled his son along the direction they'd all been going—away from the three men.

But Mark was now sprinting *toward* the three pursuers.

"Mark, what are you doing?" Rose shouted after him. Her voice echoed off the walls.

"Making sure we don't get followed," he shouted back.

"Officer Graham, wait," Rose shouted.

"Goodbye, Buttercup," Graham shouted back. Tommy cursed at him; Graham pulled him along.

G.J. was abruptly clutching her arm even as Mark reached the three men. Rose saw Mark lunge at the last man. Something very swift happened, and the man was on the ground. And then he shot the last man. Rose gasped in fright—but then Mark did something she couldn't understand: he dragged the man's limp body against the tunnel's curve, and propped him up against the curved wall, and kept the man's head above the muck.

Swiftly, Mark went through each man's pockets. Rose couldn't quite see, but it looked like he was taking their phones and dropping them into the stagnant water. Soon, Mark was gripping a second man by the throat.

"He isn't killing them," Sophie murmured.

"Rose," G.J. said, "I've been trying to tell you. I learned things. Holder is ordering a purge. He's using the fire as an excuse to declare a national emergency—martial law. He's going to round up all of his enemies, and have a lot of them shot tonight. Ordinary people, Rose, like your dad: cops who are too independent and will make trouble."

The hair on the back of Rose's neck rose. It was all happening too fast. Their group had splintered. Graham and Tommy were already receding into darkness, their curses and splashes echoing off the walls. And Mark was running back to them.

"We have to stop them," G.J. was saying. He nodded at Mark, who had arrived. "They'll shoot hundreds. They'll round up thousands more, put them on freighters, and send them to camps. His public persona—reasonable, measured—it's all a lie."

"How do you know this?" Rose tried to shake herself out of her confusion. She glanced Graham's way. Graham and Tommy were just shadows, now, nearly gone.

They'll hotwire the car and leave us stranded.

"I keep telling you, that's why they grabbed me," G.J. said. "Because I'd hacked into their private communications. I learned things. After they took me, they gave me a choice. They could take my family and send them off to a work camp, or I could work for them."

Because of your skills, Rose thought. "What did you say?"

"I had no choice," G.J. said. "I said I'd work for them. Rose, I am powerful on the inside. I figured out their systems!"

Sophie gasped.

"I was going to sabotage them from within," G.J. said. "They were going to round people up. I was going to send the secret police to the wrong houses. To empty houses."

"You can do that?"

G.J. nodded. "The freighter they have bound for a work camp? I was going to tamper with their navigation, make the ship transmit false signals to hide its location, and send it into the Island's territorial waters."

"All from a *computer screen*?" Rose shook his head.

"Bold," Mark said, but he looked doubtful.

"Psycho," Sophie said. "They'll shoot you the minute they catch you."

But G.J.'s plan got Rose thinking.

"They won't catch me," G.J. said.

"They caught you this morning," Mark said.

"What I mean is, they won't catch me until the ship is in the Island's waters. And by then, it will be too late for them."

"So then the Island can just kill you and all of the other prisoners, instead," Sophie said.

"The Island is not what you think," G.J. said. "That's another lie they've been telling us."

"Did you kill them?" Rose asked softly.

Mark shook his head. "Shot in the legs, immobilized, weaponless, without communications, and out cold. They won't stay out long. Let's get out of here." He hurried past them—

—but stopped when he realized Rose was not moving.

"Rose, are you listening to me? Hundreds of deaths," G.J. said. "Tonight is the night. Tonight is the purge. Tonight is the night Holder goes from being a leader with a fraying coalition to an absolute dictator. He does it by labeling his opponents traitors and wiping them out. We have to save them."

"Rose, let's *move!*" Mark exclaimed.

"Wait," Rose told Mark. To G.J.: "What do you propose?"

"We go to a relay station for servers," G.J. said. "I can get into the control center from any node. We place directives in the system, and before they know what's going on, in the chaos of tonight, we can rescue hundreds."

"No, Rose," said Mark. "You said that if I help you, you'd help my family get to a coyote."

"The coyotes will be among the first people they arrest," said G.J. "They're not going to want anyone escaping to another country, and telling the world what's really going on, here. You won't last the night."

"G.J., I respect you," said Mark, "but I have to get Maria, Jason, and my mom out of here. We have to escape!"

"Rose," Sophie pleaded.

In the near darkness, in the dripping water, Rose felt their eyes on her. "If we have the chance to save thousands, we have to take it," she said.

"G.J. thinks he can penetrate their system from just *anywhere?*" Mark said. "The second they realize he's inside, they will fire a rocket straight at us."

"I can convince them we're somewhere else," G.J. said. "I just have to get to a node."

"Insane," Mark said. "We have to *run!*"

"Run *where?*" Sophie demanded. "The whole city is under siege."

"We have to have a plan," Rose said, "and if we can save people, we must. Where's the closest node?"

In the dark, she saw Mark's shoulders, rise, freeze, and then collapse. For no reason, she wondered where Graham and Tommy were, now.

"Nearby. They tested my skills on their system today. When they did, I got away with some digging around."

"They let you explore their plans? Their methods?" Mark sounded shocked.

"Because they captured me," G.J. said. "They told me I could either work for them as a tech or they'd hang me." Rumor had it: Holder brought back the rope. "It's less than a mile from here."

"*What?*" Mark asked.

"It needs to be close by," G.J. said, "to run the prison. To coordinate with the freighter that will take those rounded up to the labor camps. C'mon." He walked fast now, through the muck, the odor nearly making Rose wretch, as they followed Graham and Tommy's path in the dark tunnel. "I saw an electric grid. Their diagrams give away more than they think. You see the power stations, the nodes, everything. Your mind can fill in the gaps. In fact, we should find a door in this tunnel that leads to the basement."

"And then what are we supposed to do?" Mark asked. "Sneak in, shoot anyone who gets in the way, and you and Rose reprogram the system?"

"There won't be anyone there. It's just a node," G.J. said.

"It's worth exploring," said Rose. "G.J., how long would it take for you to redirect the freighter?"

Mark fell silent, but Rose saw his hand touch his .44. She wondered what he was thinking. Did he feel betrayed? She had promised him Graham's police car, but Graham and Tommy were probably long gone, by now.

"Five minutes, tops," G.J. was saying. "All I'll do is tamper with their navigation. They'll think they're going in one direction, but if they follow what the computer says, they'll end up at the Island."

"In a foreign nation's waters," Sophie murmured.

"Free," G.J. said.

"Where is this door?" Mark asked.

"Five minutes," G.J. said.

"You're fine with this?" Rose asked.

"What choice do I have?" Mark asked. "I could leave, go home, and try to hunker down, but you said I'm on a purge list." Something about his voice made her wonder if he'd believed her. "I can stick with my original plan, but you say that's impossible."

In silence, they tromped through the stagnant sewer. Finally, Rose gathered the courage to place a reassuring hand on Sophie's back. Sophie nodded at her as if to say, *I always knew things would come to this.*

Even so, an idea was occurring to her…

…because even if they redirected the freighter, then how would they save their own lives?

Two minutes later, they found what appeared to be a utility door in the tunnel. G.J. typed a code into the keypad, and the door unlocked.

When they entered the tunnel, the automatic lights rose gradually until the gray corridor was bathed in antiseptic light.

"No cameras," said Rose, as they approached a far door.

"Perks of authority," G.J. said. He reached for the keypad to open the door.

"Wait," Rose said.

Everyone was looking at her. In the red light, she could see how fearful they looked. *We screw up, we're dead,* Sophie's face said. *And they'll interrogate our families.*

"Can you get us on that freighter?" Rose asked.

"*What?*" Sophie exclaimed. Mark looked too stunned to speak, but his hand gripped his .44.

"Can you get us on that freighter?" Rose repeated to G.J.

"Well, yeah," G.J. stammered. "But w-why—"

"Because if it's going to international waters, we want to be on it."

Mark was staring at her intensely for intensely than she had ever been stared at. It worried her; she was afraid he was simply going to leave them without saying another word.

"Rose," G.J. said, "I know this was my plan, to redirect it, but what if something goes wrong? It is a slave ship loaded with undesirables. What do you think Holder's going to do to it if he figures out something is wrong?"

"Sink it," Sophie said.

"Sink it and track us down. Kill us."

"Not if we completely take it over," Rose said.

"Can you do that?"

"I can…I can do all kinds of things, temporarily," G.J. was stammering. "I can give us cover stories and get us on."

"You're saying we can dominate it!" Rose said.

"You and what army?" Mark asked.

"We actually have one," Rose said. "We can have all the firepower we need, and we can get everyone we love out of this country."

She laid out her plan.

~

G.J. entered the keypad's code, and the door unlocked. The server room was empty. As G.J. hacked the system, giving orders to clear the way for Rose's father and his two best friends to move freely in their police cars, Rose explained her plan.

"My father's friends are ex-SEALS," she said.

"In their forties," Sophie murmured.

"Still sharp," Rose said. "They round up our families and bring them to the freighter. G.J. gives them, and us, cover identities. We are supposed to be there. Some of us are informers, others are soldiers for the regime, previously acting as cops. They board with their guns. They're a match for any member of Holder's army."

"What if they're outnumbered?" Mark asked.

"All of them have taken out whole squads singlehandedly," Rose said. "They've known each other for twenty years. Part of their training is to always know what the other man is thinking."

Mark was nodding slowly. "And you say my name was on the chief's board."

Rose nodded. In the tiny room containing the node, the only sound was G.J. typing on a keyboard. "You could try to hunker down," she said, "but where would you go, eventually?"

"To a coyote," Mark murmured, but it sounded more like a question to Rose.

"To a coyote you don't know," Rose said. "Who might just take your money and abandon your family. Or you could be with a squad of SEALS."

Mark looked away. She watched him calculate.

"All right," he said. He retrieved his phone, and sent the encrypted app to his mom's, Jason's, and Maria's phone. "We have to prepare our families."

~

"Mom," Mark said.

"How did you give me this app?" Mrs. Wingfield said. Her face was lined with worry. "If we get caught—"

"Trust me, Mom." Mark said. He hastily explained that they had to gather their things because Officer Gretton would be there in five minutes.

"Mark, slow down." Mom sounded like she might panic.

"Mom," Mark said patiently, "it's for the best."

"We can't just *leave*. There's violence all over the city. It isn't safe."

"It's only going to get worse," Mark said.

"No," Mom said. "We just need to stay home and wait for the army to restore order. The news said the army has the upper hand."

"Are you listening to me?" Mark said. "Holder's army won't protect you. They'll come after all of us. I need you to be calm. You can't fall apart like when Dad left."

Silence. He felt cruel saying that, but it had been the truth.

"Jason and Maria are counting on you," he added.

"Maria got trapped over at Emily's. She can't leave."

"We'll send someone to pick her up," Mark said.

"No!" Mom exclaimed. "Mark, listen. The…men…came over. From your…you know where. Your…friends. With the *things*." She gave him a significant look.

He could tell what she was trying to imply without saying it: Coach Bliss's people had arrived and installed a basement safe. He nodded to show that he got it.

"This solves all of our problems," Mom said. "We can't leave now. Not after this."

Mark glanced at G.J., and Rose, and realized he didn't have time to be indirect. "Mom, I just helped a crew rescued someone who disappeared. We broke a dozen laws this afternoon. There's no hunkering down and hiding out for any of us, anymore."

"You did *what*?"

Hastily, he explained. She was aghast.

"And you felt you could just make all of those decisions that affected our family *on your own?*"

"I had to."

"We're going to get killed."

"We might." Against his own rising anger, he spoke calmly. "But this is our best chance. If we hunker down, they'll sweep us up eventually. Or we can risk it and get out now."

"I can't believe this." She touched her fingertips to her

forehead.

"We can *leave*, Mom. This is the best way."

"Because you've cut off every other option." But she sounded more shocked than angry.

"This will work," he said.

"All right," she said.

He could tell she wanted to yell at him, to express everything she was feeling, but he could also tell she realized that they didn't have time for that. So he said, "I'll call Maria."

"All right."

"I love you."

"I love *you*." She sounded bewildered—somewhere between despair and panic.

"Go get my lazy brother."

"Don't call him lazy."

He hung up. Sophie asked him, "Is your mom going to be able to do this?"

Mark nodded. "Now, yes. I'll be honest: my seven-year-old sister did a better job of raising Jason and me when I was four, when Dad vanished. But she's gotten it together since then."

He called Maria. When she didn't answer, he left a text that would delete itself five seconds after she read it. Maria was preternaturally calm; she would cooperate when the police picked her up. Mark had never worried about persuading her. She would recognize Officer Gretton, and he would explain everything.

~

"Dad?" Rose said. Through the app, they made eye contact.

"Rose." He kept his voice level and his face strong, but under the surface, Rose still heard how worried he was. "Your mom is worried."

"I'm sorry." She cringed. "We rescued G.J."

"You did what?"

Rose explained.

Dad stared off into deep thought. Rose could see him playing out scenarios…

…all of them bad.

"Don't come home," Dad said. "Go to the point." The point was an abandoned house three miles from their neighborhood—ownership uncertain. Sitting in an emptied cul-de-sac, it was remote, didn't have electricity, and the closest thing to off-the-grid her father could find. In case everything went to Hell, the point would be their temporary refuge.

"No," Rose said. Before he could react, she added: "Dad, G.J. found a way out."

Her father forgot to breath. He looked straight into the camera; she felt like he was x-raying her soul. "Go ahead."

She explained her plan. He grimaced, and she knew what he was thinking: holding up at the point would buy them at most a week, after which they would be out of food. In the meantime, the authorities would review every surveillance video. They'd identify Rose and blame Mr. and Mrs. Scholl. Their family's safe life was already over.

Further, there was no other way. The authorities would intensify the border guards, and issue shoot-on-sight orders. They wouldn't be able to leave the city, let alone the nation. There was nowhere to go. Even the Black Zone would eventually get run over.

"Fine," he said.

"Dad," Rose pleaded, "don't be mad. We can get the whole family out—not just mom and my sibs. But grandma and grandpa, my cousins—everyone."

"Now isn't the time for this," Dad said. "I'll gather everyone."

"I love you."

"You're grounded until you're ninety. And I'm locking you in a room with your mother until she makes you cry. I love you."

They clicked off.

Sophie looked pale. "He didn't even yell at you."

"That means when he sees me, I am twice as dead," Rose said.

"Your mom will be beside herself," Sophie said.

"Dad will keep her calm," Rose said. "He has to."

"Finished," G.J. said.

"Already?" Sophie asked.

"What now?" Rose asked.

"We wait one minute," G.J. said, "and climb the ladder to the hatch that leads to the street. It only opens from the inside. Officer Martin will be here in two minutes."

"What's the freighter like?" Mark asked.

"The cargo decks, which are ninety percent of the ship, have been transformed into prison cells. It's full, and it holds five hundred people. They're people who don't fit in—too educated, independent, religious, something. And some stone-cold killers."

"They might be useful in a fight," Mark said.

G.J. nodded. "I say we only let them out if we have to."

"Who are we?" Rose asked.

"I've worked us all up identities as informers," G.J. said. "I made us into the worst kind of rats. We betrayed our family members to save ourselves. They summoned us because they're not done interrogating our families, and they want to use what we know against them."

Sophie looked revolted.

"What?" Rose asked.

"Nothing," Sophie said. "I'm sure it will work. It's just disgusting."

"Disgusting is the way to get in," G.J. said.

They exited the server room and climbed the ladder to the street. The sun had set. With the power shut off, all the streetlights were black. They were in the failed part of the city, where whole blocks in the former manufacturing district stood empty: five-story apartments, mills, vegetable stands. A fire hydrant stood busted, and water gushed out. Sophie hurried to it, and soaked herself.

"What are you doing?" Mark looked incredulous to Rose.

"Getting rid of this smell," Sophie said.

"Good idea," Rose said, and immersed herself.

Far away, they heard an explosion, and a tower of flame erupted. As they drenched themselves, a lone cop car roared down the street.

"Officer Martin. Officer Derek," she said, greeting the two men.

His eyes widened as they washed themselves. "What the hell?" he asked. But when a still-dry G.J. stepped near him, he waved for G.J. to step into the water. "I'll turn on the heat. You'll dry by the time we get there."

After they climbed in the car and the vent hit them full blast, Rose saw that Mark kept his eyes on Officer Derek's hands as the cop drove. Her friend's hands rested on his .44.

They twisted and turned in dark alleys and through

two miles of abandoned houses. The officer avoided the paramilitaries, other police, and the army. A direct drive to the port would have taken six minutes; it took him fifteen.

But just three blocks from the water, and then the freighter, three armed men had set up a checkpoint. "Hide your guns," Officer Derek said.

Rose gestured for Mark and Sophie to made their weapons disappear.

Derek crept up to the checkpoint. Rose's breath caught. So much now depended on G.J., and on Rose. Either the false identities G.J. had placed in the system would work—

—or they'd all get put up against a wall and shot right there.

An army sergeant twirled a finger. Derek pressed a button and their windows slid down. The former SEAL presented his I.D.

The sergeant was over 6'5" and solid muscle, wore urban camouflage, and bulletproof vest. He blipped Derek's I.D. with a scanner. "What's it like out there?" the sergeant asked.

Derek looked him in the eye. "Not good."

The sergeant sighed. "We've been stuck here all night," he said. "In the meantime, we keep getting reports of the Blues smashing shops and burning churches and synagogues."

"What we're all doing is important," Derek said.

"Yeah. Processing undesirables. I have a better solution." He closed one eye, aimed his finger, and pantomimed firing a gun. Rose suddenly felt cold. "What did these kids do?"

"Nothing. They're heroes," Martin said. "Class N informers."

"Patriots." But the sergeant looked at them like they were snakes.

"That's right," said Martin.

"At least you're not suicide bombers," the sergeant said. He locked eyes with Martin and said, "There's been some of that."

"Pathetic," Officer Martin said.

"I'd like to be nearby and just do headshots before they could detonate themselves," he said as he glanced at his screen as it displayed the false information G.J. had planted into the system. "While other guys are out there earning commendations, I'm stuck here processing whole families. Ten-year-old kids," the sergeant said.

"Probably radicalized already," Derek said. Rose wished the sergeant would just hurry up and let them through.

"Yeah." The sergeant grunted. "They do a psych profile for that. If they're not too far gone, the state separates them from their parents and put them in good homes."

"We can hope," Derek said.

"Good luck." The sergeant waved them forward.

Derek saluted, and the drove along the dark, empty road between a series of deserted shells of former businesses toward the freighter.

The ship is a small city, Rose thought as they approached the water. The freighter stood five stories high and was as long as a football field. Light blazed from a few windows.

"You never said exactly where this slave ship is supposed to go," Rose murmured.

"I wasn't able to find that out," G.J. said.

"Another country?" Rose asked.

"Maybe," G.J. said.

"Another part of this country?" she asked.

He shrugged. "I don't know any more than you do."

Which is nothing, Rose thought.

Derek parked near a building that had a retraceable corridor that led straight into the freighter. As they got out of the police car, their weapons hidden, Martin escorted them.

"Far left door," G.J. said.

Derek veered them away from a loading dock, and a checkpoint, and instead they walked along the cracked sidewalk to an open steel door.

Abruptly, Rose saw Sophie gasp and Mark whirl.

She nearly spoke, but her fingers hot to her lips instead as her shoulders bunched up.

On the loading dock, Mark watched two cops escort Sophie's parents and three siblings to the checkpoint.

Sophie's six-year-old sister was clinging to her mother. Mrs. White, to Rose, was awful at hiding her fear. Mark glanced at Rose—

—who gave him a reassuring nod as if to say, *Those cops are with us.* Part of the SEALS.

"They'll be okay," Mark whispered to Sophie.

She nodded fearfully, but Mark couldn't help but glance back.

As they frisked Mrs. White, the 20-year-old soldier laughed, and shoved Mr. White, who was still dressed for work. He was a skinny engineer. When his sixteen-year-old son got angry, and shouted something, the SEAL pulled him back.

"Will," Sophie murmured. She looked ready to cry.

And then, one by one, Sophie's family disappeared inside the loading dock.

Rose felt lightheaded as they stepped inside the

processing building. Officer Derek leading, they passed a guard, who blipped them in. They zigzagged down a corridor. On their left, in a conference room, four men and women in suits were laughing.

"Whoa!" a man cried. "Show it again!" He was drunk. The room was filled with chatter; a dozen televisions showed he news from several channels, both official and illegal.

"Keep moving," Derek murmured. He picked up his step.

"Hey. Hey, hey, hey!" said the drunk man. He surged into the hall, glanced at the kids, looked bored, and clutched Derek's arm. "Badges," he said to Derek and Martin. "You gotta see this." He tugged Derek toward the conference room.

"We're on a timetable," Derek said.

"Whoa! Big man in a *hurry*." The man had epaulettes on his jacket. Rose's anxiety spiked; she recognized him from the news. He was always standing behind the governor. On TV, he always looked stone-faced. "You don't have time for the liaison to President Holder?" he slurred.

"Respectfully, sir—"

"Shhh, shhh, shhh." The drunk put his fingers to Derek's lips. "Watch with me and I'll put you on my detail. This is show—so good." He waved fingers at the second man, who reversed one of the screens, and muted all of the others.

In silence, they watched the vice president of the nation, Hale Thompson, stroll toward his limousine. He was surrounded by men in suits and shades.

"Slow motion. Slow motion!" the drunk said loudly. A woman snickered.

As the screen slowed, the sidewalk started to crack

open. As every bit of cement erupted upward in a geyser of rubble, Thompson and his guards lost their footing—

Rose couldn't bear to watch. This was grotesque.

"Freeze it. Freeze it!" the liaison to Holder shouted. Against her will, Rose glanced at the screen. An off-balance Thompson was lost in a cloud of gray dust.

"It's a terrible image," the woman said.

"You can't see anything," someone else said.

"No. Wrong. Blood." The drunk's finger tapped the big screen. Thompson and several others were just dusty silhouettes, lost in a cloud of pulverized cement. Rubble was suspended in the air. "Play it slowly."

In time-lapse fashion, the silhouettes slowly burst scarlet until the gray cloud turned deep red, a dark mist.

"Zow! Blown to shreds!" the liaison pumped his fist.

"Axel, you're sick." The woman laughed.

"I'm creative. This was my idea." The drunk pecked her lips. "That's why you love me."

Rose was absorbing the other screens. Some were news stations, but most looked like recordings from surveillance tapes. She recognized other cities' landmarks; from these private feeds, she could see aerial views of street battles—some army and paramilitaries were fighting in urban centers, and going from office to office. Everywhere: fires.

But the official news channels showed anchors speaking calmly into cameras. By their shoulders, the screen also played footage of calm city streets, and army vehicles rolling by. The ticker tapes below said: PEACE RETURNING.

"I'm so happy to see him dead. Aren't you all happy to see that smug bastard dead?" He kept swinging his arms up until the room burst into cheers.

"'Unity ticket.'" The drunk shook his head. "How about 'scrape the pieces out of the rubble.' Do you know how big of a bomb we needed? And yet, we only took out Thompson and his private guard."

"'Private guard.'" The woman smirked.

"'Unity ticket!'" someone else exclaimed, repeating the drunk.

"Now Holder can have a day of mourning for Thompson," the drunk said, "but everybody knows he was a traitor."

"He doesn't deserve a day of mourning," someone said.

"Thank you for that," Derek said to the drunk. "We must go. President's orders."

"Of course." The drunk solemnly saluted Derek. "I just thought you'd like that."

"Yes, sir."

"After all, it's you guys who have to defend bastards like Thompson."

"Yes, sir."

"But not after tonight." The drunk downed half of his glass. "You'll never get stuck protecting a traitor again."

"Yes, sir. Thank you, sir," Derek said to the man. "We have to go."

"Of course." The drunk solemnly saluted Derek. "I did that for you."

"Yes, sir." Derek shepherded the teens back into the corridor. But Rose felt the drunk's eyes on her. She avoided looking at him, but she knew when people were committing her face to their memory. She suppressed a shudder; she had the feeling the drunk was memorizing her face, and her figure.

They took a retractable corridor onto the freighter. It

led to the third floor, which was a gigantic open space stocked with dozens of bulldozers and thousands of crates. They met with the other five former SEALs—all cops in their forties, including Rose's father's friend, Gretton. She wanted to run to him—

—but that wouldn't be wise. Instead, their eyes met only for a few seconds.

Are you all right? she asked.

An almost imperceptible nod, and his lips barely moving: *Are you?*

Yes.

Gretton: *You'd better be.*

He'd kept himself lean and muscular, as had most of his friends, but Rose's worry shifted into overdrive. On this floor alone, she counted a dozen soldiers. While she didn't think any one of them was a match for one of her father's friends, they were outnumbered and outgunned.

"The CC is actually one deck up," G.J. said. "Through a maze of corridors. It will be guarded, but your fake I.D.s should continue to work."

"Where are the people?" Sophie asked plaintively. Because they were surrounded by workmen who were making sure crates and machinery was tied down.

Abruptly, the felt the ship moving. The engines had always provided a background hum. But now, the hum increased, and the ship gave off a subtle vibration. Rose wondered: was it moving out to sea?

"Bottom two floors in hundreds of cells," G.J. whispered.

Where do we go? Rose communicated.

Up, G.J. signaled. He suddenly looked anxious. *Don't say anymore,* he added. *Not even in code.*

Rose didn't see any cameras, but you could never be

sure.

Surrounded by the six SEALs, they wove between freezers of meat and crates of vegetables and fruits. The amount of food was staggering. *Where does it all come from?* She thought. Her own family gardened, and raised roosters and hens. *If we didn't…* Well, everyone knew hunger was rampant in the city.

They reached a corkscrew staircase. "Down one floor," G.J. said.

"You said up," Rose said.

"I meant down," he said.

She watched Mark grimace. In the meantime, the hair rose on the back of her neck because the staircase allowed for only one person at a time. Suddenly, several army men were ahead of them; after three SEALs, G.J., Sophie, and Mark, three SEALs followed her—but more army men appeared behind them, and they also descended, their feet clanging on the rungs.

We're surrounded, Rose thought.

She reached the lower floor, which had thousands of boxes of goods marked from another country. Except for a blazing light that came from a central office, only dim lights illuminated this floor. The central office was made of steel walls and thick glass.

It looks bomb proof.

She felt like her body had shed all of its heat, and she might freeze until she got sick. Absorbing everyone else's mood, she felt how on edge they were. She was terrified someone would do something stupid. The SEALs were relentlessly scanning the environment, but Sophie and Mark kept taking hidden glances at G.J.

"That must be it," G.J. murmured.

The army soldiers who had come before and after

them had disappeared into the alleys between the crates. *Why?* Rose thought. They were here, and then gone. The SEALS were glancing every which way. Mark and Sophie had a level of quiet energy she had never seen. *And G.J.—*

G.J. kept stepping faster than the group, and then he'd have to restrain himself and wait. "That's the CC. C'mon." He hopped unnaturally.

The thought came unbidden. She had to let everyone know. *It's a trap,* she whispered.

And then it all happened in an instant.

~

Since they'd reached the relay station, Mark felt there was something different about G.J. Unquestionably, they'd made him suffer for eight hours in his cell. His friend's skinny, 120-pound, 5'10" frame now had welts and cuts; his jeans looked slashed with a knife, and his calf was encrusted with blood. They'd clearly beaten him.

Yet, G.J. was tenacious. He hated Holder's government. And he had a high pain threshold. If anyone could tell them *some* of what they wanted to hear, and still keep something hidden, it was G.J.

But something was off. But before Mark could figure out what, a gunshot interrupted his thoughts.

Mark saw G.J. break free of the group and sprint for the central room.

~

Gun blasts erupted. Just as one SEAL grabbed Rose by the shoulder, pulled her close to him, and into a crouch behind a barrel, she saw a second man seize up, his body arching, his .44 falling from his grip, an arc of blood gushing from his neck.

And then a spray of gunshots, some like firecrackers, others like miniature cannons. "Stay down," the SEAL whispered. Where they'd been standing, she saw a crate's boards splinter and burst as bullets tore it to shreds.

Simultaneously, the SEAL on the floor clutched his bleeding neck, and inched across the iron floor for his .44.

Someone else sprayed him with bullets. As he convulsed, Rose saw a man inside the CC fling the steel door open. G.J. sprinted inside, and the man flung the door hard. It clanged shut.

~

"He betrayed us," Mark whispered to the SEAL guarding him.

"Stay hidden." Derek whispered. He was mid-forties, white-haired, and a dad. "Let us take them out. Don't shoot any of us."

"And if you fail?" Mark said.

"We won't," the SEAL said. Before Mark could reply, the man vanished.

Between steel drums, sitting in darkness, Mark pointed his pistol forward.

All he heard was gunfire—sloppy, like that of a paramilitary.

~

Her father made Rose lie between several wooden boxes. She pointed her plastic gun forward. *Stay disciplined,* her father's voice came to mind, *because it's all going to hell.* If

Sophie or Mark came near, she didn't want to accidentally shoot either.

Abruptly, a burst of gunfire erupted, followed by the sound of wood splintering and pieces flying.

Silence.

"Which way did they go?" she heard a whisper. And then: feet scuffling.

In the otherwise eerie silence, the unfamiliar people, not the SEALs—Holder's army—seemed loud and klutzy to Rose.

Pressed against the dirty floor, the seconds dragged by for Rose. Her heart raced; she worked to steady her breathing; to calm her wild mood, to stop sweating in the dust. She felt they would hear her, they would see her, and they would learn she'd arranged to have her own family arrested and placed on board. G.J. would rat them out—and they would torture her family in front of her just to show who was in control—

Abruptly, between a crack, she saw a man fall to the floor. He didn't get up. Another set of feet—SEAL shoes— were there, and then they vanished.

The man on the floor lay still. In the near darkness, Rose saw his throat was cut, and he was bleeding out.

She shuddered and almost convulsed with fear. She wanted to shriek, but she kept it together: a SEAL had taken out one of Holder's soldiers.

And now, she made her breathing and her heartbeat very still, and she listened very intensely.

"Reid. Chuck," a soldier said. He was whispering, but to Rose, he may as well have been shouting. "Reid. *Chuck!*"

No reply.

Another man stumbled nearby. He looked every which way: his body language radiated fear. And then he saw the corpse. A gasp escaped him—

—and then his back twisted. His limbs jolted; he froze like a puppet being dangled, and he collapsed atop the other man.

His dead eyes are pointed right at me, Rose thought. She wanted to flee. But she realized: *A SEAL shot him. With his silencer.*

"Did you hear that?" someone else said.

"What?" said another.

They were nearby. She aimed her plastic gun.

~

Mark crouched between metal barrels. The SEAL, Derek, had vanished. Out of nowhere, he thought about Mom and Jason, stuck in a cell downstairs. *They are all going to die,* he thought, *because I agreed to this plan. Thank God we couldn't find Maria.*

He shook himself. There was no time for guilt.

I should see them one last time—

He heard several voices. Hastily, he plastered himself into the darkest shadow, against cold steel, to hide.

"How many are there?"

"I don't know."

Someone cursed. "How did this happen?"

"I don't know," said the second.

"Never mind. We'll have to sweep the whole floor."

Then silence. Mark wondered, *What were they doing? Pointing in different directions? Deciding who goes where?*

He'd counted six voices. *Can I shoot all six?* They were trying to be quiet, but Mark heard every scuff against the floor.

Probably not.

And then they were gone.

~

What Rose heard:

A long silence. Then, abruptly, two soldiers crying out, and thuds as they hit the floor. She felt the metal beneath her vibrate.

"Chuck! *Chuck!*" someone yelled.

And then a soldier crying like a warrior making a raid, and gunfire. Rose cringed. Their assault was wild, undisciplined. She heard bullets ping off of metal, maybe the hull, and possibly she heard ricochets—

And then nothing. The gunfire and shouts ceased.

And abruptly, Dad whispered, "Rose."

She wanted so desperately to get to her feet.

"Rose," he said. "It's Dad. Are you all right?"

"Yes."

"We got them all," he said.

Abruptly, every light on the floor came on. Rose startled. "How many?" she asked.

"Twenty. I'm stepping into your line of sight now."

She crossed herself. He appeared. He had a streak of blood across his black shirt.

"Your friend and two others locked themselves inside that Command Center," Dad said. "We don't know what they've done. If they sent for help. Whatever they've done, we don't have much time."

"What do you mean, 'Whatever they've done'?" She stepped toward the CC, glancing at Dad to make sure he thought it was safe. He urged her on even as he constantly scanned the floor for any more soldiers.

As she approached the glass walls, she saw how G.J.

looked a nauseated whitish-green. From the floor with a fresh cut across his chest, he shook his head at her, and said, something, but too fast for her to read his lips. Two other men inside were frantically working the computers.

Rose gripped the door handle, but it was locked. "G.J.!" she cried. The men inside had side arms, but they were holstered. They ignored G.J. and instead frantically talked to each other. She could read their lips.

Initiating omega, the first one said. He also looked like he might get sick.

Initiated, said the second, a pale-green.

"G.J.!" Rose rattled the door.

Looking dazed, G.J. struggled to get to his feet. Heaving for air, he gasped, *Please.* When the men ignored him, he lunged at one of them, but the much bigger man pushed G.J. to the floor.

Her father brushed Rose aside. Taking one look at the lock, he retrieved a block of plastique. He molded it on the door. "Behind the crates," he said to Mark, Rose, Sophie and the remaining SEALs, who were roved toward and away from the CC in case any more soldiers arrived from other floors—although Rose knew they'd killed of Holder's army in under five minutes. If the other floors even knew what was going on, she was sure they would not be able to handle her dad and his buddies.

Dad positioned himself behind a girder, took aim, and shot the plastique.

The explosion was terrific; a boom and the shriek of shearing metal. Rose's hands flew to her ears. Before she recovered, Dad and was already flinging the door open and rushing inside with three other SEALs.

"You're too late," G.J. said, from the floor.

"Away from the computers!" Dad yelled. The two

men raised their hands and backed up against a wall.

Rose, Mark, and Sophie came inside. Mark helped G.J. to his feet—but Rose noticed he also didn't let G.J. leave a square on the floor.

"What did you do?" Rose demanded.

The men, looking sicker than ever, exchanged glances but did not speak.

"They triggered a bomb. It will sink the ship," G.J. said.

"And you helped them *do* this?" Sophie cried.

"I tried to stop them," G.J. said.

"Why didn't you tell us this was going to happen?"

"I wasn't sure what they were going to do. I thought if I got back in the inside, I could stop it." G.J. blushed. "There was time to discuss it."

"So you chose for us?" Rose asked.

"You *liar!*" Sophie surged toward G.J., but a SEAL held her back.

"We don't have time for infighting," Dad said. "How much time do we have?"

"Ten minutes, tops," G.J. said.

Dad placed his pistol against one technician's forehead. "I am getting sick of the kid doing all the talking. How do we deactivate this bomb?"

The technician stared at Dad in absolute fear, but Rose had a feeling it wasn't from the gun placed against his forehead.

"They can't deactivate it," G.J. said.

"They sure as hell can!" Dad ground the barrel against the man's temple.

"I'm telling you I can't do it!" The pale, shaky technician mopped sweat away. "And I wouldn't, even if I could because they're going to kill our families if we let you capture this ship!"

"So, you'd rather kill everyone on board," Sophie said, "and die yourself."

"We have no choice!" the man said.

"You deserve to die!" screamed the other man. "You made us die. You made us die. You made us *die!*"

Officer Scholl gripped the hysterical man by the carotid. The man went limp, and the officer eased him to the floor.

"He was lying," G.J. said. "They have lifeboats. That's why it takes the bomb ten minutes to detonate. It's set up so that some people get to escape."

Rose and her father spoke at the same time: "Where is the bomb?" She stopped, and let him take the lead once she realized he was back on track.

"On the outer hull near the water line," G.J. said. "It's big enough to blow a hole the size of a truck in the bulkhead. They wanted the bomb outside the ship to make it harder to find or neutralize. It's by the engines."

"That way, it will trigger a larger explosion," Mark said.

"How do we remove it?" Rose asked.

"It's magnetically attached," G.J. said. "But even if you could separate it, even when it explodes, the blast will be horrific. No matter what, it will create a wave that will sink the ship."

"That's not possible," Mark said.

"Ordinarily, of course that's right," Officer Scholl said, "but the water is mined."

"'Mined'?" Mark asked.

"Holder had his navy place explosive devices deep in the water. His idea was to keep other countries out. If the bomb on this ship detonates near one of them, it will set off several of them."

"It has to be far away because of the secondary explosions," G.J. said. "Look, we have to hurry. The second the government figures out that we took over this ship, they'll trigger the nearby mines or hit us with a missile. We have to get rid of that bomb and get to international waters!"

Rose felt sick. Even though, her mind whirled. "So, we put our bomb on a life raft. We take it far away—"

"Are there life rafts?" Mark asked.

"Several," Officer Scholl said. "You'll lower me; I'll detach the bomb, motor it as far away in the opposite direction, sink it—"

Rose went white. *You'll die,* she thought, but Dad was already limping out the door and toward the stairs. Mark and Sophie shoved G.J. along as two SEALs remained behind, and aimed their guns at the two technicians.

On the top deck, two soldiers were patrolling. Panting, his upper body bleeding, Rose's father aimed. He shot each.

"Officer Scholl," Mark said, "I have to do it. With your injuries, you'll never make it down and out in time."

When her father nodded, the cold air on the top deck turned her sweat to ice, and dread sank into her. She hadn't wanted to admit it, but her father was leaving a trail of blood, and he looked worse now than five minutes ago. *Daddy,* she thought, but she pushed all emotion aside. *It has to be Mark,* she told herself. And then she realized something else.

Actually, it has to be—

"Eight minutes," Mark said. They split up three ways: Rose heading north, Mark going south, and Rose's father moving west to examine the hull. Three stories down, at the water line, Rose shouted, "I've found it!"

Dad and Mark rushed over. They took one glance at the hope chest-sized box attached to the hull. "That box?" Mark asked.

Dad nodded, and he urged Mark to hop in a lifeboat attached to the side of the ship. "Six minutes," Dad said. As he worked the controls, he handed Mark some C-4. "Just a tiny amount," he said, "but I recognize the bomb type. There should be a switch on the underside that demagnetizes the bomb case. The case will detach. You'll speed three and a half minutes out, sink the bomb, and immediately speed away. You don't want—"

"—to be underneath that bomb when it explodes," Mark said.

"I have to be honest with you—" Dad began.

"I might not make it back," Mark said.

Dad nodded. "It might knock you out of the boat. If you don't drown in the waves, you'll have to figure out which way is up, swim back to the surface, and find the life raft. Got it?"

Mark nodded.

But Rose felt unwanted emotion surging. She felt like her father was minimizing things—that the blast would be far worse than what he was saying. She looked at Mark, who looked determined. *You're sacrificing your life*, she thought. *I can see it on your face. You know this is a suicide mission.*

As the lifeboat lowered, Rose realized what she had to do. When it was twelve feet down, she snatched her father's handcuffs and key, leapt over the side of the ship, and splashed in the water.

Frigid!

Under the surface, it was dark and cold, a frozen night. She felt immediate pressure on her chest. *An icy death...* Frantically, she kicked for the surface. She couldn't see anything; she had never been anywhere more pitch-black. She swam hard for the surface. Soon, she broke the waterline, gasping.

Freezing…

"Rose!" Dad shouted in dismay. She heaved for air; she had never been so cold. She wondered if her muscles would seize up. Her teeth chattering violently, she swam for the boat, which finally touched down on the waves. She hastily gripped the side; Mark pulled her aboard.

"Are you out of your mind?" he asked her.

"I'm going to keep you alive," she said.

"I'll be fine," he said. But she saw he was lying. "How?" he asked.

"Just get the bomb!"

He motored over. The silver box looked black in the moonlight. Filthy seaweed clung to it; in darkness, it looked like it was made of rotting cancer cells. When Rose touched the metal, her fingers stung from how chilly it was. She probed through the black vines to find the switch—

—and touched cold, hard metal. When she toggled it, the box instantly fell, and she lurched, bobbled it, and pulled it into her body, and clutched it hard because she was terrified of it plunging into the water and being underneath the freighter. She fell over onto the boat's floor, the cold water soaking her once again.

"Jeez," Mark muttered.

"Go!" she shouted. She struggled to push the box off of her; it was astonishingly heavy. Gasping as she maneuvered herself, she soon sat on it to keep it in place.

Lightning fast, Mark was back at the controls, speeding out to sea, full throttle.

At first, waves splashed into the boat, soaking them both, and Rose thought they were going to capsize. She shifted so she lay atop the bomb to keep it from flying out when they bucked a wave. But then the boat turned…Mark was curving to the right…and abruptly, the waters calmed down drastically. Dazed and frozen, she slowly realized he had gone from fighting the water, and heading straight into oncoming waves, and instead had maneuvered a whole ninety degrees. Mark was letting the sea propel them far away.

Her side felt a sharp pain. She looked down. She realized she'd cut herself against the case's sharp edge. Wincing, she touched her side.

"You okay?" Mark asked.

"Fine," she said, but even in dark moonlight with dark water flying all about them, she was sure she was bleeding.

"What the hell were you thinking?" he shouted above the engine.

"About which part?" she asked.

He smiled ruefully.

"How much farther?" she asked.

"Minute and a half," he shouted, above the motor. With water flying above them, as he carefully maneuvered to stay in a wave trough, she felt he was lying. She could tell.

"Take it out two full minutes," she said. "I'll drop the bomb and we'll speed away."

He shook his head. "I'll have to help you toss it over," he said. "You'll never get it out in time."

"No," she said. "You have to get us moving fast in opposite direction. The shockwave will knock us out of the boat."

"We'll be fine," he said.

"We won't," she said. Because even in the moonlight, with his face silvery, she could tell from his voice and body language that he was lying.

"And never see Mom or Jason again?" he added unnecessarily, as though trying to persuade not just her, but also himself.

"You'd give your life for them," she said.

She watched him grimace. *Caught,* she thought. Because just moments ago, before she jumped in the water, she intuited that he never expected to live. He just wanted to save his family. But then she watched him shake off the fact that she saw right through him. *Even when we're about to die,* she thought, *you still don't want anyone to get to close.*

"You haven't answered my question," he said. "Why did you jump in the lifeboat?"

"Because when the shockwave does hit, we're both going to get thrown into the water," she said. "We'll have to find each other in the water, and cling together. One person might not survive. We have to make sure we both stay afloat, and get back to the life raft."

"You're insane," he said, but he sounded humbled. "Thank you," he finally said.

They rode in silence for ten seconds. Rose didn't know what to say. Out of nowhere, she wanted to struggle across the boat now, and kiss him. *Kiss a manly man,* she thought, *before I die.*

"Do you think G.J. succeeded in sending out a false signal?" he asked.

"Yes," she said. "He'll program something else out here—a sensor on a buoy—to broadcast the ship's signature. By the time they figure it out, the freighter will be international waters." Besides, the government would have its hands full, quelling the paramilitaries, before they figured it out.

But would they still blow the freighter up? She

wondered. They could claim anything. Other nations might be outraged—but what if Holder claimed they were murderers who had taken over a ship? She could hear his baritone: "What nation would want these saboteurs? We did the international community a favor. You would think they would say thank you."

She finished her mental count. "It's time," she said. She hefted the heavy, awkward box. In her haste, she nicked her hands on the sharp corners. Her palms stung; the box made her bleed, again. But she'd lugged and hefted the bomb. It rolled over the lifeboat's edge, hit the water, and disappeared into pitch-black water.

"Turning around," Mark shouted above the engine.

He whipped the boat around the opposite way. When they cut against the waves, gallons of water flowed on top of them. Soaked to the skin again, Rose clung to the seats. She was sure they'd capsize—

—when, abruptly, the boat righted itself in a trough again, as Mark sped back in the direction that they came from.

Under the cold, moonless sky, she crawled toward him. "Handcuffs," she said, retrieving her dad's equipment.

"You have the key?" he asked.

"In my pocket," she said, patting her zipped-up jacket.

"Do it," he said, holding out his hand.

As she bound her left wrist to his right, she asked, "Do you see the freighter?"

"Not yet," he said. "but it's due west. I'm following the constellations. Orion the Hunter," he said.

She nodded. "Thirty seconds," she said.

"It will have sunk far down," he said. "Maybe we'll be fine." But he sounded doubtful. She believed the bomb would be like an underground earthquake, and cause a miniature tsunami. She felt when the wave hit, they would be cast out of the boat. If they were lucky, they would swim to the boat.

If they were still conscious.

"Ten seconds."

"Come closer," he said. He pulled her into him. She let him.

"I don't want us knocking heads when the wave hits," he said.

"That would be bad," she said. She felt astonished at how solid he felt. He was made of dense muscle.

And then the bomb must have blown up because water exploded upward in a titanic wave, and she felt like they were about to get swept up in an unprecedented disaster.

~

Mark felt and saw a wall of water racing toward their boat. It looked like a canyon wall of sea chasing them. He clutched onto Rose; she pressed herself against him. He had one arm wrapped around her—she felt soft and beautiful to him—and one on the throttle, keeping it wide open.

The three-story wall of water raced toward them, narrowing the gap, terrifying them, until it swamped them, and they were under it, and clinging onto each other. He didn't know if the water lifted them up like they were nothing, and then rammed them below the surface, or what happened. It was impossible to tell. He had no idea which way was up, but he had the sensation of moving fast, riding along like a person lost in the rapids, except water was above and below them, as they were momentarily suspended somewhere, defying gravity. He held onto Rose, his hands holding her close, trying to keep his cheek touching hers so that they wouldn't get forced apart, and then crack skulls.

We will die this way, he thought. He'd struggled to take in as much air as possible at the beginning, but he didn't know how much longer he would last before, involuntarily, he opened his mouth and he reflexively tried to breath. His lungs would flood with saltwater. They would drown—

—somehow, they were thrust to the surface. He gasped. The last shockwave of water had passed.

"Rose," he said. His voice sounded weak to him.

She did not respond.

Frantically, he spun her back toward him. They were still handcuffed, of course. In the starlight, her eyes were closed.

"Rose!" he shouted. Nearby, he was kicking to keep them afloat. The raft floated randomly, like driftwood.

Nothing.

He kicked frantically, dragging her toward the boat. It couldn't have been long, but it felt like forever. He swung a heavy leg over the side. With a quick roll, his free arm clutching the railing, he pulled them both aboard.

He immediately began doing chest compressions. His lips on hers, he breathed into her lungs. In the starlight, she looked whitish-blue. *Please God*, he thought, although he knew from CPR class that a person turning blue was actually a good sign.

Except in this night, he couldn't really tell what color she was. She wasn't breathing. *She's dead*—

He thumped her chest. *I am handcuffed to a dead girl.* He breathed into her. *The dead girl's name was Rose Scholl*—

She gasped, water bursting out of her mouth.

"Rose," he murmured.

She struggled to sit up. Awkwardly, he helped her; he was hovering over her left side; his right hand was still handcuffed to her left.

She coughed three times. Maybe he imagined it under the pale starlight, with black waves now gently lifting and lowering their lifeboat as they floated along, going who knows where, but her cheeks looked pink.

"We're on the raft," she said. She sounded dazed.

"You passed out," he said.

"I did?"

"We capsized. We went underwater for a while. I couldn't tell which way was up. Then we were thrust on the surface and you were out."

"You saved my life," she said. She was shivering. It was cold, but he didn't care about that.

"You saved mine," he said.

"We did it," she said. "We sank the bomb. We did it! The freighter is okay."

The freighter—

With alarm, he searched the horizon. She did the same. They looked in every direction. At first, they worked against each other, both twisting in opposite directions. He braked before he accidentally wrenched her arm or sprained her wrist.

"I don't see it," she said.

"Damn it," he muttered.

"Do you see it?" she asked. She looked alarmed. She was whirling about, looking in every direction for the freighter.

"We'll just have to head west," he said. "Toward Orion."

She looked fearful, but with her right hand, she

unzipped her pocket, retrieved the key, and unlocked the handcuffs.

"Thank you," she said again. "For saving my family."

"Thank you," he replied. "For saving mine."

"And hundreds of innocent people," she said.

He clambered toward the motor. He pressed start. Nothing.

"What's wrong?" She sounded worried to him.

"The engine's flooded," he said.

"Can you fix it?"

"I don't know," he said. "I'm sure there's water mixed with the gas, now." He pressed start again.

"We have to get moving."

"I know."

"Can I help?"

"Just let me think," he said, touching the equipment. The engine would have water in it—but the tank and gas lines were intact—no leaks. *It might just be like someone poured water over a car engine,* he thought. He glanced at Rose, who was silently praying. Mark pulled the choke and pressed start again.

The engine spurted but did not catch.

"Mark, look."

Rose was pointing toward shore. He could barely make out a lonely house, standing on stilts. *She must have 20/10 vision,* he thought, because he had 20/15. Mark couldn't even tell if any lights were on; the house was just a dot.

He shuddered. How long were they underwater? How long had he done CPR? How much time had they lost? They had drifted within sight of shore.

How far away is the freighter?

"We have to think about this," Rose said.

He pulled frantically. The engine fired up.

"How much fuel do we have?" she asked.

He turned the boat around, and aimed it at Orion.

"Mark?" Rose asked.

He accelerated.

"Mark!" she exclaimed.

"What?"

"Think about where we are. What if we don't have enough fuel?"

Those were the words he dreaded. Grimacing, he opened it up.

"Mark, if we don't have enough fuel, we'll just go several miles out, and then we'll run out. Then we'll be out to sea with no food or water. How much fuel do we have?"

He hefted the tank. It was a quarter full.

"When the sun comes up—"

"I know!" he said softly. She had the mercy not finish, because he knew what she would say, *We'll die of heat and dehydration. Or Holder's people will pick us up.*

"We have to reach it," he said softly.

But when their eyes met, he realized he was being a fool. They had no idea how far out the freighter was. They had no idea if Officer Scholl, G.J., and the others decided to change directions. Ultimately, they needed to beeline straight for international waters or Holder's navy would sink them. He hoped the government didn't learn the ship had been taken over, until it was too late for them to act.

Mark slowed the boat to a crawl. "What do we do?" he asked.

When his gaze met her blue eyes, he was astonished by how beautiful she was, even though he was half-scared to death.

"What choice do we have?" she asked.

None, he knew.

"We go home," she said.

His heart sinking, he glanced back at the tiny house near the waterline. The tree line was a black outline against the night. Mark couldn't tell if they would approach a city or the natural world, because when they'd left, there were power outages all over their city, and, as the illegal news had reported hours ago, the whole nation.

"At least we got our families out," she said.

"Did we?" Because his mood was sinking. He thought they had succeeded, but they couldn't see the ship. And they had been underwater for some time. What if the government sank the freighter while Rose and he were struggling to get to the surface? How would they ever know?

"We have to have faith," Rose said.

He imagined the chance that the freighter still existed, that it was barreling into the night. Would the SEALs have let the hundreds of people locked inside of their cages out yet? But what if, instead, there were twenty more of Holder's soldiers? The three remaining SEALS would have to fight them off. *What the hell actually happened?* Mark thought. *Are Mom and Jason safe or recaptured? Or blown up by one of Holder's missile?*

And what about us? Mark thought, looking at Rose. What would they do when they reached shore? They had no food. And maybe two guns between them. Their families—gone from them. *I hope G.J. purges the state's records about our families,* he thought. But what G.J. had done—and why—was also a mystery.

Mark grimaced. Maybe they could survive for a little while, but where would they go? Wasn't it only a matter of time before they got hunted down?

In the cold, dark night, he shivered. He looked at Rose. She was being strong. He decided that he would be strong, too.

He turned the lifeboat around and powered toward the dark, unknown shore.

End of book one of
The Forbidden Trilogy

ABOUT THE AUTHOR

Tim Wuebker has shoveled snow, mowed lawns, painted houses, shingled roofs, walked beanfields, picked up rocks, delivered newspapers, detasseled corn, bailed hay, moved grain bins, rouged corn fields, done road construction, worked as a janitor, edited papers, worked in a library, wrote articles for a chamber of commerce, tutored, taught eleven kinds of college English courses, edited, done data entry, worked as a secretary, and sold books. He has also taught high school classes, including six kinds of math, five kinds of social studies, and a business course. His nonfiction personal finance book, *Money for Teens* is on amazon.

Tim loves to read, lift weights, play volleyball and tennis, use a chainsaw, experience escape rooms, and play Exploding Kittens. Back in the day, he ran 51 marathons and 500 half-marathons. He still teaches, and is at work on a new novel.

www.ingramcontent.com/pod-product-compliance
Lightning Source LLC
Chambersburg PA
CBHW021942120726
47992CB00001B/95